The Battle of Normandy

$ \top$
ck

Tom Zola

Panzers Push for Victory

THE BATTLE OF NORMANDY

Tom Zola, a former sergeant in the German Army, is a military fiction writer famous for his intense battle descriptions and realistic action scenes. In 2014 the first book of his PANZERS series was released in the German language, setting up an alternate history scenario. A different German Reich tries to turn around the fortunes of war at the pinnacle of the Second World War. Zola doesn't beat around the bush; his stories involve brutal fighting, inhuman ideologies, and a military machine that overruns Europe and the whole world without mercy. He has developed a breathtaking yet shocking alternate timeline that has finally been translated into English.

Born in 1988, Zola is married and lives with his wife and two kids in Duisburg, Germany.

London, Great Britain, June 7th, 1944

General Dwight D. Eisenhower had thrown all his staff members out of the large conference room, which left him standing alone for a moment in front of the huge map on the wall showing Northern France. All of the latest developments of the situation had been marked on the map by magnetic plates; the formed beachheads, the failed landing attempts, the battles raging at the moment. The situation of the invading troops was challenging but not hopeless.

Looking at the map, Eisenhower couldn't help but think of the brief press release he had written in case of failure. He alone would take full responsibility. Eisenhower had taken a tremendous risk in Operation Overlord, the invasion of France, despite the most massive deployment of men and material. Somehow, however, the Western Allies had to get a foothold in Central Europe. It could not be done without risk.

Eisenhower sighed deeply at the sight of the situation map. In many places, things had turned out as the critics had feared: the Allied attack forces had been pinned down by German defensive fire, had not been able to get a foothold on the beaches, and had certainly not been able to break through into the hinterland. This bitter discovery applied to most of the invasion beaches.

The Supreme Allied Commander in Europe took a deep breath and closed his eyes for a second. The silence that surrounded him at that moment was soothing to his senses. For another moment, he wanted to enjoy this silence, wanted to concentrate on the situation without being disturbed and to sort out his decisions in his mind, which he would soon have to present to Montgomery and the others.

In the East of the area of operations were the landing zones "Gold" between Longues-sur-Mer and Mont Fleury, "Juno" between Courseulles-sur-Mer and Saint-Aubin-sur-Mer, and "Sword," which stretched from the Eastern flank

"Juno" to Ouistreham on the River Orne. In these three sections, the British and Canadians had taken a severe beating. In some places, the Krauts had broken through to the beaches with panzer formations and inflicted enormous losses on the invasion forces. The Russia-proven 16th Panzer Division had driven a wedge between Gold and Sword and defeated the Juno landing troops. The tracks of enemy tanks were already touching the water in the Juno section. Among the bodies of thousands of British and Canadians, the panzers lay in wait to strike a blow against the flanks of Gold and Sword. For now, the Allied troops were sitting tight on both beaches, but Eisenhower was aware that Gold and Sword's beachheads were no longer to be held.

Further to the East of Caen, a British airborne division, the 6th, was engaged in heavy defensive action. Having failed to capture the double bridges over the Caen Canal and the River Orne at Bénouville and Ranville, respectively, the paratroopers were cut off from the invading forces on the beach. They would not be able to hold out on their own against the Germans for long. At least the British had managed to destroy some bridges over Dives and the gun batteries at Merville.

To the West, some invasion beach sections looked even worse: The attack against the stretch of beach between Vierville-sur-Mer and Colleville-sur-Mer, known as Omaha Beach, had failed. The invading forces had pushed ineffectively against German defensive fire from MG nests and modern tanks of the 5th Panzer Division, and within hours had bled to death. Despite massive Navy bombardments against the enemy's beach entrenchments, no breakthrough had been achieved at any place. Thousands of Americans were still trapped on Omaha Beach's sands, still lying unprotected in enemy fire. "Bloody Omaha" was a common saying on the ships of the invasion fleet.

Further to the West, German guns were firing from both sides at the invading army from Pointe du Hoc. The attempt to conquer the cliff had failed direly. The Rangers were trapped with their backs to the edge of the cliff. Eisenhower wanted to leave no one behind. However, he was honest enough with himself to know that this was often not possible in wartime. All hope now lay on Utah Beach, that stretch of beach between Pouppeville and Saint-Marcouf at the foot of the Cotentin Peninsula that was entirely in Allied hands. The two U.S. paratrooper divisions that had landed in preparation for the invasion, the 82nd, and 101st Airborne Divisions, had been dropped in the hinterland of Utah Beach on the night of June 5th to June 6th. Eisenhower's planners had decided to get most of both divisions across the Channel on the first night, which meant that 13,000 men had been flown to the area between Sainte-Marie-du-Mont in the South and Montebourg in the North in an extraordinary effort. At the moment, the gliders that were to provide the American airborne troops at Utah with additional material were being sent on their way because already the spearheads of the German 24th Panzer Division were pressing against the beachhead from the South. And it was already apparent that other mobile divisions of the enemy would enter that battle too – the 5th Panzer Division at the Omaha Beach area, as well as the 16th at Caen.

There was also a light Panzer Division and the infamous Panzer Lehr Division in the Normandy hinterland – not to mention the German troops in Southern France and near Calais. After all, every hour, more Allied troops landed on Utah Beach and flooded the Cotentin Peninsula. The paratroopers, who had brought in several hundred prisoners of war, including high-ranking officers, had long since joined the invasion forces on their push into the hinterland.

Eisenhower rubbed his chin, feeling the tiny stubble poking out of it. Once again, the General sighed profoundly.

The Allies' losses must already have been extraordinarily high, but they had set the frequently invoked foot on French soil, and Eisenhower would do everything he could to ensure that this step was final. So now it was necessary to support the successful Utah landing and do damage control on all other landing beaches. As many men and as much

6

material as possible had to be evacuated, Eisenhower owed that to the poor fellows who had run against the Atlantic Wall undaunted by death.

At Utah, however, the superior strike capability of the Allied forces that had already brought down Sicily should come into play. From there, Eisenhower would press ahead with the liberation of Europe.

Once again, the old General with the thinning, graying hair and the delicate features went through his plan of operation, which he had long since decided in his mind:

First, take the double bridges at Bénouville and Ranville at all costs. Besides, simultaneous attacks by the 6th Airborne Division from the East and Sword forces from the North. For flank protection, it was necessary to stay in contact with the German tanks threatening Sword Beach in order to use guided Navy artillery fire to smash those panzers. At the same time, relocating the 6th Airborne Division across the double bridges to evacuate the boys by landing crafts. Gathering all available Navy units to protect Sword. Also, focusing all fighter bombers on Sword. All Juno forces should fight their way to Sword too. If Eisenhower wanted to evacuate his men successfully, the terrain between them and their German pursuers would have to go down in an unprecedented firestorm of destruction. The U.S. General did not expect the German Chancellor to let the Allied troops escape easily, as Hitler had once allowed at Dunkirk. This time, the Allies would have to take matters into their own hands...

Second, the Gold landing beach was to be abandoned. It was a tough decision, and especially Monty would not like it. Still, Eisenhower saw no other option than to clear the tiny beachhead, which was under constant enemy fire, with acceptable losses. The fact that at Gold, a breakout from the beachhead had not succeeded, the men were trapped with the Channel in their back. This meant that any evacuation attempt would have to be within the range of German weapons. Therefore, the encircled Gold forces were to be given clearance to act on their own terms. Attempt to break out to the East towards Sword or surrender was for the brave men to decide for themselves. They were the ones lying belly-down on the sand in the enemy fire; only they could really judge the situation. On the other hand, Eisenhower was sitting in London, staring at metal plates on a wall.

Third, abandon Omaha. Immediate evacuation of all landing troops there. Yet, the German forces opposing the Omaha troops were not so strong that they could throw the Allies back into the sea. Apparently, the Krauts had their point of main effort on Caen. Eisenhower knew that his decision would cause confrontations with the British, but he assessed the evacuation of Omaha to be possible, while an evacuation of Gold would be a suicide mission in his eyes.

Fourth, extracting the Rangers from Pointe du Hoc, followed by heaviest bombardments by Navy and Army Air Forces – day and night. The enemy guns on Pointe had to vanish! They threatened not only the Omaha evacuation efforts but also all Allied operations at Utah.

Fifth, extending the beachhead at Utah at all costs. There, on the Cotentin Peninsula, the Western powers had their foot on French soil. All available forces, all materiel, all remaining vessels, and airplanes had to move immediately in Utah's direction. Eisenhower would flood the small peninsula with material and soldiers that simply had to crush any enemy resistance. He would pump the full strength of the Western powers into the Cotentin Peninsula. There the battle for Europe, and indeed the battle for the world's freedom would take place; at Sainte-Mère-Église, at Sainte-Marie-du-Mont, at Montebourg and Valognes. From there, the Allies would take Cherbourg as well as start their advance on Saint-Lô. Yet the landed troops in the area were still vulnerable and weak, but by the minute the ramps of more landing crafts were lowering as they reached the coast; by the minute tanks and trucks were rolling, men were marching, guns were pulled out of the bellies of the landing crafts. And with every minute, it became less likely that the Krauts would be able to hold France – that they would be able to hold Europe.

To Frau Else Engelmann, June 7th, 1944
(23) Bremen
Hagenauerstr. 21

Dearest Elly,

in the middle of the hours of the invasion, your letter reached me, about which I was delighted. At least I want to answer you with a few short lines and take away the fear that surely troubles you: We defeat the Anglo-Americans wherever they appear. We throw them back into the sea and do not let them gain a foothold. Day and night, my unit is moving forward. I am sure we will repel the invasion. And then we can finally hope for peace! The Allies will not try it a second time! And without them, Russia will have to give in. Everything will be fine. Please forgive me for not being able to write in more detail. Say hello to the family, give Gudrun a kiss from her father. Let it be over soon!

Your Sepp

East of Mont Fleury, France, June 7th, 1944

Throughout the night, the men of PzRgt 2 had remained on combat readiness, engaged in small skirmishes with the enemy's rearguard, who fled westward in a panic to a beach the Allies called Gold Beach. All night long, the panzers of the regiment had been on the attack. They had advanced over the dunes, repeatedly fighting enemy tanks. Every small defeat over the enemy was costly and further slowed down their advance. British and Canadian infantry with PIAT man-portable anti-tank weapons lay entrenched everywhere in small holes and hollows, waiting for German panzers.

Lieutenant Engelmann, who now was in command of the 9th Company, had lost two more panzers during the night. Anna 4 had suffered engine failure after two PIAT hits and had had to be abandoned. Of the 2nd Platoon, code-named

Berta, one tank had fallen victim to a dug-in Sherman. Two crew members had managed to dismount the burning wreck severely wounded.

Thus, after a good 20 hours in combat, the 9th Company consisted of only half its original strength, and this, although the repair units in the hinterland were once again performing miracles. Two broken-down tanks had already been repaired. The 1st Platoon, which Engelmann commanded in parallel with the company, consisted of three T-34 tanks with German Pz III turrets. Berta, the 2nd Platoon, presently had two Panzer IIIs and a Canadian Sherman, which served as a replacement vehicle for some hapless tank men. This was actually against regulations because every piece of captured materiel had to be handed in, checked, and entered into the material lists before it could be used by the troops, but who cared about that in the light of the greatest invasion in human history? The 3rd Platoon, code-named Claudia, had two Panzer IIIs at its disposal. Rita 1, the commander's actual baggage train, operated three Panzer IIIs.

20 hours of fighting, and I can count the company's tin cans on two hands, Engelmann mused, squinting into the dune-strewn foreland.

However, the German tank men were not allowed to take a break, even if fatigue and hunger battered their bodies. The enemy had landed on the beaches of Northern France with all his material and personnel superiority. The Germans had to destroy the forming beachheads, had to advance, and throw into battle what they had. The enemy had to be thrown back into the sea before he could gain a real foothold.

Further to the Northwest, on the Cotentin Peninsula, the Allies were already entrenched and started to extend their beachhead, threatening Cherbourg indirectly. The Germans had to strike now when the enemy still was weak and restricted to the beaches. Once he was granted to break through into the hinterland, the next waves of invasion forces would land on the coasts. If the Germans did not want to be crushed by the almost unlimited power of the

Anglo-Americans and their allies, they had had to strike now.

Engelmann and his men had already felt that almost unlimited power. Again and again, they had been caught in the fire of the enemy ship artillery. The grenadiers, advancing along with the tanks, were suffering tremendous losses in the terrible barrage they received all along. Meanwhile, Allied aircraft dominated the skies. Enemy fighter bombers roared closer, began to nosedive, and incessantly attacked German infantry and German tanks. With every approach of enemy planes, the fighting strength of the German troops melted away. But it was no use. There was no cover in the dunes against fire from above, and a retreat into the hinterland was out of the question. The enemy on Gold Beach had to be destroyed before he would evacuate his trapped troops. There could be no second Dunkirk. If the escape of more than 320,000 Allied soldiers had been prevented in 1940 on the beaches of very Dunkirk, who knows whether England would have been capable of an invasion of that dimension at all in those days. But there had been Dunkirk; the Germans had let 200,000 highly trained, experienced British soldiers escape – and now they had returned to finish what they had set foot on French soil for in 1939. The British landings from Caen to Longues-sur-Mer had failed – and all indications showed that the enemy had realized this – but there were still ten thousands of Empire soldiers in the area. The Germans could not let them get away one more time, or the Wehrmacht would have to face the same men again in two or four years. Maybe not in Northern France, but in the South of the country, in the Balkans, or in Norway, because the English would certainly not give up. Therefore, in the hour of the invasion, it was not only necessary to win; no, the enemy had to get such a bloody nose in his invasion attempt that they had enough for all time.

However, advancing across the bare dune sand was like a fatal running the gauntlet. Warheads from PIATs whizzed, and rifle fire hissed at the Germans from every hole and hollow. Besides, the enemy warships poured an infernal rain of fire over all stretches of beach that were under German control. They fired from a thousand guns at anything German that dared to show itself on the coast. Whole companies vanished in a matter of seconds; tanks blew up, their wrecks thrown into the air as if they were toys. Every step of the Germans, every thrust, every retreat, and every halt was accompanied by the gigantic naval guns' drumming. The Allied battleships and frigates and cruisers lay in the water off the coast, clearly visible to everyone. They formed a gigantic fleet resting on the Channel, unconcerned by any German navy that might exist. Brave German submarine commanders had achieved few successes, had sent some enemy barges to the bottom of the Channel – a drop in the literal bucket. They often suffered the same fate shortly after, since once spotted, there was no escape from the Allied invasion fleet.

The Channel was packed to the horizon with enemy ships of all sizes. Engelmann began to sweat at the sight of the sheer gigantic fleet that the Allies had gathered for their invasion. In front of this backdrop, the battle was sitting twice as heavy on the stomach.

If the Germans encountered enemy forces, they immediately had to charge against them; otherwise, the enemy would radio for a hellfire that would cause military units to evaporate as if they were raindrops in the blazing desert sun. The Germans had to seek the grueling close combat, again and again – they had to throw themselves into the deadly enemy fire, while every combat was accompanied by the Allied battleships lying in mute threat in the water.

The mere necessity of clearing the beaches of the invading troops forced the German units to stay close to the coast. However, an escape into the hinterland would also be utterly useless for another reason: The enemy navy's guns reached far beyond the shores and could still strike with precision even 20 kilometers out in the hinterland. And the enemy's artillery observers seemed to be lurking everywhere; they crouched in their hiding places, having been dropped by parachute the night before the invasion, and let rain down a shelling that seemed to originate directly in hell on German troop concentrations, on bridges, on barracks, on German howitzers. Engelmann felt as if all of Northern France was on fire.

Also, since nightfall, enemy planes had been flying attacks with such ferocious intensity that the German forces in the area melted away like ice cream in the midday sun. Again and again, the enemy fighter bombers blocked the view into the sky, swooping down onto the German panzers and destroying several of them. AA gun crews of the Wehrmacht fired to a fare-thee-well; however, they hardly had a chance to hit the maneuverable low-flying planes. The Luftwaffe's strange arrow-shaped fighters, which had protected Engelmann's company from Allied Double-Tailed Devils the previous evening, however, had been the first and last German aircraft the lieutenant had seen since the beginning of the invasion. Additionally, there were numerous enemy bombers. Formations that seemed to be endless flew into the hinterland. These days, the Allied forces might have gathered more steel over Northern France than the Germans had spread over the whole of Europe.

As if this was not enough, reconnaissance planes of the enemy were flying their courses high above. Usually, after such an aircraft's appearance, it took only a few moments until once again, well-aimed artillery shells from the ship's guns were raining down on the Germans.

Now, also, the constant roar of propeller engines penetrated the background noise. Engelmann, who was fighting his way meter by meter through the dunes of the Normandy coast with the vehicles of his company, narrowed his eyes to a slit and looked up at the sky. From the Channel, three enemy fighter bombers were already rushing closer again. In a blink of an eye, they were over the battalion's tanks. They flipped sideways over one of their wings and dove. Like eagles hunting mice, they dashed towards the tanks.

"Go, Hans! Go, go, go!"

Engelmann banged against the lid of his hatch while his

13

tank Quasimodo gave a creaking howl. The tracks gnawed their way through the soft sandy soil, slowly struggling forward. Thick clouds covered the sky, single raindrops found their way to the earth again and again.

"Siggi! The platoons should fan out. Fan out wide, man!"

Too late! The tanks of Berta and Rita 1 had moved up too close, standing together between the dunes like a colony of emperor penguins. The voice of Master Sergeant Kranz, the former SS soldier and platoon leader of the 2nd platoon, was heard over the airwaves, becoming hectic. A trickle of a second later, the low-flying aircraft released their bombs and went up again. The explosives dropped down among the group of German panzers. The detonations made a deafening noise, throwing up massive amounts of sand.

Engelmann's breath stopped for one moment. Spellbound, he leaned forward and stared through the small eye slit at the tanks of his company.

"Berta reports no losses," Stendal shrieked in delight. Seconds passed, the panzers slowly separated from each other.

"Rita 1 no losses either," Stendal finally reported. For a moment of relief, Engelmann relaxed, exhaling in liberation. At that second, a shell went astray, smashing violently into Quasimodo's turret. The ricochet buzzed away.

Sparks flew across the tanks' steel skins, as from the front, from the side, from everywhere, the well-hidden British and Canadians fired with everything they had. The III Abteilung, which in cooperation with a grenadier regiment was clearing up this section of the coast, had to remove one pocket of resistance after the other in bitter efforts.

The tanks of the 11th Company – Engelmann envied its commander for his 17 Panzer IVs in the modern variant H – advanced South of the 9th. Meanwhile, in the further hinterland of the coast, the 10th Company's panzers, as well as those of Stollwerk's unit, proceeded. Together they pushed in on the enemy beachhead, which reached just beyond Longues-sur-Mer. From the west, too, the Wehrmacht troops were engaging the enemy's landing site.

Again the endless shell hail of the ship batteries came in.

The first salvo struck close to Stollwerk's tanks, ripping the earth out of the ground as high as a house. The shock waves tugged at the panzers, pushed them around, twisted them, and sometimes even knocked the weighing tons tanks over as if they were made out of cardboard. Finally, Captain Stollwerk's tank was severely damaged by a nearly hit.

For a moment, a foul curse from Stollwerk dominated the radio frequency.

Meanwhile, the three P-38 fighter bombers of the enemy flew a large circle in the sky. Through his eye slit, Engelmann recognized that the pilots would make another attack. Once again, he ordered via Stendal his forces to farther fan out. Slowly, the 9th Company vehicles struggled their way through the dunes, with the infantry in their slipstream. When the fighter bombers dove again, the grenadiers threw themselves to the ground with hectic movements.

Autocannons echoed through the battle roar; all three planes were firing on the German Sherman, apparently furious that the Wehrmacht was using the Canadian vehicle for their purposes. Clanking sparks jumped over the steel of the battle tank. Fountains of sand and small bushes splashed around the Sherman, which tried to escape at full speed. The crew was lucky: no bullet penetrated the steel or shredded the tracks. The enemy planes turned away, and the Sherman continued to move. Suddenly, however, three Canadians, who had been hiding in a foxhole, revealed themselves. They were only 30 meters away from the Sherman, behind it. One of the Canadians was carrying a PIAT. He ducked and hammered the gun's monopod into the sand. The tubular anti-tank weapon with the spiky warhead was thus ready for action. In the next moment, there was a bang. The red-hot shaped charge missile bounced against the Sherman and caused a darting flame. Thick, black smoke developed.

Full of rage, Engelmann struck with his fist against the steel of his tank. Shallow fire from the grenadiers hit the Canadian PIAT shooter moments later. The other two threw up their hands.

The panzers of the 9th moved on. The tankers did not have to worry about the two Canadian prisoners of war because they were immediately welcomed by some grenadiers. Four landsers kept the two Canadians in check with their carbines. Then a young second lieutenant entered the scene, stomped towards the prisoners of war, and pulled out his pistol. Before they understood, the Second Lieutenant pressed the pistol against the first Canadian's temple and pulled the trigger. The man collapsed. The officer did the same with the second POW. When the two executed men stained the light sand with their blood, one of them still twitched constantly so that the second lieutenant used his pistol again on him. After that, he and his men moved on without further ado. Engelmann didn't notice anything of this scene, as he was focused on the area in front of him.

The forces of the Wehrmacht pushed forward bit by bit. The British and Canadians had no choice but to retreat. Rumors presumed that at Mont Fleury and Longues-sur-Mer, landing crafts were already busy evacuating the failed invasion troops. This had to be stopped as soon as possible.

More planes appeared in the airspace, 15 or 20 fighter bombers. They carried the blue-white-red cockade of the Royal Air Force. Gunpowder emerged between the maneuverable aircraft when a German 20-Millimeter anti-aircraft gun began to shoot at them. The AA gun's firings clattered across the battlefield.

Engelmann wiped the sweat from his forehead with agitated movements. His tanker cap was sticky, his hair wet. On the radio, reports were pouring in. Meanwhile, Münster chased Quasimodo up a narrow hill. A PIAT warhead sizzled through the air without hitting a tank. The grenadiers positioned a machine gun that then spat long bursts of fire up ahead. However, the fighter bombers in the sky did not seem bothered by the Engelmann's company in the dunes. Easygoing, the planes flew over the lieutenant and toward the hinterland. There, also, the battle was raging. The thunderous impacts of the ship's artillery roared over the high dunes in the rear so that even Engelmann could hear the numerous detonations inside his tank. He stretched up, opened the lids, and looked to the South. Somewhere behind the chain of dunes, Stollwerk's company, among others, was fighting. The enemy's naval guns were continuously giving the German tankers and grenadiers a beating there. The impacts threw earth, rubble, and bodies so high into the air that some were hurled over the dunes. And now, right there, the approaching fighter bombers were also swooping down on the tank companies. Engelmann saw the bombs being released from under their fuselages and tumbling toward the earth before disappearing behind the dunes. He watched the wings of the steel birds spitting rockets before the planes veered. As the bombs and rockets went off with mighty blasts, the 20-Millimeter AA gun fell silent – forever. The only German weapon in this section that could effectively fight aircraft was history. The fighter bombers were already preparing for their next attack.

Engelmann gritted his teeth. Long lines of enemy bombers appeared on the horizon, humming louder and louder from the hinterland, finally hovering over the beach and making their way back to England. The whole airspace was filled with them, with the so-called Flying Fortresses plus a sufficient number of fighters for protection. The firmament was literally covered with planes – with planes of the enemy. The steel behemoths darkened the sky.

Oh, Lord, give us strength..., Engelmann whispered. In the distance, the first buildings appeared. They belonged to Mont Fleury, a tiny coastal town. Against all odds, against all losses, against all attacks, the III Abteilung continued to move towards this tiny town, where the decisive battle for Gold Beach was to take place.

Bern, Switzerland, June 7th, 1944

Thomas Taylor's gunshot wound in the shoulder had initially bled heavily. He wore dark cloth pants with suspenders and a white shirt, on which the seeped lifeblood shimmered in a bright red. After Luise Roth had shot him, he had hurried out of the apartment stark naked, disappearing into a narrow side street, which was covered in absolute darkness because of the ordered blackout.

Taylor had had to grope his way through the darkness and had finally reached a backyard. There, he had gotten dressed and had taken a rag from a clothesline rope, which he had since pressed against the bullet's entry wound to compress the tissue. With his fingers, he could also feel the exit wound in his right shoulder blade. Although Taylor could hardly care for his injury without the appropriate bandages, he was lucky in the end: the bleeding stopped on both sides after some time.

Taylor had to be careful because, under increased activity, the wounds could easily tear open again, and he had already lost a lot of blood. However, he could not afford to be cautious because he was being chased – mercilessly. The entire Swiss police force seemed to be on his heels.

Temporarily, it had seemed as if everything would turn out well once again: After Taylor had reached the clothesline rope, he had collapsed in a moment of weakness. The fresh gunshot wound burned as if his skin had been peeled off, and vinegar poured over him. Blood poured out of the holes in his body in large amounts. His eyesight became weak and colorless; his sense of smell disappeared. His heart hammered all the way up into his skull. His thoughts raced. Emotions flooded his chest. Anger and sadness, pain, and hatred; all of these were fueled by vast amounts of adrenaline coursing through his veins. Finally, Taylor was not able to stay on his feet. His knees buckled; he simply collapsed and hit the pavement.

Taylor couldn't tell how long he had been lying in the backyard next to the clothesline rope – minutes... hours? Not with the best will in the world, he didn't know. At some point, however, the screeching sirens snapped him out of his trance. They were muffled sounds, rising and falling again, and they covered the whole of Bern. Air-raid warning!

18

Taylor prayed to God that the Americans would mistake Bern for Stuttgart that night and cover it with a real bomb carpet because, in such chaos, he would be able to escape from the city unnoticed. The warning sounds quickly died away again, and humming airplane engines could not even be heard in the distance. What remained of the background noise were the shrill sirens of the Bern police. Luise must have called them.

Taylor had had to pull himself up by the pole of the clothesline rope to get to his wobbly feet. At first, he almost fell over again, having to cling to hung towels, which he stained with his bloody hands. The sirens came closer, closer, and closer.

The pistol in Taylor's hand felt heavy. He could hardly hold it. His fingers trembled, his eyes twitched constantly. Unbearable pain pounded in his shoulder. But at least he could stand. Slowly he put one foot in front of the other, step by step. He staggered out of the backyard, staggered across the dark street. Suddenly he slammed into a large metal object, the impact almost knocking him off his feet. Taylor groped into the darkness, felt the metal of an automobile. It had to be Luise's old Maximag, parked opposite the apartment. Quickly, Taylor peered behind him and up the front of the building. All the lamps in the apartments had correctly been switched off – even in "his" apartment, which he had left in the twilight of dawn. What might have happened to Luise? Was she still there? Crying, desperate... Taylor had to shake like a dog to get rid of suddenly arising, disgusting thoughts.

For a moment, it crossed his mind to use Luise's car, even though he knew how stupid that was. Switzerland was not as desperately poor as it had been a few years ago, but many raw materials, including oil products, were still rationed. Luise always had enough fuel for the car through her father's friend, but far and wide, she was the only one with that privilege. The yellow sports car would stick out like a sore thumb on the empty Swiss roads, where more and more carriages and strange inventions like wood-powered trucks were being spotted again.

Taylor ducked into a narrow alley and hurried away. The surroundings around him sounded strangely muffled. Meanwhile, a shrill beeping had burned itself into his hearing. At that moment, Taylor's excellent memory helped him immensely. His mind was still working as it should. He could even now call up a detailed map of Bern and the surrounding area in his mind. He had to hurry. Somehow he had to get to the Reich, to France, or Italy.

At first, his path led him out of the Aare bight, away from the light sandstone buildings and the old town's arcades. Then he followed the course of the river for about 500 meters until it turned North. Taylor's course, however, continued to the Northwest. In the black of night, he crept through the modernized Länggasse with its large row houses and industrial quarters, finally reaching the Grosser Bremgartenwald, a natural park on the edge of the city center that had so far been spared from the Plan Wahlen. Deciduous and coniferous trees grew there. From here, Taylor's destination was once again the Aare, which, after making a few detours North of Bern, turned to the West at the border of the Grosser Bremgartenwald to the North.

Already in May 1943, shortly after Taylor's arrival in Switzerland, he had begun to make preparations just in case. He knew that if he ever had to escape quickly, he could not be seen on the main roads, so the bridges over the Aare were also off-limits. Therefore, he had hidden rubber dinghies at two spots on the riverbank; a little further away from Bern, he had also set up a total of eight hiding places over the time, where food, clothing, equipment, and 9-millimeter rounds were waiting to be collected.

Wounded, exhausted, chased like a fox on a fox hunt, he struggled through the Bremgartenwald. Somewhere among the tall trees, his strength failed him; he leaned against a trunk, sat down, and his eyes immediately fell shut. It was only the shrill shouts echoing through the undergrowth that awakened Taylor. Whistles were twittering among them. The darkness of night was already giving way to the day. For the moment, the world lay covered behind a gray veil.

Taylor heard them shouting clearly – the policemen who

seemed to be close on his heels. In long chains, they combed through the forest, shouting orders and reporting loudly. The boys were not particularly careful, but they did not have to be. They were in the majority, and they were well-rested; they had to assume that the German fugitive stood no chance. A faint smile trembled on Taylor's lips.

Arrogant Swiss! he thought. *These better traffic constables have no idea who they're dealing with!*

Groaning, Taylor straightened up, pushing himself to his shaky feet with the help of both arms. He weighed the pistol in his hand – he had seven rounds left.

Enough for at least ten Swiss, he tried to encourage himself, *as stupid as they are!*

"You guys! Over to the left!" Sharp shouts rang through the forest, unmistakably the Swiss dialect. Taylor peeked out from behind his log. He could see them. Policemen in dark uniforms were marching through the forest. The undergrowth cracked and crunched wherever the long chains of police officers moved through the woods. They were 200 meters away from Taylor, but apparently, they had not yet spotted him. More shouts rang through the air. Someone was giving orders loudly.

Bloody beginners! Taylor's features twitched before he turned and put one wobbly foot in front of the other. He groaned softly as he worked his way down a narrow slope. The Aare lay before him, the water shining between the trees. But the shouting and the rustling behind him got louder and louder.

Taylor clenched his teeth, swallowing the sharp pain that shot through his shoulder. Stitches in the side kicked in. His heartbeat pounded in his temple, but he forced himself to keep going. The voices and sounds behind him drove him on.

While Luise was at work, Thomas Taylor had regularly passed the time by intensive running training. At the same time, he had always used his laps to check all his little hiding places because if he needed anything in an emergency, it would be fatal if one of his stashes had been looted. Only last Friday, he had made sure that the rubber dinghy at this place of the Aare was still hidden well camouflaged by branches and canvas bags cut into strips. The boat, already inflated and ready to go, lay a little above the bank in a small hollow. It could not be seen from the hiking trails that ran through the Bremgartenwald. As long as the river did not have a severe high water level, his rubber dinghy should be safe.

His pursuers caught up. Panting, Taylor slid down the slope, limping toward the hollow with the boat. His left hand held the pistol, which became heavier and heavier. He could feel it getting all warm, boiling in his injured shoulder. The wounds had opened up from the exertion, bleeding terribly again. Taylor pressed the blood-soaked rag against it. He groaned. Pain, as if red-hot coals had been tipped into his shirt, raced through his body. Sweat was pouring out of all his pores. He was losing far too much fluid. Taylor was aware that he would not be able to keep up this chase much longer. He needed a break; he needed food. Otherwise, the policemen would soon pick him up off the ground. Taylor kept running. The growing stitches in his side tortured him. Each painful stitch knocked the air out of his lungs. His pulse pounded – pounded loudly. The hammering, the indescribable, eternal *pokpokpokpokpok* settled over his thoughts, over his senses. The pounding and beating of his heart determined everything at that moment.

"Stop! Freeze!" it roared through the forest in Swiss German.

In a flash, Taylor turned around, raised his gun. He fired without having a target. The recoil of the Parabellum knocked him off his feet. Taylor fell, sliding down the last few feet of the slope. He screamed horribly, brought himself back to his feet with a roar. Now he was on a narrow forest path, behind which the slope continued down to the river bank.

Agitated voices echoed through the forest.

I told you: traffic constables! Taylor thought as he groaned and started to move. Lukewarm blood oozed from under the rag.

If he was lucky, the policemen now lay under cover for a few seconds before they realized they were out of danger. That was valuable time, which Taylor desperately needed, but he knew that the way back into the Reich would be a long and hard one. Once he was out of the Bern area, the town police's dilettantes would be the least of his problems; for then, the Landjägers would start hunting him down. Unlike the town policemen, the Landjägers were militarily organized, well-equipped, and excellently trained gendarmes. They would put Taylor to the test with all his skills.

Landjägers or not! Taylor tried to distract himself from his unpleasant situation with casual comments in his mind. *After all, they are just Swiss!* Again, a sardonic grin tried to fight its way to the surface, but this time it didn't succeed. Taylor's face was too contorted and disfigured by the pain and exhaustion.

In front of him, there was the place where he had hidden the boat. It was perfectly camouflaged into the natural environment. Further down, the forest merged into a muddy waterside interspersed with shimmering green duckweed. The thick trunk of a white willow was half in the water at the bottom of the hollow, warding off the current. It thus transformed a small part of the bank into a body of standing water covered with a whitish film.

Taylor reached the hollow. It took a huge load off his mind to see the boat lying intact in front of him. Quickly he looked up the slope. There was still not a single policeman on the hilltop, but they were already moving again. Taylor could hear their shouts, their footsteps, their relentless advance.

Roaring like a bull, Taylor pulled the boat into the water, climbed in, and grabbed the wooden paddle. Immediately, he thrust the paddle blade into the water, and grudgingly guided it back to give the boat a push. Rocking, his rubber barge headed out into the river, was caught by the current and was swept westward. That's how Taylor had worked it out. His next stash was a few hundred meters downstream on the opposite side of the River Aare. He would gain enough time to loot his stash by crossing the water since the next bridge was quite a bit further to the East. Taylor had also considered the current, so he would have to arrive at the other side of the river relatively precisely at the same spot where his stash was if he could drain enough strength from his weakened body for the paddling. But it just had to work!

A distant gunshot rang through Taylor's thoughts. Immediately he ducked down into the boat as if the rubber walls would offer him protection.

Silence.

No more shots followed. Taylor listened intently to the roar of the current. His pulse beat kettledrums inside his head. He held his breath. He heard nothing. No shouts, no more gunshots. Slowly, he leaned forward, poking his head out over the rubber of the boat. He couldn't spot any policemen at the waterside. Quickly, Taylor grabbed the paddle, plunged it into the water. He had to make sure he got to the other river bank! Moaning and groaning, he fought the biting pain. Fatigue had taken hold of his body, pushing him down, trying with all its might to dominate Taylor's senses. It tried to persuade him to just lie down in the boat and go to sleep – enjoying the rising sun that was already shining warm rays down on Switzerland. However, he struggled through the turbulent current, jumped into the water just before reaching the other side of the river. He let the boat drift away because he would not need it anymore. Taylor struggled up the embankment. His eyesight had gone entirely colorless; his stomach burned, his hands shook. How long would he be able to endure such a chase?

Determined, he put one trembling foot in front of the other. A paved path led parallel to the river along the bank. A large open space, enclosed by forests, stretched across the terrain on this side of the river.

The Swiss Plan Wahlen also affected the Bernese countryside: The open space was covered with carrots planted in long rows, their green tufts sticking out of the ground. Narrow footpaths interrupted the endless rows of carrots.

There were two farms a few hundred meters away to Taylor's left. They were his destination.

Some ten meters away from the farms, large buildings with red gable roofs emerged from the ground. There was a small cluster of beeches on the field, which, with their pot-bellied growth starting right at the trunk, looked like green drops of water pointing up to the sky.

Taylor limped over to the beeches. Meanwhile, soft but steady siren wails filled the air again. He might not make it to the edges of the forest, which were many hundreds of meters away in every direction from his position. Taylor felt his body was reaching the limit, that he was on the verge of collapse. He couldn't take it much longer. The thought of food, ammunition, and bandages waiting for him in his stash spurred him on once again, making his limbs take a few more wobbly steps.

Taylor thought desperately. He could not afford to lie down among the beeches, for the policemen would sooner or later search every millimeter of these grounds. Taylor had to reach the nearest forest.

Fuck the pain, he told himself. He had to hurry, had to do his best. He had only minutes before the police would arrive. The confidence in getting something to eat noticeably motivated him and activated his last reserves of strength.

Puffing, Taylor made his way through the dense undergrowth of the beeches. In the middle of the trees, he had buried the large wooden box. He reached the spot... and froze. A hole in the ground was where his box had once been hidden. Taylor felt dizzy; he had to crouch down, or he would have collapsed. Gasping for air, he closed his eyes and tried to get his breathing under control.

Seconds passed. The sirens became louder and more distinctive. Taylor's eyes opened abruptly. He grasped some branches of beech and pulled himself up. His shoulder was burning hideously. Taylor had gotten over the initial shock, and he had to move on. He was about to leave when a Swiss voice made him freeze: "Get off my property!"

25

Taylor squinted through the wavy leaves of the beeches. He sighted the outline of a man in a bright red shirt and soiled work pants standing between the cluster of beeches and the front farm on the carrot field. He had folded his arms and now whistled loudly between his teeth.

"Are you deaf? Get out of here!"

Again Taylor weighed the gun in his hand. "Shut up, you son of a bitch..." he muttered in apathy, struggling out from between the beeches and onto the field.

The Swiss froze as Taylor revealed himself. With open mouth and flickering eyes, he glared at the bloodstained and armed German. Taylor raised his pistol, pointing it with his trembling left at the man, who stood rooted to the spot. The Swiss did not move at all.

But Taylor did not pull the trigger.

Only six rounds left, he calculated his chances and possibilities in his head. Instead of shooting, he threatened the man with a shaky voice in High German: "Make sure you get away, or I'll blow your head off!"

Taylor lowered the pistol. The man spun around in a flash and sprinted toward the farm in a panic. He frantically yanked open the front door, disappeared into the building, and thunderously slammed the door shut.

The sirens were loud now. Very loud. They were close.

Taylor gritted his teeth before limping on. His eyes peered at the edge of the forest behind the field, which was some distance away. His whole body craved a drink of water. Why the hell had he crossed the Aare without drinking some of its cool water?

With his pulse pounding in his throat, Taylor started to move. Meanwhile, the sun in the firmament was blazing brightly. Scorching rays burned down on the earth. Taylor was sweating. A real flood of salt water poured over his face. He licked up what he could catch with his tongue, but the salty liquid only made things worse. His mouth became sticky, his tongue swelled. It was suddenly like a felted, thick sweater in his mouth. Taylor started moving again, trying a mixture of limping and running, not noticing a hand stealthily opening a farmhouse window and flipping open the shutter to the outside. A rifle barrel slid out over the window ledge. It was aimed straight at the staggering Taylor.

The shot echoed. Taylor could literally feel the hot breath of the bullet, which missed his head by millimeters. He immediately threw himself to the ground but instantly cried out in pain. He heard the clacking sound as the shooter repeated his rifle. Taylor raised his gun and fired a shot blindly in the direction of the window from which he was being shot at.

Five more rounds, his thoughts raced.

Again the Swiss fired. Taylor roared in triumph as the projectile tore through a carrot plant next to him.

"Why the hell does every fucking Swiss have a piece?" he hissed, pulling the trigger of his gun. The bullet shattered glass; the shooter ducked under the window ledge.

"It's about time we put this filthy country under German administration!" Taylor struggled to his feet. The click of the rifle's breech echoed from the farm, but the gunner was nowhere to be seen. With both hands on his P08 – his shoulder aching like hell – Taylor aimed for the window.

"WHAT THE FUCK?" he bellowed in a fit of spite that made him momentarily tune out his unfortunate situation. "Are you suddenly scared?"

At gunpoint, Taylor staggered toward the window. Noisy sirens accompanied his march. Maybe he had a minute left before the police would appear on site.

Taylor was in a rage. When he was halfway to the window, he fired. The bullet slammed into the room behind the window – a kitchen. Tin pots flew to the floor with a clatter.

The last few meters to the window, Taylor ran. Panting, he reached the ledge, but then his left foot slipped into a small hole in the ground, and he fell over. He screamed; the pain was so terrible. Immediately he pressed himself against the wall under the window. His twisted foot was suddenly very hot and pulsated.

"Fuck," he moaned. *Three more rounds!*

Gently and noiselessly, the barrel of the rifle slid over the window sill above him. Taylor stared upward with a grim expression. The gunman was looking for him! The muzzle of the rifle moved from left to right, then back again. The wood of the rifle stock scraped quietly across the window sill. Seconds passed. Taylor clearly heard the sirens wailing from the East. He had 30 seconds left – at the most. The gunman behind the window pulled his rifle back again, so the barrel was no longer visible to Taylor.

The German spy pressed the warm steel of his gun against his forehead, thinking feverishly. If he wasn't hurt, he'd jump through the window, grab the guy's gun, and beat his face to a pulp with it. But in his condition, he wouldn't even be able to stand up to a little girl in close combat. Taylor finally looked to his right and saw the front door to the building. Slowly, he pushed himself toward the door; his body always pressed against the building's walls. But it was too late. A police car, gleaming in the sunlight, roared down the street with a deafening wail of sirens. Taylor raised his pistol and pulled the trigger. Sparks sprayed across the body shell, and the driver stepped onto the brakes. The car turned over with screeching tires. Simultaneously, the doors burst open, and four policemen jumped out of the vehicle on the side facing away from Taylor.

"Give up!" an unsteady voice was heard from behind the car.

"Very funny!" Taylor groaned, pulling himself up by the doorframe, pressing the handle, and falling into the house. He slammed hard on the stone floor with his healthy shoulder, slamming the door into the lock with his feet while falling. As fast as lightning, he turned in the direction where the shooter must be.

Thomas Taylor found himself in a narrow hallway. A wooden stool stood in one corner, a crucifix hung over the door. All sorts of framed photographs were displayed on a small shelf opposite the entrance. A doorway led into the next room – the kitchen. Taylor could barely hold up his gun. Heavy as a tank, the Parabellum seemed to him, trembling in his hand. Outside, more cars sped up, came to a screeching halt. Car doors were slammed. Boots stomped across the street.

With a graceful movement, the gunman, the man who had tried to chase Taylor off the property, emerged from behind the kitchen doorframe. He immediately aimed at the German. But Taylor was quicker, crooked his finger, and fired. The bullet pierced the rifle's wood, was thus affected in its trajectory, and whizzed away upwards. It grazed the Swiss man's upper right arm before hitting the ceiling of the kitchen. The man cried out. His rifle fell to the stone floor. The Swiss immediately held his wound with his left hand and threw himself under cover behind the doorway's frame. His rifle remained in Taylor's field of vision, only two meters away! Frantic shouts echoed outside.

One round left, Taylor counted with rattling breathing, while his eyes and the muzzle of his gun did not leave the doorway. He felt the cold of the stone floor take possession of his body. His shoulder throbbed like hell, his foot twitched, swollen up thick.

I hate Switzerland, Taylor thought.

Pointe du Hoc, France, June 7th, 1944

Throughout the night, both sides had attacked each other with sporadic machine gun and mortar fire. The Americans were helplessly trapped. Perhaps 100 of them were left, but the Germans did not know for sure. In any case, the Americans had their backs to the wall. They defended the cliff's outermost trenches; behind them, the rock face steeply dropped 30 meters.

Now daylight had reached Northern France. From the East, weak rays of sunlight shone down on Pointe du Hoc. The sky was cloudy.

Less than 100 meters separated the trenches of the Germans and the Americans. Because of the short distance, the U.S. troops could not use their air superiority or the naval guns waiting to smash German targets. Nevertheless, the German tanks remained in the cliff's hinterland out of range for the enemy warships.

Berning and his men – Weiss, Reuben, Hege, and a few others – crouched in a narrow trench, careful not to stick their heads above cover. An alarm post, currently manned by the 1st Squad soldiers, kept watching over the enemy's activities on the other side with a scissors telescope. Otherwise, the motto was "wait and see," because while the Yanks were consuming their few supplies, the gunners and soldiers of Berning's unit were receiving fresh rations twice a day, plus ammunition and bandages when needed. The pro-German Frenchmen, who had stayed at the farmhouses in the hinterland of the cliff for the first two nights, were meanwhile over at the company of the 352nd Infantry Division in the trenches. They were fifteen men, carrying old hunting rifles. Better than nothing. Spellbound, the Wehrmacht soldiers waited for the enemy's next move, for the American was in a tight spot in this standoff, not the German. The division's HQ suspected that the enemy would try to evacuate in the night to come.

Let 'em piss off, Berning grumbled in his mind. *Better than more fallen because of even more fighting.*

Meanwhile, in the hinterland of the cliff, the German 155-millimeter guns thundered. They could not be operated from their prepared firing positions on the cliff due to the Americans' presence. Still, their shells nevertheless reached the invading troops west of Colleville-sur-Mer without difficulty. Since the day of the invasion, the firing boomed repeatedly; the crews had fired without rest at the enemy. Meanwhile, bush telegraph rumored that the enemy's venture was turning into a disaster for him.

A U.S. reconnaissance plane, which looked very much like the German Fieseler Storch, was making its rounds up in the firmament, calmly observing the situation on the cliff.

"Arrogant Yank!" Hege spat out and looked hatefully into the sky. The Americans had been able to destroy all German anti-aircraft guns during the attack on Pointe du Hoc, so the plane could circle the sky completely undisturbed. German planes were not to be seen.

"One would think this is their country!" Hege's face was contorted into a stubborn grimace. He lit a cigarette.

"Well," Reuben interjected, "it's not really our country either." Hege looked at the private first class blankly.

"What did you say?"

Reuben leaned over to Hege and spoke directly into his ear: "I said that this is not our country!"

"What is our country?"

Reuben waved it off. "Forget it, buddy," he shouted and smiled.

"I wonder what the Yanks are doing over there," Berning pondered, drawing lines in the ground with a stick. He thought of his old comrade Bongartz, whom he had left to die in Olchowatka. The bluish face of the suffocated lance corporal accompanied him every day and still tightened his throat. Anger about himself, but also grief, had a stranglehold on his thoughts. Berning would never be able to forgive himself for Bongartz's death. He had killed so many people in this war, but this one dead man, whom he had not even killed himself, weighed on him more than anything else.

"Starving," Weiss grinned.

"Yeah, yeah, they'll starve," Reuben confirmed, nodding. "By the way, have you heard that some NCOs are supposed to have disappeared from the 453rd Regiment?"

"Nope." Weiss shook his head. "Disappeared how? Did the brothers break?"

"Not a clue. They're just gone."

Time passed. The landsers took turns at the scissors telescope. It remained quiet. Not even spoiling fire was shot from over there. Probably the Americans were quite low on ammunition.

At some point, Master Sergeant Pappendorf crept through the communication trenches and reached Berning's squad's positions.

"Unteroffizier Berning, over here!" the master sergeant screeched. Berning groaned silently, but he pulled himself together and squeezed past Weiss and Reuben. In his head,

31

he reflexively replayed the night of the invasion to his mind's eye, when Pappendorf had sent him into every damn enemy fire – out of sheer spite, Berning was convinced.

"Jawohl, Herr Feldwebel?"

"Berning!" Pappendorf's lips twitched diabolically. "You want to earn the Iron Cross, don't you?"

No, Berning would have preferred to say. *I just want to stay here and survive. I don't give a damn about medals!* But he did not dare to speak his real thoughts. Instead, his heart leaped through his torso, at least that's what it felt like. Berning had a bad feeling.

"Of course, Herr Feldwebel," he sighed with tired eyes.

"I knew it!" the platoon leader was delighted. "I can count on you!"

On the ground, Pappendorf spread out a sketch of Pointe du Hoc that he had pulled out of his map pouch. All the trenches and positions were marked on it.

"If we don't do anything, the enemy will disengage from us during the night," Pappendorf explained. "That's why I volunteered to carry out a special mission from the company commander in order to nab that gang."

Berning was petrified. Special missions were his specialty, according to Pappendorf.

"I immediately thought of you." Pappendorf bared his teeth like a predator. Apparently, he had not yet forgiven Berning for what had happened with Rommel. The master sergeant visibly enjoyed putting Berning in charge of a possible suicide mission.

"Look at the sketch."

"Jawohl, Herr Feldwebel."

The Americans' trenches stretched along the edges of the cliff at one point. In the area directly in front of Berning's position, another communication trench led off in a transverse direction from the Americans' trenches but stopped after a few meters. The end of this very trench pointed directly at Berning's squad and was perhaps 70 meters away from it – 70 meters across open, flat terrain.

"That's where I want a machine gun!" Pappendorf's index

32

finger tapped on that transverse communication trench. Berning's eyes got wide and wider.

Is he serious? He was upset, shocked. He looked up, looked directly into Pappendorf's small eyes, which flickered wickedly. The master sergeant was serious!

It is not a suicide mission; this is a death sentence, Berning concluded. A thick lump tightened his throat. He had to stand up against this order, had to defy Pappendorf!

The master sergeant, however, continued to chatter cheerfully: "Grab three men, Herr Unteroffizier. Then come to me, pick up a machine gun, so that you can finish off the Yanks in close combat. On a yellow flare, we'll throw smoke grenades into the front area; then, you jump over. Make yourself comfortable in that communication trench over there, and get your teeth into it. From there, you can work your way into every corner of the cliff. Let the Ami try to get away from there again!" Pappendorf nodded at Berning with a severe expression.

Berning was paralyzed. He could not believe what was being asked of him. He had to open his mouth NOW, had to say something!

"There... there... there are at least 100 Americans in the trenches, Herr Feldwebel," he stammered.

"Hence the machine gun. Any further questions?"

Berning stared at his platoon leader, whose face had become a statue of iron determination.

"We're counting on you, Unteroffizier! You have ten minutes." Pappendorf nodded once more, turned around, and disappeared. Left behind was a trembling, anxious Berning. He returned to his men with a feeling in his stomach as if a ladies' team were holding a bowling tournament inside.

*

Hege had fought terribly against the order; Reuben and Weiss also cursed. But in the end, they had all realized that there was no way to avoid it.

Now, Berning, Reuben, Weiss, and Hege were lying in

33

readiness at the edge of the trench with an MG 42, submachine guns, and loads of hand grenades. With tense muscles, serious expressions, and a bad feeling in their bones, they waited for Pappendorf's flare signal.

"We're not going to survive this," Weiss whispered. Reuben nodded frightened.

"We'll make it, men!" Berning reassured them with little credibility. A fire of despair raged within himself, which caused him a tremendous stomach ache.

Then the flare rose above their heads, and chosen landsers threw smoke pots into the forefield. These burst open with a soft bang. Within seconds, a white wall of fog built up.

"Now go!" Pappendorf roared. Berning hesitated for a moment. But then he gave the order to engage. The four men climbed up the trench wall and charged into the fog. At once, they heard the firing of the Americans' automatic guns. They heard the whirring of the projectiles, which dashed through the fog. Berning and his men continued to advance. The sergeant's breathing hammered. His eyes narrowed. He sucked the acrid fog into his lungs so that a nauseating coughing urge spread through his throat. He should have had his men put on gas masks!

Berning heard his soldiers behind him. Their breathing wheezed, their equipment rattled. Their metal-soled boots skittered over the stony ground. In long strides, they sprinted through the mist. The very next moment, they unexpectedly slipped out of the white veil, standing in the middle of open terrain - in the Americans' field of vision! Berning spotted the enemy positions - 40 meters ahead! The fog had not spread out wide enough! Berning stopped.

Oh no, he groaned in his mind as he saw what felt like a hundred enemy muzzles aimed at him. With a tremendous burst of fire, the Americans opened up on them. Hege immediately grabbed his stomach, letting out a sharp scream. His machine gun fell to the ground, shattering, and his hands turned red.

"Retreat!" Berning roared. He heard the sound of bullets barely missing him.

"Back in the mist!"

Berning and Weiss each grabbed one of Hege's arms and dragged him behind them. Together with Reuben, who had taken the machine gun, they ran back into the wall of artificial fog. Hundreds of bullets were after them. With Berning in the lead, the Germans fought their way back through the fog, some of it already covering their platoon's trenches. When all at once their own positions in front of them emerged out of the thick white mash, Berning almost fell into them. Immediately he jumped down and pulled Hege behind him. The lance corporal did not utter a sound anymore. He was passed out, his eyes twisted. Blood gushed from his abdomen. Reuben and Weiss jumped into the trench after him, where they immediately took cover.

"Medic!" Berning roared at the top of his lungs. He pressed both hands on Hege's wound. Bubbling sounds emanated from the latter's throat. "Where is the godforsaken medic?" the sergeant asked a nearby private first class, who could not take his eyes off the blood. Now, however, he nodded and disappeared. Already Pappendorf was standing next to Berning.

"Unteroffizier Berning!" the master sergeant snorted angrily.

"Jawohl!" Berning yelled, without taking his eyes off Hege.

"JAWOHL, HERR FELDWEBEL!" Pappendorf raged. "Do we have to start all over again!?"

That was the moment when Berning was about to jump up and smash Pappendorf's face. Infinite rage overcame him. He was fed up with this shitty behavior for good! At the last moment, however, he pulled himself together. After all: He ignored Pappendorf's last statement and also his question. Berning also did not say the requested "Herr Feldwebel." Instead, he silently attended to Hege, pressing both hands on his wound. He tried to stop the terrible bleeding somehow. Pappendorf was shaking.

Pappendorf was about to explode. Several moments passed in which Berning could not bring himself to say "Herr Feldwebel," in which he paid no attention to Pappendorf at all.

"Berning! WHAT ARE YOU DOING HERE?" Pappendorf bellowed angrily. "Move out of the trench IMMEDIATELY AND COMPLETE YOUR DAMN MISSION!"

"No," Berning groaned.

Still, the blood gushed out from under his hands. He bent over Hege to apply more pressure to the wound. The lance corporal lay unconscious, no longer showing any reaction.

Weiss squatted at Hege's head and chattered at him, "Hege, you don't want to go that way," he pleaded. "Come on, buddy. You're still a virgin. We wanted to change that after the war! We wanted to go to Hamburg together! Please, buddy!"

Reuben plucked a bandage from his haversack with trembling fingers.

Pappendorf had frozen into a statue of incomprehension. His eyes narrowed to small slits. His hands formed fists. His body trembled under the tension. Desperately Berning paid no attention to the master sergeant.

"What did you just say?" Pappendorf whispered in a menacingly, calm voice.

Berning, however, cried out, "No, damn it!". He yelled as loud as he could. Then he looked up, looked directly at Pappendorf. "Bauer's hit!" Reproachfully, he pointed at Hege. "I don't have a machine gunner anymore!" Berning stopped abruptly, for slowly – very slowly – Pappendorf's hand moved to his pistol holster.

"What kind of Bolshevik shit is this you're pulling!?" the master sergeant assessed. Pappendorf looked in all directions, spotted a very young private first class watching the scene from some distance, and whistled at him.

"Jawohl, Herr Feldwebel?" the said private reported panting.

"You are now the machine gunner of Unteroffizier Berning." Berning glared at Pappendorf with a desperate look. The private first class, on the other hand, got all wide-eyed.

"I have no MG training, Herr Feldwebel," he reported meekly. Such a thing could happen when training was shortened further and further in order to supply the

36

battered Wehrmacht with fresh personnel.

But Pappendorf grinned maliciously. His hand rested on the pistol holster. His fingers played around its black leather. Berning did not dare to say anything. He waved over another private first class, instructing him to take care of Hege. With clenched teeth, the man pressed both hands on Hege's stomach wound.

"Never mind!" Pappendorf announced in the meantime. "It's like a rifle, only faster! Now get going, Berning! Get out of the trench, or I'll lose control!"

Berning looked at Weiss and Reuben for help. Both stared back with widened eyes.

"... I..." he stammered incoherently. He searched desperately for a way out.

"WILL YOU HURRY UP!?" Pappendorf roared suddenly, hurling his moist pronunciation into Berning's face. The sergeant blinked but jumped up and clutched his submachine gun. Hesitantly, Reuben, and Weiss did the same. The very young private first class grasped the machine gun hesitantly. Fear was in his eyes. His hands clasped the weapon completely clumsily. It was obvious to Berning that he had never had any contact with the MG 42. Still, Pappendorf preferred to fill the platoon's free time with tactics lessons and theoretical teachings about tank offensives.

"I'm counting down from ten now, Unteroffizier..." Pappendorf whispered, not taking his hand from his holster.

Berning was helpless. He had no choice but to dash back into this hell. He looked over the edge of the trench. All that was left of the wall of fog was a thin, transparent haze.

"The smoke is gone," he reported trembling.

"IS IT MY FAULT THAT YOU OAF ARE SO SLOW?!" Pappendorf screamed. "No one told you to come back here!"

"...but..."

"Don't expect me to waste three more fog pots on you!"

"... what? We should..."

"TEN."

"...you can't..."

"NINE." Pappendorf's fingers opened the holster.

"... that... that..." Berning tossed his head left and right. His heart flickered. His stomach turned over. Weiss and Reuben and the very young landser looked like guinea pigs who knew what the scientists were about to do to them.

"SEVEN!"

Berning grasped his submachine gun again. Briefly, he thought of simply killing Pappendorf. But that would only lead to his death by hanging. Once again, he took a quick look over the edge of the trench. Immediately thin fountains of earth burst up in front of him. The smoke was gone. They would not even make it out of the trench alive.

"SIX!"

"On my signal, men..." Berning whispered in a broken voice.

"FIVE!!!"

Berning, Reuben, Weiss, and the young landser got ready, tensed their bodies. The private first class fiddled with his machine gun so that it rattled.

"FOUR!!!" Pappendorf's fingers touched the grip of his pistol.

Berning exhaled loudly.

Well then, he encouraged himself in his mind.

"Stop the attack immediately!" Company commander Balduin's voice suddenly sounded. The first lieutenant had appeared out of nowhere in the platoon's trench and was standing behind Pappendorf. In his hands, he held a pair of binoculars.

"Watched the whole thing from behind," he said in a stern voice. The words put a grin on Berning's lips.

"We have no chance of success here. BUT: Outstanding performance, Feldwebel Pappendorf. You and your platoon can be relied upon! Do not shy away from the greatest danger! For this, you deserve the respect of the entire company, Herr Feldwebel."

Berning's grin disappeared.

"Thank you, Herr Oberleutnant," Pappendorf replied to the praise.

"See that Bauer gets to the casualty assembly place," with these words, Balduin disappeared. Hege was quietly babbling to himself, his eyes closed.

Pappendorf's gaze, however, focused solely on Berning.

Bernese countryside, Switzerland, June 7th, 1944

Taylor focused his battered senses on the rifle lying two meters away from him on the tiled floor. Outside was a hustle and bustle. People rushed about. He heard shouts. More and more policemen were streaming toward the farmhouse from all sides. Taylor was trapped, and to get out of the trap, he needed firepower.

Two meters... only two meters was the distance between him and the rifle. Two meters that became an almost impossible distance for the severely wounded Taylor. The Swiss carbine K31, the local conscripts' standard armament, held six rounds, if he remembered correctly, so at least four rounds were still resting in the weapon. Taylor, on the other hand, had only one round left in his pistol.

Carefully he stretched out his arm, his teeth crunching, swallowed the pain that tortured him. His ankle was thickly swollen, his shoulder burned like hell. Shiny, fresh blood stuck to his shirt.

Even with his arm outstretched, he was still a good meter away from the carbine. The Swiss weapon was out of reach. And behind the door frame, this scumbag was still squatting.

Taylor's panting breathing and hammering pulse lay like soundtrack music over the background noise. Still, he could hear the Swiss man, who remained on the other side of the wall, breathing heavily. Outside, more vehicles were approaching. Dozens of men audibly took up positions. The policemen were loudly considering how to proceed.

Bloody hell, Taylor realized for a brief moment the whole

mess he had gotten himself into. The exhaustion paralyzed his mind, made his thoughts slow down. The immense blood loss made him tired. His field of vision had lost color saturation. His skull was throbbing, boiling, and turning turkey red. Taylor was no longer capable of coherent fathoming. Only that rifle defined his mind; only that rifle revealed itself to him as the way out of his situation. All his senses – his whole, battered body – focused on that one gun, its wooden buttstock scarred by Taylor's projectile. But there was still the heavy breathing of the Swiss man hiding behind the door frame.

Gently, very gently, Taylor pushed himself across the cold tiles. His limbs ached. He stretched his right arm as far as he could. Centimeter by centimeter, he worked his way toward the rifle. Suddenly he stopped, literally frozen in motion. Behind the wall, a strong, moaning sound was heard.

How badly had Taylor hurt this Swiss bastard? Could the man still fight back? Would Taylor even be able to stand up to a fight by himself? He stared at his foot, which seemed to be the size of a soccer ball. Taylor's blood had already spread all over the hallway. His cheeks and forehead were white as a sheet, trembling, shaking. His lips were quivering, bluish. He had to stay awake! He had to get through this!

Taylor continued to work his way toward the rifle. Centimeter by centimeter, he pushed his shuddering hand forward. Finally, he felt the bare wood. Taylor grabbed it, pulling the rifle toward him. Sighting, he grasped the K31 with both hands and examined the rifle.

The breech was made of metal and resembled that of the K98, but apparently, the cocking handle had to be pulled straight out to the rear instead of turning it. Either way, Taylor would get a shot out of the thing...

Outside, the frantic activity of the policemen increased audibly. Taylor thought: *These better school crossing guards could storm the building at any moment.*

"You smart-aleck Schluchtenscheisser!" Taylor addressed the Swiss man behind the wall in clear High German. To emphasize his threat, he slammed his hand against the rifle breech so that it clicked metallically. "You are in a real fix!" Groaning, Taylor pushed himself up, his face marred by pain. He tried to prop himself up as best he could, but for all intents and purposes, he was just a pile of misery – after all, a pile of misery with a gun. But what could he do? How was he going to get out of here? Adrenaline and fear coursed through Taylor's body, controlling his thoughts and actions. Pure instincts ruled him.

In the next moment, something happened that Taylor had not expected: the Swiss man slowly came out from behind the door. He presented himself in the doorway, his eyes fixed and his face grim. He stared at Taylor. Long, bloody streaks were visible on the Swiss man's wounded arm.

"You have no chance of getting out of here, Swabian," the man said with his head held high.

Taylor was about to reply when a tinny voice was heard outside, apparently amplified by a megaphone: "This is Martin Durant, deputy commander of the Bern police. The house is surrounded! We know who you are! Surrender and come out with your hands up. You have two minutes; then we'll come in!"

Let them come! Taylor thought, unable to fully comprehend his unfortunate situation. Finally, he opened his mouth, roaring at the top of his lungs: "I have a hostage!"

Had the policemen heard that? Taylor listened outside, his eyes never leaving the Swiss man standing in front of him. There was no answer from this Durant.

All right! Taylor thought. *That'll keep them busy for a while.*

The Swiss, however, put an abrupt end to the idea of escape that had just formed in Taylor's mind.

"I will not be taken hostage," the man hissed.

The Swiss didn't give Taylor time to think but let actions follow his words. Determined and apparently unafraid, he took a step toward Taylor, never taking his eyes off him. A confident, aggressive flicker crossed the man's face. Taylor shuddered. He struggled a step backward, bumping the back of his head against the wall. His arms cramped, his hands shook as if they were electrified. The carbine vibrated terribly in his hand. Slowly but firmly, the Swiss pushed himself along the wall toward the door. Taylor stared at his opponent. He was doomed to inaction. Carefully he pulled his carbine closer because, with a long gun, he needed a certain distance from his opponent. Otherwise, the Swiss could overpower him in a flash. The Swiss, however, did not seem to be looking for a fight... he wanted to leave.

"Stop!" Taylor uttered in a fragile, hoarse voice.

The Swiss shook his head, pushed himself further and further along the wall. He had almost reached the door.

"STOP!" Taylor screamed, but actually, he was instead pleading. The Swiss didn't even look at him anymore. Confident of victory, he stalked to the exit and flung open the door. Taylor thought he saw a grin on the man's face.

"STOP, MAN!" Taylor roared with the last of his strength. The Swiss, however, went.

Scheisse! Shit! Fuck! Taylor's mind tried to catch a comprehensive train of thoughts. Without the man, he was done for. And that very man just threatened to disappear from Taylor's field of vision, running off all at once like a wild animal.

Taylor's head was empty at that moment. His situation, possible consequences, ways out... every thought had given way to a dark, empty void. Taylor raised his rifle, fired.

The Swiss stopped and grabbed his chest. A blink of an eye later, he collapsed. Immediately, the policemen were in a state of turmoil. Footsteps sounded everywhere. Panicked shouts reigned the area. They were coming!

Taylor's hands balled into fists. His eyes narrowed. He heard the policemen approaching the house from all sides, so clumsily did they proceed. At this moment, two men in uniforms dragged the shot Swiss out of the line of fire.

New thoughts flooded through Taylor's mind. He couldn't help but think of the political impact a captured German spy, murdering his way through a neutral country, might have in the world – how Germany's wartime enemies, trying to hide behind a righteous cause, would exploit his case for propaganda purposes. Taylor, however, would not allow himself to be made a political hostage. He would spare himself and his country this ignominy!

It was over, Taylor now knew. He had maneuvered himself into a mousetrap in which his options for action had melted down to one. Quick as a flash, he turned the carbine, put the warm metal barrel in his mouth. At that moment, Taylor knew no hesitation, no stopping. His mind told him to pull the trigger. And he did.

A metallic click was heard. No shot rang out. For a moment, Taylor remained in complete astonishment. Then he took the carbine muzzle out of his mouth and began to laugh. Taylor laughed loudly and resoundingly. That damned Swiss hadn't even completely loaded his gun!

Taylor let the rifle fall to the ground with a clatter. He still had the pistol! He reached for his P08 as two policemen sprinted through the front entrance with their guns raised. Taylor raised his gun. Too late! The policemen thought he was going to shoot at them. So they fired. Taylor collapsed in the hail of bullets.

Outskirt of Mont Fleury, France, June 7th, 1944

The sun, shining only sporadically between the gray clouds, descended leisurely to the horizon. Meanwhile, the defeat of the British and Canadians in this section was about to happen. While the enemy still held the Sword Beach to the East, the positions of the Western powers at Juno and Gold had been put under massive pressure by endless German counterattacks. Longues-sur-Mer was no longer in Allied hands, and from there, the Wehrmacht units charged eastward to conquer the tiny coastal village of Mont Fleury.

More than 8,000 prisoners of war were taken at Longues-sur-Mer, and a total of 17,450 British and Canadians had been taken prisoner since the beginning of the invasion.

Mont Fleury was in enemy hands, the last Allied bastion of Gold Beach. The British and Canadians fought grimly, apparently wanting to give their fellow soldiers fleeing with boats fire protection to the last round. Thousands of pieces of wreckage had washed up on the beaches throughout the afternoon; shattered barges protruded from the shallow water. Meanwhile, the Allies were mobilizing everything that could swim to evacuate their troops. Transport ships of all sizes raced to Mont Fleury's beach under German fire, loaded soldiers and materiel, and zigzagged away again, somehow trying to squeeze through the German bombardment.

The Wehrmacht concentrated on the departing boats because the Germans did not want to sink empty barges; they wanted to kill enemy soldiers, wanted to prevent a second Dunkirk. By the minute, boats were being torn to shreds, ripped apart by four batteries of eight-eights that had taken up positions on the beach East of Mont Fleury. The Allied fleet had to watch this spectacle helplessly; the commanders of the battleships and cruisers did not have the heart to intervene. Only every third ship made it out of the German antiaircraft gun's hellfire in one piece. Countless sank, dragging kicking bodies with them into the depths. The enemy's fleet, still dominating the horizon, also began to move. Slowly the mighty warships glided apart.

For Engelmann, who was waiting with his company in the dunes off Mont Fleury for the order to attack, the sight of the enemy's ships moving away was a real treat. One glance over at the eight-eights was enough for him to know why the Allies' bombastic vessels of war -- built to dominate the world's oceans -- were heading away, because: Once the AA guns were done with the fleeing invasion forces, they would turn their attention to the main fleet, would fire at anything within range. But the enemy fleet was not allowed to fight back.

Once again, Engelmann glanced over at the anti-aircraft guns, which were thwarting the enemy's escape with muffled blows. War sometimes brought out perfidious ideas – it made people turn their innermost being outward, which otherwise lay hidden and suppressed by a rule-bound society. The war, which, far from ideologies and nations, became a raw struggle for his naked existence for each individual, brought out man's true essence. Any attempt to impose rules on this elementary struggle was counteracted by the real armed confrontation. It was absurd to believe that specific international laws could restrict the brutal and fierce fight for the survival of ordinary soldiers – ordinary people. Whoever lay in the trenches, in the artillery fire of the enemy, no longer believing that he would ever see his homeland again, whoever witnessed the violence that the enemy brought upon his comrades, inevitably had to fear that he himself would become a victim of such cruel violence. He had to fear that projectiles the size of their thumbs would eat through his entrails, that brute blast waves would tear off his limbs, that hateful men would drive their bayonets into his stomach, that the hands of an enemy heated in battle would grip his throats and squeeze it tight. Those who feared such things no longer cared much about rules; they did what they thought they had to do to save their skin; they slaughtered the enemy most viciously, and they also developed a hatred for those who had surrendered; they often even developed a hatred for those who did not take part in the war at all, but only spoke the same language as the enemy. The war brought out only the worst – only the most human – sides in the men involved.

In this world war, a struggle that surpassed the Great War in its intensity and cruelty, not only men fought for survival. No matter who had sparked the fight, who had brought the most guilt upon themselves, in this war, ideologies, ideas, and finally, nations were also fighting for survival, in addition to the soldiers. The German Reich was fighting for its right to exist. Whether it had earned this right or not was irrelevant because, in the end, the strongest nation would win, not the one that deserved it.

And again, this struggle for naked survival brought out perfidious ideas.

Engelmann looked at the eight-eights, which were

equipped with armored shields and kept firing and firing at a steady pace.

The lieutenant looked at the approximately 140 prisoners of war kneeling in large squares in the sand between the eight-eight guns of each battery, guarded by soldiers with machine guns. These POWs were the life insurance for the guns.

Engelmann wrinkled his nose. It may be that the warring nations boasted that they were conducting the battle following the regulations of international law, but on the front lines, the reality sometimes looked different. Engelmann disliked methods such as the abuse of prisoners as human shields. He was disgusted by them. But there was nothing he could do to stop it – and secretly, he was pleased that the Allied forces were going down the drain.

In Engelmann's field of vision lay the coastal village of Mont Fleury. White ruins rose from the dunes, blocking the view on the beach. German explosive shells struck, throwing up earth and rubble. A thick cloud of smoke hung over the village. Dozens of fighter bombers filled the sky. The agile little Thunderbolts, dangerous tank destroyers, swooped down again and again. Engelmann thanked the Lord that they hadn't targeted his company so far, but he also knew that each dive further thinned the German panzer force. There seemed to be no match for Allied air superiority, and there was still not a single German aircraft in sight.

The artillery fire hammering into the village now changed. The gunners fired smoke shells in preparation for the Germans' decisive attack. Twice the British and Canadians, entrenched in Mont Fleury's ruins protecting the evacuation site, had already thwarted a German advance – but now the last resistance was to be broken. Enemy forces squatted in the rubble of the village with PIAT AT weapons and sticky bombs, but tanks were still there, too; Shermans, Churchills, and some of a new and potent type. Within minutes, Mont Fleury disappeared in a cloud of artificial fog. White smoke formed a thick cloud around the collapsed houses.

To the West of Engelmann's vehicles, Panther panzer's engines roared to life. The Schwere Abteilung -- heavy tank battalion -- would enter the village together with a regiment of grenadiers, while the II and III Abteilungs were to block all access routes to Mont Fleury. No one should escape, and the fog would let the invading Germans do their work undisturbed by enemy planes.

The Panzer V Panther, weighing just under 40 tons, was not actually considered a heavy main battle tank. The term was General Guderian's idea, who tried to increase the Panther's psychological value on both sides. He wanted to ensure that the Reich's latest tank development was perceived as a heavy, invincible combat vehicle.

"Von Burgsdorff has given the order to attack," Stendal reported in his South Tyrolean dialect. "The Schwere Abteilung is on the move!"

Soon after, a fierce battle sound emerged out of the fog. When the haze cleared after some time, German assault troops under the Panthers' protection had entered deep into the village. Thick, black smoke was rising from the wrecks of Allied tanks. But also, two German panzers lay shot to pieces in the streets of Mont Fleury.

Meanwhile, on the Allied part, a headless flight began in the direction of that narrow beach stretch, which lay directly behind the village. Boats continued to race back and forth in shuttle traffic. The eight-eights carried out a real clay pigeon shooting.

Engelmann's company stood ready to intervene at any time. Battalion commander Meier had ordered the 9th Company, the last unit equipped with Panzers III on the Western Front, to be used only for reconnaissance purposes. Therefore, Engelmann was to get close to the enemy if necessary, establish contact and keep an eye on him. Direct tank combat, however, was to be handled by the Panzer IVs and Panthers.

Hours passed, and night had fallen on Normandy. The sea sparkled in the light of the stars. Dozens of enemy planes were still circling in the firmament, but they were hardly able to do any harm at night. Suddenly, the 9th

Company and the 12th Company were ordered to move by radio. Some enemy tanks tried to break out of the encirclement in a southeasterly direction. They were thus heading directly for Engelmann's position, presumably an act of desperation in the face of defeat. Engelmann was to reconnoiter the enemy forces, and Captain Stollwerk – commander of the 12th – would then engage.

Well then, Lieutenant Engelmann sighed. He peered out of his turret hatch to the left, where Stollwerk's tanks started to move. Only seven panzers were left to the Captain after the hellish bombardment by enemy naval artillery and fighter bombers. But Stollwerk did not think of holding back. His tanks rushed forward mercilessly, rolling over the soft sand of the dunes. Already the 12th had moved in front of Engelmann's unit and was chasing toward the village. The engines of the 9th also came to life. Engelmann ordered to take up the pursuit of Stollwerk without fail. With a frown, the lieutenant gazed into the blackness of the night, which was penetrated by orange-colored fires in Mont Fleury and the faintly flashing blackout lights of the tanks.

While Quasimodo worked his way through the soft sand, his steel brothers of the 9th Company following him, Engelmann was annoyed with Stollwerk, who had rushed off immediately instead of coordinating first. The lieutenant was afraid that Stollwerk – bearer of the Iron Cross 1st Class – wanted to upgrade his medal. He hoped he was wrong because nothing was more dangerous than a tinsel-obsessed officer.

Flares rose above Mont Fleury. Tracer bullets hissed glowingly through the alleys; the screams of the wounded echoed across the dunes. The flares hovering in the sky like artificial suns gave the sandhills outline-less surfaces on which gloomy shadows were broken. Engelmann leaned forward; then, in the dim light of the flames, he recognized shadowy shapes standing at the entrance to the village, which could well be tanks. More flares rose, and Stollwerk's panzers were suddenly brightly illuminated. Muzzle flashes lit up the shadowy formations. The sand was thrown into the air between the German tanks.

Engelmann counted 19 enemy tanks that started to move, rolling into the dunes.

"Hans, speed up!" he yelled to his driver, then he gave the same instruction over the radio to the platoon leaders. In the forefield, one of Stollwerk's panzers stopped abruptly, spewing smoke. The meager remains of the 12th came to a halt and fired nearly simultaneously. Stollwerk's Panzer IV in the variant with the long barrel certainly had potent firepower. Against the backdrop of Mont Fleury flickering under the fighting's heavy fire, two of the enemy tanks fell apart at once.

"Stupid son of a bitch!" Engelmann groaned, banging his fist against the steel of his copula. At the same time, he cursed the fact that his company mainly was still using Panzer IIIs. Since von Witzleben had taken over the government, tank production figures had dropped slightly, which was why the Wehrmacht lacked modern combat vehicles at every corner. For this reason, Guderian had refrained so far from taking the Panzer III out of service.

This meant that Engelmann once again had to drive very close to the enemy in order to destroy him; once again, he had to put himself and his men in great danger. So much for the 9th Company not having to take part in tank duels! *Damn you Stollwerk!* Engelmann criticized his fellow officer in his mind.

The panzers of the 9th Company engaged the village, but the enemy had done his homework. Machine guns, nestled in the buildings on the outskirts, started cackling. Truly, they could not penetrate the armor of a tank, but they could blind them with well-aimed bursts of fire, forcing the commanders to go under the hatch, which in the darkness led to near disorientation. Sparks danced across Quasimodo's steel skin. Engelmann slipped into his copula, closed the lids.

"Berta, put those MGs out with HE rounds!" he yelled into his throat microphone.

"Copy that," Kranz's voice sounded on the radio.

"The rest stays with me." Leaning down into the belly of the tank, he ordered, "Siggi, AT round!" Lance Corporal

49

Jahnke nodded and slid an anti-tank round into the loading device. With a clack, the breech slammed shut.

Still, enemy machine gun salvos pounded against the steel of Quasimodo. Inside, the firing echoed as a deafening thunderstorm.

Berta's vehicles stopped, aimed at their targets, fired. Where the machine guns' muzzle flashes were, explosions ate through the buildings. More flares rose, casting their light like spotlights on the battlefield. Engelmann realized that Stollwerk's tanks were under heavy fire farther ahead. If something wasn't happening soon, the 12th Company would cease to exist. Meanwhile, the enemy tanks had moved up to form a steel front. Engelmann had never seen this type of tank, which he could now observe quite clearly for the first time against the firestorm in Mount Fleury. They were clunky but flat. Their silhouette was extremely low. And they seemed to be rectangular, with no sloping or rounded shapes. These tanks looked almost like German Tigers. And now they engaged!

A violent jolt coursed through Quasimodo as the pressure of a nearby impact tugged at the tank. At that moment, Berta fired another volley. The impacts continued to shake the village buildings visible in the flickering glow of war, but they failed to cripple the enemy machine gunfire completely. Tracer bullets raced through the darkness like fireflies on an arrow.

Engelmann tried to estimate the distance to the strange enemy tanks with his eye, which was extremely difficult under the circumstances. His panzers had almost closed in on Stollwerk's position. The captain had ceased his raid and was now trying to position his remaining tanks advantageously among the dunes. Another Panzer IV was already out of action. After several hits, the turret had become wedged; the main armament now pointed rigidly in front of the tank and toward the ground. Engelmann estimated the distance to the strange enemy tanks at 500 meters.

"Rita 1, this is Anna," Engelmann whispered in a hoarse voice.

"Listening," the company sergeant major returned.

"Come to a halt, and engage those tanks."

The Panzer IIIs of Rita 1 acted as ordered. They stopped, then they fired. The blast waves from the shots tore violently at their turrets. The shells hissed glowingly at the enemy tanks, making it possible to get a good look at the shots. Engelmann's gaze followed two rounds that dashed toward an enemy tank. Both hit. One simply disappeared; the other bounced like a tennis ball and darted sparkling toward the sky. There was no visible effect on the target.

So get closer, the Lieutenant growled in his mind, cursing at that moment all those who had been involved in the development and production of the damned Panzer III. *Damed 5-centimeter gun! Why don't they send us off with a horse and lance right away?*

Suddenly there was a crash and a roar. Quasimodo shook itself. The tank men inside clung to the fittings. They had taken a hit in the hull's front, but the Russian construct proved to be tough. The projectile had not penetrated the armor.

"All tanks except Berta move now! Reduce the distance to the enemy tanks!" Engelmann gasped into his microphone.

Meanwhile, Stollwerk was taking a severe beating, but the strange tanks were also firing on Engelmann's company. The impacts were close to his panzers, then suddenly, the platoon leader's tank of Claudia broke down. Smoking, the panzer came to a halt. At the same moment, Berta fired another series of shots. Once again, Mont Fleury's buildings were violently shaken, but the machine gun fire still did not cease.

"The engine's dead, but we're okay! Turret working," Kranz reported in a calm voice. More impacts dug into the dunes between Engelmann's tanks, hurling the white sand and flat bushes. The lieutenant wiped the sweat from his brow, feeling the violent hammering of his heart.

Fourteen enemy tanks dominated the forefield. Within the blink of an eye, Stollwerk lost another tank. A jet of flame hissed out of the open turret hatch. The British unleashed an incredible hellfire that just about swallowed the two

51

German panzer companies. These were on the verge of going down in it.

"Gottlieb, contact battalion command!" Engelmann screeched in a raspy throat. The heat stood like a thick mush inside his tank. Stendal changed the frequency to which Engelmann's headphones were set with a quick movement of his hand.

The lieutenant heard a crackle in the loudspeakers and immediately started to speak: "Brunhilde, this is Rita." Internally, Engelmann had stuck to his code name "Anna," but for external communication, he had to use the company's code name, which was "Rita."

Again, Berta's panzers, now well behind, fired deadly explosive rounds into Mont Fleury. The enemy's machine gun fire had weakened considerably. The strange tanks of the enemy, however, continued to fire from all guns. Again and again, the ground piled up just beside one of Engelmann's vehicles. Well hidden forward observers, who were located somewhere in the village, proved to be brilliant at illuminating the German tanks by constantly firing flares.

Stollwerk's unit was struggling to survive. The Panzer IVs maneuvered between some high dunes, desperately trying to escape the AT shells bursting between them. Only two panzers were still fully operating. Stollwerk himself had had to dismount from his vehicle and was lying in the sand with his pistol at the ready. Another of his tanks had received a hit on the left track. It now turned desperately in circles to not become a too-easy target and at the same time somehow get the English tanks in front of its muzzle.

"BRUNHILDE, THIS IS RITA!" Engelmann roared into the microphone as seconds passed without a response.

"Brunhilde," Major Meier finally spoke up, commander of III Abteilung.

"YES, THIS IS RITA! WE ARE UNDER HEAVY FIRE AT THE EASTERN SIDE OF THE TOWN. Enemy tanks in strength 14 at least! 12th Company almost completely out of action! Need support, IMMEDIATELY!" Münster looked up at his commander with a puzzled expression, but the lieutenant didn't notice. Instead, Engelmann listened to Meier's reply, "Stay out of this, Rita! Those are Cromwell tanks – brand new tin cans from the Tommys. They'll shoot you down in flames!"

You don't say!

"Get into position, keep moving. Continue to attract the attention of the Tommys! The 10th from south-southwest on the way." Of course, the British could have listened in on the radio transmissions, but there was often no time to conceal communications in combat. Engelmann had the orders transmitted to the other crews via Stendal. His panzers made a full-speed stop, then jerked backward and took hull-down cover among the dunes. As they did so, they continued to fire at the enemy. Fat tracer rounds whizzed through the night against the background of the burning Mont Fleury. Those Cromwell tanks swallowed the shelling like candy, while around the 9th Company, the whole landscape flew apart. Stollwerk's tanks were no longer visible in the flickering light of battle; dark clouds of smoke shrouded their position.

"Brunhilde to Rita and Wels. Keep your heads down; we have a surprise for the Tommys!"

Engelmann did not have time to think about the nature of the surprise. Already there was a terrible hissing in the air, and then the rockets of a Nebelwerfer battery of launchers came hurtling with a tremendous roar. These rockets, which swooshed in large groups through the night sky with long tails of fire, fell between the Cromwells and near the outer buildings of Mont Fleury. Them detonating puffed up the noise of battle into a cacophony of destruction. Meanwhile, more and more rockets hammered the enemy into the ground. A thick wall of sand and dirt settled over the British positions.

For the moment, all enemy fire had died. The rockets would probably not defeat the Cromwells, but the concentrated fire at least petrified the enemy for the moment.

Meier, a good officer in Engelmann's eyes, had perfectly coordinated the combined arms effort. No sooner than the last rockets had fallen in front of Mont Fleury, the fog of sand began to clear, and the dark formations of Cromwell tanks shimmered through. Then 16 Panzer IVs of the 10th Company rushed onto the battlefield. They caught the British on the wrong foot.

The enemy needed a few moments to realize that he was suddenly being shelled from the side – it was those moments that sealed his defeat. When the Cromwells swung their main armaments in the direction of the newly approaching German tanks, half of them had already been blown to hell.

Twenty minutes later, the battle was over. Some Cromwells lay abandoned among the dunes. Others produced thick pillars of smoke that partly covered Mont Fleury.

"Good work," Meier praised over the radio, "take up positions immediately to block further breakout attempts. 10th return to the initial position. We'll wait until the Schwere Abteilung has cleaned up along with the infantry."

Engelmann had his tanks take up advantageous firing positions in order to be able to fend off any further escape attempt. At the same time, he himself drove over to Stollwerk together with Anna's other panzer. Perhaps they could help transport the wounded to the rear echelon. He also wanted to check on his officer comrade and finally coordinate with him.

When Quasimodo reached the tank wrecks of the 12th – blazing fires illuminated Stollwerk's position – the captain was climbing into one of the two remaining panzers that had not yet broken down or shot to pieces. Immediately he put on his tank helmet and linked up with the company frequency of Engelmann's unit.

"Josef!" the captain's voice was coming over the airwaves. "Three enemy tanks have gone back to Mont Fleury. I'm not going to wait here for them to come back. I'm going after them! Are you with me?"

Engelmann shook his head slowly. "I think," he replied coolly, "Brunhilde has given clear instructions."

"Whatever you say. For my part, I'm not made for

watching." The short conversation ended with that, while the engines of Stollwerk's two remaining Panzer IVs howled. Already the tanks were moving. More rockets from the smoke launchers chased over Mont Fleury and hit the sandy beach behind it. At night, the shells looked like planes caught on fire and crashing. Two lone Panzer IVs were rolling towards the inferno.

"Man, the captain, is a real son of a gun," Münster stated admiringly. Engelmann, however, shook his head. There was an evil fire burning in his chest.

Bénouville, France, June 7th, 1944

Master Sergeant Schneider knew that the British would try to get out their fellows from the 6th Airborne Division who were encircled on the other side of the Orne. The enemy invasion seemed to be turning into a disaster for him. The British, who had come ashore between Longues-sur-Mer and Caen, fought grimly for every square meter. Looking at a map, it became clear that they were trying to keep a corridor open for the paratroopers, who could only reach the British beachhead via the double bridges at Bénouville and Ranville.

Once again, Schneider had visited all the emplacements of his diminished squad. The grenadiers of the crazy captain defending the bridges were on high alert; accordingly, machine-gun nests they had dug all around the periphery of the double bridges and reinforced with sandbags were manned by four men each. The rest of the soldiers waited for their turn in the surrounding buildings or alarm posts on the strip of land between the Caen Canal and the Orne.

Schneider was satisfied with the condition of the defenses. Nevertheless, the loss of good comrades still weighed heavily on the minds of his Brandenburgers.

The grenadiers of the 9th Company, who had been bluntly used up during the British paratrooper attack like firewood thrown into the stove by their commander, that dimwitted captain, had suffered severe losses. They mourned dozens of casualties, which made the morale of the already discouraged elderly men shrink immeasurably.

Schneider even feared that the old men would desert at the next enemy contact, which was an attitude that unfortunately could be transferred to most men of the Infantry Regiment 744, at least concerning the units that were in charge of defending the bridges. The NCOs and officers of that regiment, on the other hand, appeared to Schneider as wannabes who knew the war only from the Wochenschau.

In France, it had taken its toll that for von Manstein's operations in 1943, the mass of battle-hardened soldiers had been pulled out of the units in Northern, Southern, and Western Europe in several waves. What remained were mostly the greenhorns, those in poor health, and the old Reichswehr soldiers – once just old enough for the Great War, now too old for this one.

Schneider repeatedly noted with unease what kind of indolence had formed in these units over the years. The soldiers had lived in France like a bee in clover. While the landsers on the Eastern Front trudged through deep mud, sometimes sinking in the mud and sometimes in snow, and had to endure life-denying temperatures for weeks in a dark hole, there were parties in France with French girls, the wine was drunk, sports tournaments were held, and the summer was allowed to be spent on the beach.

Schneider shook his head. He crossed the Canal Bridge to the West to take a look at the road.

No one should be surprised if something like the crazy captain is the result, he finished his train of thought.

"Mary, mother of Jesus!" a scratchy voice suddenly raged. Schneider stopped and listened into the darkness. Then, in the building that housed the 9th Company HQ, the door was yanked open, and a man leaped outside. Schneider recognized from the lanky movements, with the arms always swinging back and forth like electric eels, that it must be the said captain.

56

"Those darn Frenchmen!" the officer grumbled.

Speaking of the devil, Schneider mused, approaching the captain at a quick pace. Elegantly, he swung his Sturmgewehr 44 over his shoulder.

"What's wrong, Herr Hauptmann?" he asked hastily.

"Ah, Feldwebel!" he was delighted to see Schneider stumble out of the gloom in front of him. "You've come at the right time!"

"I hear that a lot." They both grinned, their teeth shining in the darkness.

"The damned underground has become active again!" the Captain cursed with clenched fists, which he raised up and down like a child who didn't get his way. "They must have cut off all communications between us and Ranville."

Schneider rolled his eyes, but the captain could not see that in the darkness.

Ranville is on the other side of France, he thought to himself, while the officer continued to rage: "I no longer have a connection to the Chief of the 12th from over there. I can't get your Fritze on the phone either. And the Regiment commander is pestering me!"

"Is he here?"

"No, calling again and again. I've already sent some messengers over, but I don't need to tell you what it's like with my grenadiers. They're so old I'm afraid they'll die of natural causes on the way!" The captain turned around in a circle with his arms flailing, constantly whining something about: "Oh God, oh God, oh God, that's a pretty thing!"

Schneider grinned; he had to think briefly that the captain, too, was no longer precisely one of the younger ones. At the same time, he nodded.

"You can count on me, Herr Hauptmann." Schneider tapped himself against his field cap.

"Ha! I knew that right away!" With both hands, the officer hit Schneider's shoulders, causing him to sway briefly.

The madman not only has a power of order, but he also has a powerful punch, Schneider thought, shaking his head before turning away. He was beginning to like that crazy guy somehow.

At a quick pace, Schneider made his way to the Canal Bridge. Of course, he did not help the captain out of his duty to obey. No, Schneider was pursuing his own intentions, respectivley, he would prefer to have the fate of the bridge's defense in his hands rather than in those of this grandpa grenadiers.

No connection to Ranville? That did not sound good. After all, there were no boy scouts with guns East of the Orne. The British paratroopers were professionals who would prepare their attack sufficiently instead of simply storming the bridges while shouting hurrahs. Schneider hurried. He rushed past the grenadiers' heavy machine guns, crossed the Canal Bridge, and finally reached the area of responsibility of his men. Among the bridge house ruins, Schumann and Schütz had made themselves comfortable under a canvas tent and were stuffing themselves with pumpernickel and canned meat. The Dschibril brothers, whom Schneider had received from Huber as compensation for the high losses in his squad, also lay hidden under the canvas. Yusuf was sleeping, while Mohammed was chewing on a dry slice of brown bread. The two guys from Libya refused pork for reasons incomprehensible to Schneider and the others. Then they were just unlucky on days like these when the rations consisted only of bread and canned pork. But still, the Dschibrils always found something in the German food about which they complained loudly. Calvert and Moseneke guarded the MG in the roundel emplacement on the other side of the street.

"I'm going to jump over to old Fritze and check out the situation," Schneider called out to the boys as he passed by the ruins. In the darkness, the men peeked out from under the tarpaulin as dark figures and nodded while munching. Schneider, on the other hand, now started moving briskly. He was not at all pleased that the connection to Ranville had been interrupted.

Maybe you're just driving yourself crazy, old boy, he said to himself, speeding up his pace more and more.

In front of him, the land disappeared in complete blackness. Dark areas shifted in front of his eyes. The waning moon was covered by gray clouds that night, which left Northern France without any glimmer of light. Schneider could not even sense the Orne Bridge in front of him. Nevertheless, he was running because as long as he could feel the asphalt under his feet, he knew that he would not run into any obstacles. Schneider was brave enough to run even in complete darkness. When he had made half the distance, he stopped abruptly, listening into the night. There was nothing. Insects chirped, the Orne gurgled softly. But otherwise, the scenery was quiet. Slowly, Schneider took a few steps forward. He held his machine carbine tightly because a lousy premonition was spreading through him. Once again, Schneider concentrated his gaze on the total darkness. Had he just heard something in front of him?

Suddenly there was a bang. A glaring flare rose into the sky, causing Schneider to freeze. The fluorescent projectile moved radiantly like a bright star along the firmament and brought light across the Orne Bridge. The flare had been fired from somewhere on the right bank of the Orne, where Fritze's men, among others, were located.

But when Schneider took a glimpse at the bridge, which looked like a gloomy steel skeleton in the flickering shadows, he held his breath for a moment. A hot stab raced through his heart.

Dozens of British were on and even in front of the bridge with guns at the ready. They fanned out to form a skirmish line. In the unexpected glow of the flare, the enemy soldiers were frozen into pillars. With their circular, canvas-covered steel helmets, the Tommys looked like ghostly monsters of the dark. Before Schneider could form a clear thought, a machine gun opened up where the flare gun had gone off before. It cut down the British with rapid fire bursts. The men threw themselves to the ground; some were hit in the bullet storm and knocked over like skittles. It could only be the Brandenburgers of the 3rd Squad who had opened fire, for what was lashing at the Tommys in deadly staccato was an MG 42. The grenadiers, however, were equipped with MG 34s. Schneider could hear the difference in the firing

59

sequence at any range. The successive shots became a long, rattling sound in the case of the MG 42. It was precisely this sound that lay threateningly over the background noise, in which the desperate cries of the British were almost drowned out.

It took seconds for the Tommys to get over the shock, but then they returned fire from all guns. Bren MGs roared, Sten Guns blazed. Countless muzzle flashes twitched through the night. The Allies, who, like the Russians, relied heavily on automatic weapons, were generally superior in firepower to any German unit. The MG 42 was the exception, but due to the enormous rate of fire, the ammunition was gone faster than the landsers would have liked. Besides, the high rate of fire put enormous strain on the material. Therefore, the shooter fired short, well-aimed bursts of fire at the embankment of the Orne, scattering salvos of deadly bullets again and again into the British. A second flare shot into the sky, but then the British also fired their flare ammunition. All at once, the battlefield was lit up like a soccer stadium. A wild gunfight turned into targeted attacks. More British stormed across the bridge.

Schneider had to assume that the enemy had somehow overwhelmed the grandpa grenadiers in Ranville. This was not good – and Fritze was mercilessly outnumbered with his two squads. Suddenly, thunder roared across the battlefield. Near the MG 42, an explosion flared up.

The damn Brits have once again brought their whole toy box with them!

Schneider turned on his heel and raced back to the Canal Bridge. Fritze would not last long without reinforcements.

The master sergeant rushed down the street with long strides, sidestepping, several times accompanied by the breeze of a projectile whizzing around. Schneider passed the roundel emplacement, where he was pleased to find that Calvert and Moseneke were on their toes and already observing in the direction of Ranville. He informed them about his obversations with quick words, then dashed on over to the destroyed bridge house. Schütz, the Dschibrils, and Schumann had already suited up. They wore field belts and steel helmets, plus Gewehr 43 and 44.

"There's trouble over in Ranville," Schneider spluttered.

"Already noticed," Schumann replied.

In brief words, the master sergeant gave away a sitrep.

"Mannerheim!" he then ordered. "Over to Wolle and tell him what I am up to: I'm going ahead with my squad to screw Fritze out of there. Wolle has to take over the bridge defenses on his own and is also to man our roundel MG nest because I'm going to get Jack and Fourie now. You'll be back in two minutes!"

"Jawohl," Schumann answered curtly, followed by a nod, though he pronounced the "jawohl" at the end very quickly so that it sounded more like "jawoll." Schumann was strong in running, immediately sprinting away. He disappeared into the darkness.

Yelling, Schneider gathered his squad. When Schumann returned, the Brandenburgers immediately started to move. Calvert carried the machine gun, and the other squads all were equipped with automatic rifles, which gave them quite a bit of firepower to counter the damn Sten guns of the British. Schneider hurriedly explained his plan while he and his soldiers ran towards the battle that took place in front of Ranville. Fritze's machine gun had apparently moved further inland on the spit of land between the Canal and the Orne because from there, tracer bullets were now cutting through the slowly receding darkness in a beating rhythm. The day broke.

When Schneider had moved to within 100 meters of the fighting, he put out his hand, hissing a "Halt!". Immediately, his men crouched down, securing a small perimeter around their squad leader in all directions.

Only a few tens of meters in front of them, the English faction had taken up positions. They were located north of the road that connected the two bridges. From there, they engaged Fritze's machine guns. Glowing projectiles darted from right to left and from left to right across the roadway.

The Tommys devoted all their attention to the German MGs. To all appearances, the Brandenburgers lurking in the darkness remained hidden from the enemy.

Good for Schneider.

"Listen up!" he whispered. "Half-left in front of us is a narrow hollow next to the road. We'll take up positions there. Surprise fire on my command!"

"Looks like someone's already made himself at home out there." Calvert pointed roughly in that direction. As if on cue, a British Bren MG spewed fire from where Schneider actually wanted his squad to be. The relatively slow rattle of the Bren mingled with the thunderous noise of battle, the bullets chasing like burning arrows toward one of Fritze's machine gun position.

"Shit, you're right! Thanks," Schneider returned.

"You're welcome, honey." Calvert showed his teeth.

"Yusuf, Mohammed. The machine gunners are yours! Shut down the British, and then pull up the Bren. On three short bursts of fire, we'll move up. Keep the MG going, so the Tommys don't notice anything."

The two brothers each pulled out a long dagger. The blades gleamed faintly in the glow of the crescent moon. Yusuf rejoiced like a little child.

"Allāhu Akbar", the Libyan whispered, and a threatening twitch played around his features. A blink of an eye later, the Dschibrils had vanished into the gloom. Schneider looked at his men, who were no more than shadows in the receding darkness, one by one.

"There go the maniacs..." Calvert remarked, looking after the Dschibrils.

"I don't want anyone to speak ill of our Dschibrils," Schneider stated matter-of-factly. "Muslims are great anyway."

"Germany would need a lot more people like that," Schütz tossed in. "I'd rather have them than the narrow-minded Catholics." The others nodded in agreement.

Suddenly, the Bren fell silent. Only a few seconds later, someone fired three short bursts into the sky, after which the gun hesitantly took up the firefight with the German machine guns, but Schneider could tell from the tracer bullets that the Bren was aiming much too high. So the Dschibrils were at work.

62

"Splendid comrades!" Schneider exclaimed before giving the order to march to his squad. Instantly the soldiers dashed across the road and reached the hollow. They jumped in and brought up their weapons in a flash, pointing the muzzles in the direction of the English.

"Heat them up!" Schneider bellowed, drawing his flare pistol and releasing a projectile into the sky. Yusuf, lying at the Bren, swung the machine gun around and pulled the trigger. At the same time, the Brandenburgers' other weapons went off. In one stroke, massive surprise fire slapped the enemy. The British, lying about 80 meters away, fell into a state of shock for seconds. They then responded and started firing at the hollow where they had just had a machine gun position and where Schneider and his men were now crouching. Hellishly hot bursts of fire flew around the Brandenburgers' heads.

Among the Tommys, however, there were some who had been hit. In the slowly shimmering light of the approaching day, men rolled across the ground. Pointed screams filled the air.

Schneider jumped over to Calvert under cover of the hollow, grabbed him by the belt, and pulled him down to cover, where he handed him the flare gun and holster.

"Take over here! I'm running back to the bridge!"

"Do you have to take a shit or what?"

"I'll see that I get to that captain! We need his men here to kick the Tommys out of Ranville."

"Are you sure? Are we talking about the same captain here? Not that he has his greandiers marching up in two lines. The first line reloads, the second line fires, or something like that. He's just going to put them all in the grave if he has them lining up against the Tommys." Calvert shook his head. "No, we'd rather deal with them ourselves than watch that maniac sacrifices his men."

"Leave it to me. I guess I get along with him pretty well, and maybe I can do something to influence him. Anyway, we need more men around here!"

"Yeah, well, tell them right away to bring their walking sticks so they can make it to Ranville, as well." A nasty grin crossed Calvert's face. Schneider continued, "Send out the Muslim brothers. Tell them to get in touch with Fritze. Keep the enemy tied up as long as you can. I'll be back as soon as possible."

Calvert nodded, turned to the men, barking orders.

But Schneider started running. He raced along the road toward the West. Behind him, the battle roared. In the approaching daylight, he could already faintly make out the Canal Bridge's outlines and the buildings behind it.

Suddenly, in an infernal din, great fireballs twitched over the buildings beyond the canal. The street and surrounding land were torn open under the impacts. Flares appeared in the sky. Just at that moment, an explosive round shredded one of the grandpa grenadiers' MG nests. Screaming men were whirled through the air like dolls. The only German anti-tank gun, lying in a sandbag position on the riverbank, fired exactly one shot before it too was silenced by a detonation.

The German bridge defenders scurried around like voles. Only one did not run. One stood there like a rock while the world broke in two around him. He just stood there, looking north, while thrown-up dirt trickled down on him.

At least it's not hard to find him, Schneider thought to himself. He adjusted his helmet, then leaped toward the bridge. He dashed under the metal superstructure of the crossing, hurtling straight into the roar. A voice in his head told him to turn back and seek shelter somewhere, but damn it, Schneider was good at keeping his weaker self under control. He reached the crazy captain, who raised his arms amid the conflagration, standing there like Satan himself.

"Ah, Feldwebel!" the officer's voice laughed through the roar. He was bleeding on his cheek, where a tiny splinter had pierced through the top layers of skin.

Schneider threw himself on the ground in front of the officer. "Get down here, man!" he abruptly barked at the captain.

The officer waved it off with the calmness of a train ticket salesman. Wiping his bleeding cheek, he said: "Slowly, boy!

64

I'm still collecting for the wound badge in gold."

"EVERYTHING IS BLOWING UP IN OUR FACES HERE!" Schneider pressed his body against the ground with all his might. He may have defeated his weaker self, but he didn't want to die at any price. The captain, on the other hand, remained calm: "That shows that you lack experience! This isn't the first time I've been through this, you know," he shouted against the roar and thunder of the drumfire. "You know, back in 1916 in..."

Schneider jumped upward, grabbing the officer by the scruff of the neck. With a mighty tug, he brought the man down before bending over him.

"We don't have time for stories!" he gasped. "The enemy artillery is taking the bread out of our mouths!"

"Ha! No artillery, boy! No artillery! These are British tanks firing!"

"WHAT? They're here with tanks?"

"Yup. Have taken the north of Bénouville and are now pressing against the bridge." The captain pointed north, where Schneider made out the outline of a wooded area in the darkness. Gray boxes slid between the trees. Lightning flashed where the enemy tanks fired.

"Must be Comets and Crusaders," the captain mused aloud, barely audible amidst the hellish noise.

"What the fuck? We're screwed if they show up here with massive tank forces."

"No, no, my friend. My panzers are already moving. Wait and see!"

"Your panzers? YOUR PANZERS? These Czech jalopies can't even..."

Schneider, whose anger threatened to overtake his mind at that moment, suddenly cut himself off. The ground, on which he was lying prone, began to vibrate violently all at once. Despite the explosions that tore up the earth around him, despite the blast waves that swept over his body like invisible fists, despite the burning splinters that screeched through the air, Schneider felt with unmistakable clarity the constant rattling that had gripped the ground.

A gigantic tank peeled out of the darkness in the West.

The monstrous steel colossus pushed its way deliberately up the road to the bridge, rolling within a few meters of Schneider and the captain before turning North and slowly driving toward the British tanks. Behind this armored behemoth, a second immediately appeared, followed by a third. Schneider stared open-mouthed at the giants. These things were over ten meters long and three meters high. An immovable, sloping turret with an enormous barrel was enthroned on top of the oversized hull. Immediately, the British tanks launched themselves at the German giants. AP rounds slapped against the hulls of the colossi. Whirring, they were knocked off and hurled into the air; others detonated against the armoring without producing any effect other than scratching the steel. When the most forward colossus fired for the first time, a tremendous shock wave swept over Schneider, tearing his helmet from his head. If only he had closed the strap! On the British side, one of the tanks was hit in the side. The detonation force lifted the tank and flung it onto its back as if it were made of plastic.

The captain suddenly had a grin on his face that reached up to his ears.

"Got new tanks..." he boasted.

"...I see..." Schneider marveled.

"It's the new Schwere Abteilung 666 with its Ferdinand II. 12.8-centimeter cannon, 230-millimeter armor in the front. Music to your ears?"

"A little..."

"Oh yeah. Tigers are also here. They will kick up a fuss now!"

"Then surely you can do without some of your men?"

"Why? Because of Ranville?"

"Yes! Did you get any report from there yet?"

"Well, sure. Connection's back!"

"I ran over there especially for you!"

"Yes, that was earlier. Now is now, Feldwebel. Ha! Change of situation! You know that!"

The artillery fire against the German positions near the bridge had ceased entirely. Instead, the enemy's shelling rattled toward the Ferdinand IIs, which swallowed the raining down explosive rounds as if they were rotten apples.

The captain jumped up, brushing off his uniform.

"So, will you give me some of your men?" Schneider asked, still completely taken aback by recent events. "You can stay here yourself," he added quickly.

"Oh, give me a break! Come in, have a coffee..."

"MY PEOPLE ARE IN A FIREFIGHT AT RANVILLE!" Schneider interrupted him. He had no time for the captain's games.

"Feldwebel, you don't know the whole story. We made a feint on the Tommys over there. They're done."

"You... I... oh, THIS IS TOO STUPID!" Schneider waved his arms in a rage, then he pulled himself together and raced back across the bridge.

Behind him, the Ferdinand IIs made short work of the enemy tanks. Dozens of the British tin cans burned and lit up the battlefield.

Schneider, however, felt an infernal rage in his belly. After all, the lives of his men were at stake! In such situations, he could not take a joke, then he was not up for stupid games. His choleric streak did the rest.

It all ends sometime, Schneider said to himself as he sped back. He had sprinted half the distance when he noticed that no more shots were fired at the Orne Bridge.

He ran on. In front of the hollow where he had left Calvert with the rest of the squad, Schneider made out a number of figures strutting around seemingly without a care in the world.

What's going on here? Schneider stood still for a moment. He gasped roughly, and then he jumped in great leaps over to the hollow where his men were lying. He dived into it, plopped down on his bottom.

Schneider was suddenly frozen to the spot. A surprised twitch crossed his face. On the floor of the hollow, the Dschibrils squatted on their strange little carpets. They bent toward the East, murmuring. Beside them, Calvert lay on the floor, rolling a cigarette.

67

"You look like you've seen a ghost," the South African grinned.

"What's going on here?"

"Oh, the Soutpiels have been taken POW."

"What?"

"Suddenly, a dodgy second lieutenant arrived with his armored infantry. He eliminated the Tommys. Had apparently been a prepared trap, only nobody told us." Calvert grimaced. "Same as always, because we're just the appendage. The Swede and the others are out front with Fritze, by the way."

"Oh?" Schneider let himself fall backward. He landed with the back of his head on the cool dirt floor and wiped the sweat from his forehead.

East of Colombiers-sur-Seulles, France, June 8th, 1944

Lieutenant Engelmann squinted through the dense canopy of leaves that hid his company from the eyes of enemy pilots. Thin, white clouds drifted across the firmament. U.S. Thunderbolts roared around up there, looking for prey. Again and again, the American fighter bombers made their rounds over the patch of woods where the III Abteilung was hiding. A low, steady hum reached Engelmann's ear after a while, coming from the North and approaching rapidly. The lieutenant's hackles raised, his fingers tightened around the edges of the turret hatch so that the finger's knuckles looked whitish. Bombers were approaching! Engelmann said a quick prayer in his mind that the four-engine Liberator bombers with the glass turret in the nose, which appeared on the horizon, would drop their bomb load somewhere else. And he was lucky: The 120 planes, which darkened the sky for the moment like a solar eclipse, flew over the positions of PzRgt 2, eventually moving on into the hinterland. Engelmann's luck would be the bad luck of others, for somewhere these vast birds of steel would open their bellies, somewhere they would drop hundreds of bombs on German formations – would wipe platoons, companies, battalions off the map within seconds. Already, the Wehrmacht's losses from airborne attacks were indescribably high. After the Germans had nevertheless advanced relentlessly during the first two days of the invasion in order, following Rommel's defensive concept, to throw the enemy back into the sea before he could establish himself on the French coast, a change in thinking now occurred. The armored units, in particular, had been hit hard, and now the Wehrmacht's mobile forces in Northern France were to be prevented from entirely disintegrating; thus, troop movements by day had to be avoided. Enemy air superiority was visibly paralyzing the Germans – and indeed in areas where the enemy did not have set a single foot on the ground. Since the beginning of 1943, enemy air superiority had become apparent on all fronts, and now the German soldiers in France really felt what it meant to have lost the battle for the skies.

The large group of Consolidated B-24 Liberators floated leisurely away. With them, the hum of the engines grew quieter until it could no longer be heard. The pilots had their eyes on the ground, searching for targets. Only in the morning of that day, the Allied air forces had caught one of the division's supply convoys, which should have been supplying the regiment with rations and ammunition. Most of the trucks had been shot on fire; then, the loaded explosives had blown up. Sixteen men fell, 33 were wounded. Thus, the aircraft with the white stars or the blue and red cockades on their wings were not only responsible for the Panzer Regiment 2 having to hide in a forest during the day, but also for the fact that ammunition and supplies were at only 45 percent – not to mention the men's rumbling stomachs. Nevertheless, the regiment had received new marching orders.

Engelmann looked down from his copula at the camouflaged T-34 hull of Quasimodo. All around him, his company's tanks lay in waiting position in a dense forest. It had been a genuinely Sisyphean task to maneuver the tanks into the grove under cover of darkness. Now the steel beasts stood there calmly, covered with leaves and branches, waiting for their next mission. The tank men crouched in their panzers or had crawled under them. No one dared to utter a word or otherwise make any noise. All senses were focused on the airmen who owned the skies. All work on the tanks had been completed, and the men were supposed to be resting, sleeping if possible. But with the muggy air carrying an immense humidity that made the uniforms stick to the bodies, sleep was almost impossible to think of. However, once night had fallen, there would be no more sleep any time soon, for then the regiment would roll toward Cotentin Peninsula. There the Americans had established their army and threatened to expand the beachhead, which they had been flooding for two days with vast quantities of soldiers and materiel. There the enemy stood at the gates of Carentan in the South and just before Montebourg in the North, thus controlling a section of 20 kilometers in length. And this he seemed unwilling to give up, for if the air raids in all other sections of the Normandy were already fierce, the skies over this particular successful landing section –Utah Beach – were littered with enemy planes that rained down a devastating hellfire on the German defenders without pause. The Americans had their frequently invoked foothold on French soil on the Cotentin Peninsula, and they were not about to take it back under any circumstances. The battle was fought with extreme severity by both sides. If the Allies were defeated, years of planning and an all-time expenditure of resources would have been in vain. However, if the Germans lost the battle for Normandy, another land-based front would soon have to be defended with troops from the North Sea coast down to the Mediterranean. Defeat in France would mean Germany's overall defeat. Another land front, only a few hundred kilometers from the Reich's borders, the Wehrmacht, already stretched to breaking point across Europe, would not withstand.

Engelmann sighed. He had realized how wrong his

70

preferred strategy had been and how right Rommel had been with his motto of striking the enemy on the beach and throwing him back into the sea by any means necessary. In fact, the lieutenant initially came down hard on Rommel's defensive concept, which involved positioning the mass of the units directly on the coast.

Engelmann had shared Field Marshal von Leeb's view that it was necessary to let the enemy come to be able to defeat him in the hinterland – where the naval artillery could no longer strike. To defeat him there with superior panzer units. The lieutenant had quickly learned that the enemy's naval guns were terrible but nowhere near as deadly as a sky infested with enemy fighter bombers. And those aircraft could appear virtually anywhere in France.

So if the Germans had let the enemy invade the beaches in peace first and then let him come into the hinterland for the fight, there would soon be no superior German armored units, Engelmann had understood. The Allies' numerical material superiority, which poured over the Cotentin Peninsula at that very moment, dwarfed even that of the Russians so that the Germans would quickly face a ten- and twentyfold enemy preponderance.

Moreover, the Americans were equipped with the latest technology. German landsers were amazed at the spoils of war they were making these days: Radios as small as palms, maps worked into silk cloth or paratrooper dummies that automatically fired blanks. And now the enemy was on French soil – had at least formed one beachhead, which Rommel wanted to avoid at all costs. Now it was a matter of pushing in there quickly before the Yanks could establish themselves lastingly.

But there could be no question of speed when the advancing Wehrmacht units had to leave 15 hours of daylight unused. Otherwise, they would be smashed by the enemy air forces.

Meanwhile, Allied pilots did their utmost to track down the Germans even at night. They continuously illuminated the roads, paths, and fields of Normandy with flares. The panzers of PzRgt 2 would have a real running of the gauntlet ahead of them when they set off for Carentan the next night.

Meanwhile, doubts troubled Engelmann. Doubts that it was already too late, that the Americans had irrevocably taken hold of the few kilometers of French ground they occupied. Rommel did not want to move combat-effective forces from the Pas-de-Calais area and march them toward Cotentin Peninsula, even though every man was now needed at the U.S. beachhead to beat off the enemy attack. Apparently, Commander-in-Chief France-Benelux was not yet fully convinced that the Normandy invasion was the enemy's main and only invasion effort.

Engelmann bit his lower lip. His stomach was also rumbling terribly; he had shared the last remnants of his chocolate with the crew in the morning. Of course, that had not made him full.

After all, Allied landing attempts had been defeated everywhere else. At Colleville-sur-Mer – code name Omaha Beach – an American attack had been repelled in unbelievably bloody conditions. 4,600 dead GIs lined the shore there, and close to 12,000 men had been captured when Allied evacuation efforts had become impossible due to Wehrmacht units that had broken through. Omaha Beach had become a bloodbath for the Americans, but the defenders had also had to pay their toll. Under long-lasting bombardments from the sea and the air, all German strongpoints in the Omaha section were horribly battered. Further to the East, the British and Canadians also had to admit defeat. They had attacked in alliance with free French, Belgian, Polish, and Luxembourg troops.

The beachheads from Longues-sur-Mer to Saint-Aubin-sur-Mer had been destroyed, more than 26,000 men had become German prisoners of war. At Ouistreham, just outside Caen, the enemy was still fighting grimly, having broken as far as four kilometers inland in places. But the Allies had realized there, too, that the landing had failed. The enemy in front of Caen was no longer fighting for a beachhead; he was fighting only to enable the evacuation of as many troops as possible. The British attempt to capture the double bridges at Bénouville and Ranville had also failed. Thus the remains of the 6th Airborne Division were trapped. It was a matter of time before the last resistance of the airborne soldiers was broken. Then Normandy West of Carentan would again be entirely in German hands, even if there were still scattered paratroopers and commandos buzzing around everywhere in the hinterland, presumably supported by the local population. But the Wehrmacht had to live with that, and it would cope with it. The only critical and decisive thing that happened on Cotentin Peninsula, and that was precisely where Panzer-Regiment 2 would intervene. Branches cracked next to Engelmann's tank, then Stollwerk knocked against Quasimodo's hull with a broad grin on his face. After another insane day's work by the repair units, the captain once again had three Panzer IVs at his disposal.

"Well, Josef? Still happy with that thing?" He laughed mockingly. Engelmann nodded curtly. What wouldn't he do for a Panzer IV?

"Do you know how the landsers call your tin cans?" Stollwerk teased.

"No."

"Racial defilement." Stollwerk showed his teeth.

"I think I'll stick with Quasimodo," Engelmann replied coolly.

Now Stollwerk's face became distorted. "What's eating you, old friend?" he asked bluntly. "Looking at you, one would think we were losing the war, so dark is your expression.

"I fight with a 5-centimeter gun against the most modern tanks of our time. What do you think I should look like? Like this?" Engelmann put on a wholly wryly smile.

"Don't take everything so seriously, Josef."

"We're at war, and bullets are flying around my head. What exactly shouldn't I take seriously?"

"Well, just that! Relax, clear your mind. You always act as if the war would be lost tomorrow."

"It's not won tomorrow, either."

"We're working on it."

"Mhm."

"Please! Don't tell me you can also find something bad about the situation here in France? We have defeated the invasion! The enemy has got his fingers burned; he won't try this trick again."

"The circus is not over yet. The enemy is still holding on to some sections of the coast."

"Oh, cosmetics, Josef! Pure cosmetics! We'll give it another good whack in the next few days, and then the Yanks on the Cotentin Peninsula will also run away."

"Whacking? Like you did at Mont Fleury? How many of your men fell there?"

All of a sudden, Stollwerk's face darkened. He narrowed his eyes, and his lips formed a grim line before he asked, "What's your problem, Josef?"

"My problem? Am I the one who throws himself recklessly into the enemy's fire? The one who needlessly risks the lives of his men? And I'll bet Meier wasn't thrilled with your solo effort at the end of the battle either."

"Oh, Meier," Stollwerk waved his hand, "is a man without format. We must finally understand what is at stake here in principle. Therefore, only a drive for action and the utmost severity are appropriate. We must not grant the enemy anything, but instead, the completely wrong signals are being sent from Berlin. Meier! That is an officer of the Witzleben brand. Humanism, clean war! These gentlemen fool themselves with such ideas – and they are doing lasting harm to the German people. Meier! Pah!" Stollwerk spat out indignantly. "The old troop officer lacks the necessary guts... just like you."

Engelmann listened, while Stollwerk continued slowly. He seemed to choose every word carefully, emphasizing every syllable: "You should finally understand that we are at war. No advance without risk. No victory without losses. This is how the game works!"

"Yes. And if a man is killed in your company, do you tell it to his mother, his wife, in the same way?"

"Yes!" Stollwerk glared at Engelmann like a predator. "Yes, just like that. That's the price, Josef."

West of Trévières, France, June 9th, 1944

The battalion was on the move. At half speed, the tanks pushed through the darkness of the night. Engelmann drove over the hatch, listening into the darkness. Through the camouflage light, he faintly made out the Panzer IV's outline in front of him. Behind Quasimodo, the tanks of his company rattled. In a long convoy, the unit moved along a well-maintained road that led past Isigny-sur-Mer and across the Vire river directly to Carentan.

"Ebbe, put the Abteilung on my ears," Engelmann demanded. Nitz confirmed and switched the radio accordingly. To Engelmann's delight and, at the same time, regret, Nitz had sneaked out of the military hospital, showing up at the company's panzers just before dark. Nitz had been severely wounded after his tank had taken a direct hit on the first day of the invasion. A pain-distorted expression, which in the past had always appeared when the master sergeant's back pain got bad again, was now permanently on his face.

Engelmann would have liked to order Nitz to return for medical treatment. In the end, however, the lieutenant could not bring himself to do that. The tough Nitz was older and more experienced than Engelmann, and all the men of Quasimodo's crew put together. So the lieutenant did not want to presume to make such a decision over the master sergeant's head. Secretly, Engelmann hoped that it was not false pride that had driven Nitz back to the unit. The master sergeant should actually have the necessary sense of responsibility to decide for himself whether he was still an enrichment or rather a burden for his comrades.

However, Engelmann no longer had a tank he could give to Nitz, nor could he dismiss any of the commanders. So Engelmann's decision was to reassign Nitz as his radio operator. To do this, Stendal had to go into the replacement. Though, that was nothing much because the young Sergeant would be assigned officer aspirant in a few days. As soon as there would be vacancies at the officer training course in Wünsdorf, Stendal would leave the unit anyway.

Engelmann had reorganized the company in addition to this personnel change: The platoons Claudia and Berta no longer existed, but Anna – now led by Kranz – and Rita had four panzers each again. If Engelmann's tank as the company command vehicle was added, his unit consisted of nine panzers, some of which were damaged. That was almost half a company again! And with their Panzer IIIs and T-34 misfits, they would undoubtedly have been able to impress any enemy tank unit in 1934.

Engelmann bit his lower lip. He almost had to laugh at such thoughts, but only almost, because basically, it was anything but funny to have to compete with a Panzer III against the most modern tanks of the Allies.

Engelmann listened into the night. Every now and then, he heard the enemy's planes circling the skies, searching for prey. Again and again, they dropped flares that conjured up colorful shapes in the sky. The German tank men could only hope to remain hidden in the dark.

"Just look," Ludwig marveled through his optics. "The whole sky is full of Christmas trees." Allied flares sailed down on parachutes, which their pathfinders dropped as markers for bomber targets. The night over Normandy glowed in bright colors.

Engelmann's eyes focused on the tank's outline in front of him, one of Stollwerk's unit. The captain's vehicles formed the tip of the Abteilung's convoy.

The trip was long and tedious. Engelmann's thoughts soon slipped away to home, when there was a terrible hissing in the forefield before a ball of flame tore the darkness apart. Immediately, the convoy stopped, the tanks rushed away from each other, off the road. Already the guns of Stollwerk's panzers were thundering. There was a flash of lightning to the right of the road. Screams were heard. Tank MGs rattled. Confused messages rang through the airwaves. Nobody seemed to know what was going on.

"Rita?" Stollwerk's voice was heard.

"Listening," Engelmann replied in a strained voice.

"Enemy infantry on right side of the road with AT

weapons. Breakthrough not possible, two of my panzers have thrown their track." Stollwerk had also been able to rearm to four panzers thanks to the repair units. "Need fire support! Half right, about 75."

"You get it!"

Engelmann ordered loading a high-explosive round before briefing Ludwig. They had to fire at random because lighting up the battlefield would attract every damn fighter bomber in the area. Ludwig pressed the trigger. The fireball of the projectile ate through the night.

"Ebbe, have the company fire half right at ten o'clock. Range 90. Hit or miss!"

"Half right, 90!" Nitz groaned, tormented by pain, then his words roared into the radio operators' transmitting equipment. Engelmann's company opened up as instructed. So did Stollwerk's panzers. A real inferno erupted in the area to the right of the road. Tongues of flame licked skyward, bushes and trees blazed up. Machine guns salvos chopped between them. After two minutes, the tanks stopped firing. The suspected enemy position was ablaze. Tree trunks lay across, a man wrapped in flames ran away screaming. Then several figures with raised hands appeared in front of the sea of flames.

"Rita?" Stollwerk chatted in delight.

"Here," Engelmann replied.

"Are you covering the forefield? I'm taking prisoners."

Engelmann made sure Ludwig had his hands on the coaxial MG and had the rest of the company briefed through Nitz.

"We have the weapons up against the enemy," Engelmann finally reported.

Dimly, he could make out what was happening in front of Quasimodo. The lids of Stollwerk's tank opened, then several men climbed out with pistols at the ready.

Engelmann counted seven POWs, who stood out as dark figures in front of the flames. By their helmets and equipment, he recognized that six of them were American paratroopers. The seventh figure wore a civilian dress, cloth pants, and a shirt too big for him. The man was probably a fighter from the French underground.

While the prisoners of war were being sorted, Stollwerk was already climbing back into his tank. Soon after, his voice rang out over the radio, "Wels for Brunhilde." Engelmann had had the Abteilung frequency tuned into his headphones and was listening.

"Brunhilde here. What the hell is going on?" Meier demanded to know. What made him a good commander was that he let his subordinates do their job first instead of immediately demanding reports or intervening from far away. After all, in the middle of a battle, one had more important things to do than report to one's superior.

"We got six prisoners of war. Yanks," Stollwerk's voice crackled out of the speakers. Engelmann frowned. "On top of that, I have two 13-12 with 08-03." Engelmann didn't need a translation from Nitz for that. He knew Stollwerk was referring to his immobilized panzers.

"Good work, Wels. To all: enter 04-01..."

Engelmann could not translate at 04-01 in his head, with the radio notebooks changing at irregular intervals. It took Nitz less than five seconds to provide the information without being asked: "04-01 is hull-down positions," he whispered. Engelmann nodded. Meier's voice continued to drone over the airwaves, ".... Commanders gather with me. Let's see about getting our heads down and treating the prisoners. Igel supports Wels with the 08-03s. And hurry! In an hour, it's getting bright!"

La Roche-Guyon, France, June 10th, 1944

Field Marshal Erwin Rommel entered his command post at La Roche-Guyon's chateau for the first time since returning from the military hospital. A whitish, long scar gleamed on his forehead. He had not yet fully recovered, complaining about headaches.

Moreover, he had had to skip the celebration of his wife's

birthday because of the enemy landing.

The sand-colored mansion with the black gabled roofs was situated on the bottom of limestone rock, on the top of which rested the remains of the old castle. Its terraces, where Rommel liked to promenade, offered a magnificent view. On the other side of the castle, the Seine ran in curving ways through the wooded countryside of Northern France.

The catacombs beneath the mansion were anything but peaceful at the moment. Telephones rang every minute, officers stumbled about, glancing at the large maps set up and drawing on them the situation's current developments. The old, rough masonry held a dusty, stuffy air in its rooms and corridors that made the men cough. Sweat and dirt on their skin combined to form a sticky, gray mass. Dim light bulbs dangling from the ceiling filled the command post with gloomy light. Major General Bodo Zimmermann, a tall man with short, slicked-back hair that had grayed at the sides, glanced after Erwin Rommel, who disappeared around the next corner to take a call. Finally, Zimmermann turned with an offish expression to a map of Normandy and the Cotentin Peninsula.

By now, the first British units had probably also landed on the peninsula. The Allies held a strip 22 kilometers wide, into which they pumped more soldiers and more tanks day and night. They had captured Montebourg, and powerful formations of Shermans were at the gates of Valognes. The beachhead was still unstable, and the enemy troops were no more than a small expeditionary force. Yet their landed forces were not strong enough, their soldiers not dug in deep enough, and their tanks not numerous enough that the Wehrmacht would not be able to push them back into the sea.

Of course, the enemy had already landed more than 115,000 soldiers between Carentan and Montebourg, but the Germans were still in the numerical majority. It was mainly due to von Manstein, who had been able to free up units from the Eastern Front to fight the invasion of France by smart frontline corrections and deceptive maneuvers – and who was now suffering the consequences. The day before, on June 9th, a large-scale, long-planned offensive by the Soviets in the southern and central sections of the Eastern Front had started, perforating the German lines to the hour and crushing the defenders beneath them. The Wehrmacht did not have much to do against the Red Army – it was even on the run in many places! Stalin and Eisenhower had truly coordinated perfectly. But for Zimmermann, Rommel's new chief of staff, Russia was a minor matter at that moment. The major general had his own war to fight in France. With eyes aching from overtiredness, he looked at the last remaining enemy beachhead of any significance on the situation map. Zimmermann thus directed his gaze to the Cotentin Peninsula.

Rommel threw everything he had at the enemy. Infantry divisions raced toward the beachhead from all sides. German panzers rolled through the vast orchards of Normandy, pushing toward the Allies.

On paper, the Yanks and British didn't stand much of a chance. They were landing about 20,000 men a day, according to reconnaissance estimates. Even if they could hold their beachhead for another ten days, they would not come close to matching the strength of the Wehrmacht troops facing them. But, as in any battle, there were some unknown variables in the calculation: How successfully would the enemy fleet, which sailed around the English Channel as if it were on a cruise, intervene in the battle for the coast, and how badly would the German forces suffer from enemy air superiority? Moreover, how skillfully could the Wehrmacht use its numerical advantage on such a tiny front line? These were the questions that concerned Zimmermann and all the other men in the catacombs of the castle.

Although the first successes were achieved and the Allied advance was stopped, these were still too fragile achievements. A well-placed attack from the Allied battleships' mighty guns could cause companies to disappear within seconds, not to mention the immense combat power of enemy aircraft. These were even capable of wiping out battalions, regiments. If they were lucky, they would shoot every single tank out of a division. In short, enemy planes and ships could destroy any German victory; could ultimately lead to the success of the enemy invasion.

Behind Carentan, however, the enemy advance had been stopped, and in front of Valognes, the Wehrmacht's strong anti-tank forces were a real obstacle. These were the first initial successes, which had to be consolidated and eventually expanded.

It's about time to improve our chances, Zimmermann muttered to himself. As if on cue, a beaming Rommel hurried around the corner with a note in his hand. The smile looked somehow strange on the otherwise serious Swabian face, but hopefully, it meant something good. The major general contemplated his chief's Knight's Cross for a moment or two, which sparkled between yellow and red collar patches in the dim light. Rommel's voice brought Zimmermann back to the here and now, with the field marshal joyfully waving the note: "I've just had the Chancellor on the phone again, Herr Zimmermann. He has put the Höllenhunde under my command!"

By all means, this is great news! Zimmermann nodded joyfully. The Höllenhunde – the hell hounds – had the potential to crush any enemy gatherings.

"Ha! And von Witzleben wanted to use these flying bombs against London!" Rommel shouted triumphantly in his Swabian dialect. "But I was able to make him believe that the American beachhead is big enough and therefore suitable as a target.

"How many Höllenhunde are at our disposal?"

"374 are ready for firing on the Somme, and more are on the way. Speer, the daredevil, has increased production in the last few months."

"What are your orders, Herr Feldmarschall?"

"Stop all attacks. At 2100 we will begin shelling. All available artillery batteries additionally give them a beating they'll never forget. Our units at the frontline should ready for attack. What is the status of Panzer Schwimm Regiment 31?"

"The commander reports full combat readiness in the area of responsibility."

"Tell me, when will the 5th and 16th arrive at the frontline?"

"The 5th is already on-site with the majority of its troops; the 16th will be in parts from dawn."

"Must be enough! We must not give the Americans time to rest. Tomorrow, at 1200 sharp, I want the Hell Hounds to stop; immediately after that, all troops attack. Tanks to the front, push in the beachhead with fast raids, and break through to the coastline. The bastards won't even know what hit 'em!"

Northeast of Isigny-sur-Mer, France, June 10th, 1944

Engelmann was sound asleep when the sharp, bloodcurdling scream of a cruelly tortured soul cut through the air. The lieutenant's eyes snapped open, and he jumped up. He almost hit his head on Quasimodo's underfloor. Next to him, Nitz also was awakened by the fierce scream that defined the soundscape as a long-drawn tone of agony. In a mixture of pain and confusion, Nitz looked around. Engelmann had no idea what was going on. Just as he was about to struggle out from under his tank – Jahnke and Ludwig were also slowly awakening and stretching out under their blankets – Engelmann noticed that one of the sleeping places was empty.

"Where is Münster?"

Nitz shrugged his shoulders. The scream became overly shrill, and it pierced Engelmann's marrow and bone. Suddenly, a tank engine howled, laughter reached the lieutenant's ear.

With a leap, Engelmann jumped out from under his panzer, wriggling into his tanker suit. Regardless of his disheveled appearance, Engelmann dashed off toward the sounds. The now high-pitched, shrill scream did not stop. All the noise came from the direction where the 12th Company had taken up position -- Stollwerk's company! Engelmann hurried through the woods. He leaped across a swath, smashing through the undergrowth in long strides. Sweat poured out of his pores, flowing in long streaks down his forehead. The sky, which could be seen through the treetops, was cloudy.

With every step, Engelmann got closer to the terrible scream. In front of him, he saw the outline of a tank camouflaged with branches. Another roar of an engine filled the air. Engelmann fought his way through thick brush, pushed his body through a row of bushes – and froze.

With eyes wide open, he looked at the gruesome scene before him: Stollwerk's tank stood between the trees with its engine running, the captain's driver looking out of the open hatch. However, the left track had caught a man's feet in civilian clothes and crushed them to ground meat. With the rattling engine, the steel track of the vehicle weighing tons paused on the man's feet, crushed into a fleshy pulp, and the man screamed terribly. That man, wearing cloth pants and a shirt too big for him, was tied lengthwise to a board, only his arms swinging free. And Münster stood over him with his legs wide apart!

Engelmann was shaking all over.

Münster fixed the man's hands while a sergeant of Stollwerk squatted next to the victim speaking in French. Stollwerk himself had his arms crossed, standing a few meters away, and seemed extremely satisfied.

"What does he say?" the captain wanted to know.

"He's just screaming," the sergeant replied.

"The guy should finally open his mouth!" Münster roared in a vile tone of voice.

"Relax, Feldwebel," Stollwerk replied, grinning sinisterly, "he'll talk." The captain signaled to his driver, who nodded and stepped on the gas. The tank engine hummed, and the tortured man shrieked in a mangled voice as the tank jerked. The next trackpad slammed down on the man's

83

shins, shattering them before the steel, weighing tons, crushed flesh and tissue as if they were insects. The man howled at the top of his lungs. Münster seemed to have real trouble keeping his wildly flailing arms in check. Stollwerk's sergeant talked relentlessly to the poor guy, who would never be able to walk again.

"What's wrong, Josef?" Stollwerk asked at that moment, snapping Engelmann out of a kind of trance. "You look so pale around the nose," the captain added provocatively.

And really: Engelmann was pale like a corpse. Nausea overwhelmed him. He swayed. He briefly supported himself with his hands on his thighs to avoid falling. For a moment, he almost threw up. He caught himself again, straightened up. Bloodshot eyes stood out from his suddenly ashen face.

"What on earth are you doing here, Arno?" Engelmann asked in a clear, distinct voice, containing a threat. And before Stollwerk could answer, Engelmann, addressed Münster: "Feldwebel Münster!" he ordered in all clarity. "Get away from that man at once!"

Again he turned to Stollwerk: "Leave that man alone now!" he demanded with an iron-hard undertone in his voice. Münster's gaze caught Engelmann's deeply shocked face for a moment, then he turned to Stollwerk in search of help. The latter put on a smile.

"I'm not going to leave that man alone," Stollwerk stated with disdain. The two officers faced each other. Hostile glances, scrutinizing their respective opponents, met.

"HAVE YOU LOST YOUR MIND? Do you realize what you are doing here?" Absolute shock lay in Engelmann's voice.

"Yes, old friend, I am well aware of what I am doing here."

Münster remained in uncertain immobility, while Stollwerk's sergeant, unperturbed by Engelmann, clenched his hand into a fist and pounded it against the Frenchman's head. Immediately he let more words in French rain down on the man, who had entered a kind of delirium.

Tankmen approached the scene from all directions, but

they kept their distance. Meier was not present, taking part in a meeting with the division staff at that hour. Engelmann and Stollwerk were, therefore, the only officers on the site.

"No." Engelmann shook his head, dismayed. "NO! You... you are torturing this man to death? What are you?" Engelmann stared at his counterpart with a razor-sharp look. "This is an outrageous war crime, which you..."

"NO!" Stollwerk screamed suddenly. "NO, Josef! I've been so waiting for you to say that because you're so wrong! Is this man wearing the uniform of a regular armed force?"

Stollwerk pointed to the tortured man.

Engelmann's gaze followed the pointing finger, focusing on the poor guy. The tracks that had driven his feet and lower legs into the ground glistened red. Chunks of tissue stuck to the trackpads and links. This time Engelmann could not pull himself together. He spat beige brown chunks and biting stomach acid, staining his uniform.

Stollwerk burst into a diabolical laugh. "What's the matter?" he taunted Engelmann. "What do you think the people look like that you've been shooting at with high-explosive ammunition, you fool!"

With great difficulty, Engelmann swallowed the rest of the vomit and wiped his mouth, trembling.

"If we let this bastard live..." Stollwerk pointed threateningly at the Frenchman. "...he will sooner or later attack us again from behind. We must eradicate this gang-like plague of France once and for all! It is a matter of the German People's survival, so don't give me that humanistic, sissy crap that's going to be the downfall of us all if we're not careful!

"Feldwebel Münster!" Engelmann's voice thundered. "I command you to let go of this man, dammit, right now...!"

"YOU DON'T!" Stollwerk roared, then turned to Münster: "You don't move from the spot!" Münster seemed at odds with himself. He glared at Stollwerk and Engelmann in turn.

"Münster, I just..." Engelmann started, but Stollwerk immediately interrupted him: "ARE YOU DEAF, JOSEF?" he spat. A tone of superiority dominated his voice. "Look at

85

your uniform, and then look at my shoulders! Think very carefully about who is giving orders to whom!"

Engelmann clenched his teeth. During Meier's absence, Stollwerk had the power of command. And Engelmann knew what the penalty was for disobeying orders or rebelling against superiors. But was he allowed to be stopped by regulations when he witnessed such injustice? Or was it even his duty as a loyal soldier to obey his superior in the certainty that he would make the right decisions? Engelmann hesitated.

"Josef," Stollwerk said suddenly in a calm voice. "Lie down, old friend. You look tired." The captain smiled mockingly. Engelmann stared back, stunned. His lips twitched. His eyes were glassy. His hands were trembling. Unsure how to act, he could do nothing but stare at his fellow officer.

Münster also seemed to think. Meanwhile, the torture victim had fallen silent. His chest was still rising and falling, but he had passed out.

"Haupt... Hauptmann," Münster suddenly stammered. "Can someone else perhaps take over here? I would also lie down now."

Stollwerk cast Münster a nasty look. "No, you stay here!" he determined.

"But..."

"I thought you wanted to see how we did it back in Poland!"

"Yeah, I guess..."

"Then you'll stay here!"

"Jawohl."

Engelmann watched the scene with his mouth open. Slowly, he turned around, took the first step toward his own company. His head was empty. Trembling and internally shaken, as if worms ate his guts, he made his way back.

"Well, Sergeant?" he heard Stollwerk say behind him.

"The Frenchman sang like a boys' choir," the person addressed explained in a matter-of-fact voice.

"What a pity. I thought I could even get the fourth verse

of the Horst Wessel Song out of him." The man's grin was audible in his words.

"Arno!" Kranz, who had appeared out of nowhere, hissed. "Stop that, Kamerad! In the name of God! Everyone's looking already."

Engelmann halted hesitantly. There was already a certain distance between him and the horrible events. He turned around slowly and saw Kranz going to Stollwerk like a tiger. Dozens of uncertain pairs of eyes watched the scene from all directions. Kranz stood menacingly in front of Stollwerk.

"Let it go, Peter." Stollwerk waved it off.

"No, I'm not going to let this go!"

Kranz was furious. Reproachfully, he pointed at the tortured Frenchman. "Why, Arno? Why?"

"Good heavens!" Stollwerk groaned. "Has everyone gone crazy now? There lies no benefactor of humankind under the tracks. There lies an enemy of the Reich, and that's exactly how I'm treating him!"

"Don't make it worse, Arno!"

"WHAT? WHAT, Peter? That almost sounded like an order, OBERFELDWEBEL!"

"Take it any way you want, but stop your inhumane doings!"

Engelmann watched the scene with an uncertain look. He felt that Kranz could need some support.

"Oberfeldwebel Kranz, step away from my tank immediately!" Stollwerk spoke in a highly official voice.

"No way!"

"Are you refusing my order?"

"YES, I refuse your fucking order! I'm not leaving until this man is under medical care."

Engelmann kept his distance.

"You refuse my order in front of two witnesses? Do you know the consequences?"

"Jeez, Arno!" Kranz was furious. "I've experienced enough shit myself. I've let myself be made a henchman of death often enough! War! Yes, yes, war, alright! But this?" The master sergeant pointed at the Frenchman with an angry wave of his hand. "This is disgusting. This has nothing to do with war."

"Yes, it does!" Stollwerk barked. "IT DOES! IT DOES! IT HAS EVERYTHING TO DO WITH WAR!"

"Yes, and when the French find him, they'll grab one of us. Then they'll put him through the wringer! And when we find the body, we'll set fire to one of their villages. Well, is this going to go on forever, until you can't get out the door without fear of being killed?"

"Yes, Peter. If it's necessary, yes!"

Engelmann stared at the fighters with wide eyes, but he did not move or intervene. He had already lost against Stollwerk...

"You're off your rocker, aren't you?" Kranz blatantly flipped the captain the bird. "You're such a disgusting prick that you make me vomit!" the master sergeant added in a shaking voice. The opponents glared at each other.

"Did you forget where you came from? Whose uniform you used to wear?" Stollwerk roared.

"Did YOU forget where you came from?"

"We're both SS men!"

"WE ARE GERMAN, DAMN IT! We come from a civilized, modern society!" Kranz's words resounded through the forest. "But you act like a goddamn bushman from Africa!"

With that, for a moment, he had silenced Stollwerk.

"With your behavior, you're disgracing the SS! We were an elite unit, but men like you have turned us into murderers!"

"Well?" the captain hissed, pausing. "How about now, Kranz? Are you the nice good guy who's going to report dutifully? So I can get my just punishment?" Stollwerk seemed confident of victory. At least his voice sounded like it. Kranz, however, shook his head. "I'll let your conscience take care of that. And now, in the name of all good spirits, I beg you to leave the man alone. Don't make it worse!"

Stollwerk gave his driver a furtive glance, then said indifferently, "Finish him off." Immediately, the driver proceeded. The track rolled mercilessly over the

Frenchman, dismembering his body and pressing the chunks of flesh and fragments of bone into the ground. Organs and tissue mass were pressed out of the body by the tracks so that the flesh burst from the man's chest and flanks before these body parts were also caught by the trackpads and crushed under it. At the last moment, Münster jumped to the side. His hands clutched torn arms.

"If you like, take him to the doctor," Stollwerk sneered. Kranz, however, shook his head in anger.

"You are disgusting me!" the master sergeant said, stomping off with a red head.

Engelmann knew that there was no point in reporting the incident. Meier was an honorable man, but with an old National Socialist like von Burgsdorff at the head of the regiment, the report would at the latest "ooze away" at this level. Even if the complaint reached higher levels, it was highly likely that nothing further would be done. Stollwerk was very popular with the landsers and was a master at wrapping his soldiers around his finger or threatening them subliminally. No one would remember this incident if it came to questioning, or they would immediately tell a story favorable to Stollwerk. In the end, it would be a testimony against testimony. Reich President Beck could ramble on about his doctrines as much as he liked; if the wrong people were sitting in the right places, nothing would happen. So Engelmann kept at it: He would accept the matter, would do nothing further. With a sinking feeling in his stomach, he went back to his tank. He couldn't forget what he had seen, and also Kranz's performance.

*

"Yes, gentlemen," Meier stated, clapping his hands together, "what do you say?" The Abteilung commander had gathered the commanders in the dim light by his command tank, where he had spread out a large map of Normandy on the front hull. Stollwerk had greeted Engelmann at the beginning of the meeting as if nothing had ever happened, and even now, the captain did not show anything. The others, of the ranks of staff sergeants and master sergeants, acted normally, although they had undoubtedly also heard what had happened.

However, Engelmann knew that there was a lot of support within the Wehrmacht for severe and harsh actions against the enemy. How else could orders like the Commissar Order have been implemented – at least partially – in Russia?

"While I was away, the good Herr Stollwerk did not remain idle," Meier meanwhile rejoiced. "He personally reconnoitered Isigny and came upon the fact that the criminals of the Marquis are hiding seven NCOs of the 253rd Infantry Division in the cellar of the town hall. They have been missing since the first day of the invasion. Besides, two American liaison officers are said to be there."

Stollwerk nodded without batting an eye. Engelmann could only wonder how ice-coldly Stollwerk lied about his findings' origin – and everyone played along with the game! Engelmann was stunned. He felt powerless.

"The Frogs planned to execute and horribly disfigure the comrades, then effectively place the desecrated corpses near German units. This is one hell of a disgrace." Meier shook his head in incomprehension. "This very night, a special operation will be set up to free the Germans and capture their tormentors. My dear Herr Hauptmann..." Meier slapped approvingly on Stollwerk's shoulder, "...I'll make sure you didn't do this for nothing." The battalion commander smiled broadly. Stollwerk nodded.

Engelmann suffered severe inner conflicts. Stollwerk's deed remained the dominant issue in his mind. The knowledge gained through it might save the lives of some comrades. With the hatred the French underground had for the German occupiers, the abducted NCOs might face a fate as cruel as that of the Frenchman that morning. Was it righteous to kill one man to save the lives of seven? This question troubled Engelmann at heart.

"Whatever," Meier continued, abruptly snapping Engelmann out of his thoughts, "the enemy is assembling his armored forces in unknown strength at Carentan, so there the decisive battle must be enforced at any cost. Once we have smashed the enemy's armored forces and captured Carentan and Sainte-Mère-Église, the Americans will have their back to the sea. Then, gentlemen, the Anglo-American invasion has failed. Therefore, I want you once again to impress upon your men explicitly the importance of the forthcoming operation."

Engelmann tried to concentrate on Meier's briefing with all his might, but the thoughts in his head were going nuts.

"The division intends to reach the southeastern outskirts of Carentan this night. We move into the ordered deployment areas and keep our heads down. At twelve o'clock tomorrow, we will enter Carentan in alliance with the 24th Panzer Division. The 24th will break through enemy lines on our left flank and advance to Sainte-Mère-Église and Valognes. In reserve are still the 5th Panzer Division and two infantry divisions, which will occupy the captured ground. As soon as you have reached the initial positions, keep in touch with my staff. I will try to pick up as quickly as possible all important information from our neighbors and higher command. I will soon announce the time and place of my issue of orders."

"Attack at twelve o'clock?" the master sergeant, who was currently assuming command of the 10th, asked. "What about enemy fighter bombers?" Engelmann had not even thought of this obvious question; he was so out of it.

"Rommel has assured us of sufficient fighter protection for the entire area of operation." The Abteilung commander looked at his men. They all had serious expressions at that moment.

"Let's hope those aren't just platitudes," Meier murmured. The other men nodded tensely.

*

In the night, the tanks rolled across the Vire, heading for Carentan. The flashes of thundering guns flickered on the horizon. But for the tankers of PzRgt 2, the war would not continue until the following day, at twelve o'clock, when the sun was at its highest, and the enemy fighter bombers were best able to detect their targets.

Icy silence reigned in Engelmann's tank. Since the incident with the Frenchman, Münster had not exchanged a word with Engelmann apart from what was necessary for his duties. Nitz, Jahnke, and Ludwig seemed to sense the trouble between their commander and the driver. They, too, remained silent.

Thus, with depressed hearts, the tankmen moved toward their goal. They reached the deployment area for the assault on the Allied beachhead without further incidents, while the sky was once again filled with colorful flares floating toward the earth on parachutes.

La Halte du Vey, France, June 11th, 1944

The countryside surrounding Carentan offered difficult terrain for tanks, mainly because retreating Wehrmacht troops had flooded the drained swamps around the village shortly after the start of the enemy invasion. Now Carentan was belted by flooded fields and wet meadows in which any heavy vehicle would inevitably have gotten stuck. The narrow Douve river meandered through this marshland and wound its way around Carentan. There were only two ways in for the German attack forces: From the East via the access road that led from Isigny-sur-Mer to Carentan, passing the transverse Vire, and from the Southwest from Sainteny.

It was incomprehensible to Engelmann that the Anglo-Americans had assembled their armored forces at Carentan, of all places, assuming that reconnaissance had insufficient knowledge of the enemy's real strength. Were the Allies speculating on being able to hold the narrow access roads long enough to land sufficient troops so that they could eventually break out of their beachhead?

The fact was, the 5th and 16th Panzer Divisions had to pass through the bottleneck of Carentan to reach the American landing zone. Simultaneously, the 24th Panzer Division advanced over the second main road, which led to Valognes via La Haye-du-Puits. Failure at Carentan would also mean the end of the 24th Panzer Division's advance, which would otherwise expose its flank. With massive enemy forces on every kilometer of the front, it was also essential for the German attackers to operate in the tightest of spaces and to proceed only in combined arms.

Engelmann's tanks had taken the lead of the Abteilung, which at the hour was pushing westward through La Halte du Vey. In front of Engelmann, the Vire flowed through the countryside from North to South.

Two crossings west of La Halte du Vey had to serve the entire regiment. Otherwise, a detour of several kilometers to the South would have had to be accepted. For this reason, two nights ago, the men of Pioneer Battalion 16 had taken over the securing of the bridges.

Engelmann's Quasimodo rolled ahead of the long convoy of tanks and other military vehicles, while on its left flank, the neighboring I Abteilung approached the second bridge. The I Abteilung hold ready as a reserve.

The problem was that the Schwere Abteilung 503, which temporarily reinforced the division, could not use the bridges with its Tiger tanks. Only in the early morning, an advance party had judged both bridges to be impassable for the super-heavy steel giants, which weighed almost twice as much as a Panzer IV. The Tigers had no choice but to take the southern bypass, where the sappers had built a panzer crossing over the Vire River. Unfortunately, the place for that crossing was poorly chosen because one had to use unpaved roads to reach it. Thanks to the floods, the tanks had to drive at a snail's pace. Anyway, it was no use; moving the panzer crossing would have taken much more time.

Engelmann had stuck his upper body out of the commander's s hatch and was looking up at the cloudy sky. Not a single plane was in sight – not a single Allied plane, but not one of their own either.

Well, as long as it stays that way, he mused. Ahead of him was a fork in the road, each way leading to one of the two bridges only a few hundred meters apart. Broad fields and meadows offered a beautiful view of the terrain to the tank officer. Single trees rose here and there. Engelmann cleared his throat. The tinny echo coming from the loudspeakers showed him that his throat microphone was working. The bridge was directly in front of him, a wide concrete structure built across the Vire, about 50 meters long. Holes in the piers and cracked asphalt on the bridge itself testified that American infantry had tried several times in recent days to get a hold of the crossing. On both sides along the bank, German soldiers lay in makeshift emplacements, and North of the road, some buildings stood together in which the pioneers had also taken up residence. Half-tracks were parked there, as well as a motorcycle and many boxes of supplies.

Squads of bushes, at this point man-high, with thick, light-green leaves, grew on both sides of the road and the meadows. Hedges, which had been planted in long rows like lined-up soldiers, grew behind the buildings. Engelmann spotted several apple trees with juicy fruits hanging from their branches near a homestead with a wooden barn in front of it. He was getting hungry. Once again, the suppliers had provided his unit with nothing but stale bread and canned sausage. Was it so hard to provide a hot meal? At least once a day?

A second lieutenant from the pioneers jumped out of the thicket just before the bridge. He stood in the middle of the road and waved to Engelmann, beaming with joy.

"Panzer halt at the man in front over there!" Engelmann shouted.

"Jawohl, Herr Leutnant," Münster muttered.

"Combat mode, Hans," Engelmann reminded him after a moment's hesitation. A quiet "Jawohl" was all Münster replied.

For a moment, a thousand thoughts rained down on Engelmann, but then he shook himself like a wet dog. He didn't have time for this shit! Engelmann forced himself to look ahead, where the second lieutenant was waiting impatiently.

"I'm now contacting the local troops, the rest keep eyes and ears open," Engelmann said into his throat microphone. Behind him, Kranz peeked out from the copula of his Panzer III. The master sergeant tapped his headphones and gave a thumbs-up.

Kranz's vehicles moved to the right and fanned out on the field.

He has his boys under control, Engelmann had to admit. A touch of envy mingled with his thoughts. He shook himself again. He had to concentrate on the essential things.

As ordered, Quasimodo came to a halt in front of the pioneer officer. The squeaking of the tracks stopped, only the steady hum of the 500-horsepower Maybach engine was heard.

Engelmann looked to the South, where at some distance, the Panzer IVs of the I. Abteilung – that unit had the Panzer IV in the long barrel variant exclusively – were taking up positions in front of the other bridge. What would Engelmann have given to have such a panzer under his butt again?

In a fit of sheer rage, he inwardly cursed von Witzleben and all the other fools who had had a finger in the pie in the decision not to take the Panzer III out of service but to let the troops "use it up." The fine gentlemen from Berlin should have put themselves in the last Panzer IIIs and used them up in combat with enemy Shermans and Cromwells! Engelmann snorted, then suddenly, he stopped.

What is going on? He didn't understand himself anymore. If he was usually bold and circumspect, now his emotions were boiling up inside him as if he were a hothead. Engelmann felt his pulse pounding in his throat. His cheeks had heated up, sweat beaded on his forehead. With a pinched face, he concentrated all his senses on the officer in front of him, who wore a gold signet ring on his finger.

"Moin moin, Kamerad!" the sapper officer, who must have come from the far North of Germany judging by his dialect, greeted him. "Are we finally making the American

95

get a move on?" The man rubbed his hands together, a smile of anticipation on his face. An MP 40 dangled from its shoulder strap.

"Looks that way," Engelmann grumbled. "What's the situation, Herr Leutnant?"

The pioneer ignored the question. Instead, he eyed Engelmann's tank with a displeased look.

"My goodness! What kind of a tin can do you have? Is that supposed to be that Panther everyone's been chattering about?"

"Yes, of course," Engelmann replied with rolling eyes. "I - command – a – Panther..."

"Bit small," the Second Lieutenant wondered. "Always imagined them bigger."

Engelmann's fingers tightened on the edges of his hatch.

"Look," he hissed, "let's leave it to official business, eh? The bridge is passable for my panzers?"

"Well, yes, it is. The way is clear."

"And over there?"

"Lies the 3rd of us."

"How far can you observe from over there?"

"To the outskirts of La Blanche."

Engelmann peered over the bridge. Over there, behind the sparsely vegetated embankment of the Vire, he recognized another wildly overgrown meadow with a bump running across it. Thanks to this, he could hardly make out a tiny French village a good 300 meters away.

"La Blanche is the one-horse town over by...," the pioneer explained, pointing a finger across the bridge.

"I know," Engelmann snarled.

"Yeah, sorry I opened my mouth!" The pioneer officer got snotty. Engelmann again wondered about himself. He couldn't wreak his anger, pent-up for whatever reason, on others! That was uncomradely.

"No, please," Engelmann returned ruefully, looking like a dog that had shat in the apartment. "Please excuse my behavior." The pioneer nodded curtly.

"I've had a rough couple of days," Engelmann explained himself.

"Okay! It's forgotten." Already a broad smile was coming back to the pioneer's face. Engelmann nodded gratefully before turning the conversation back to the essentials: "How about charges? Have you checked out the piers and the shore?"

"Don't worry, man. We sappers weren't born yesterday!"

"Did you check them today, in case enemy commandos were here during the night?"

The pioneer laughed in a stilted manner. "Please," he proclaimed. "How should that be possible? There's a company on each side of the bank, and we've got eyes like a lynx and ears like an elephant, I can tell you."

"Well, then!" Engelmann was not unaware that the I Abteilung's foremost tanks were moving across the other bridge to the South of him.

"Panzer, go!" he now also yelled into the steel belly of his vehicle before calling both platoons over the throat microphone. He ordered Rita to stick immediately to him, while Kranz was to cross the bridge last. Meier's orders were for the 9th Company to assemble in front of La Blanche to wait for the 10th's panzers. Under their cover, the 9th was then to capture the village in order to provide sufficient space for the remnants of the battalion. During the night, an outpost of the pioneers had already knocked off an enemy scouting party stalking the Northern edge of the tiny village. Whether the Americans were now at La Blanche was unclear. At the very least, however, their armored forces still appeared to be far behind the village. At Saint-Hilaire-Petitville, a tiny village in the East of Carentan, the enemy tanks' masses seemed to be gathering for the decisive battle. They blocked the narrow access to Carentan there, for north and south of the main communication road, the terrain was so swampy that it could not be passed. Air reconnaissance further revealed that at Carentan itself and on the narrow causeway leading from there through the flooded fields up to Saint-Côme-du-Mont, other mechanized forces were on the move to reinforce the American ring of blockades protecting the beachhead. The enemy poured approximately all of his armored units not engaged in combat with the 24th Panzer Division in the northwest into the Carentan area. A tremendous material battle in a confined space was in store for both sides. The enemy supplies were lined up like on a string of pearls for miles across the access causeway – they formed one single, iron snake. Every fighter bomber pilot dreamed of such a target. Still, for reasons unknown to Engelmann, the Luftwaffe held back its bombers. Lieutenant Engelmann hoped that at least the promised fighter aircraft would show up because the Panzer Regiment 2 also made a prime target on its approach to the enemy.

Quasimodo started to rumble. Slowly, his tracks moved toward the bridge. Engelmann looked over the forefield from the copula. Beneath his monster of steel, the Vire was rushing along. Where the current broke at the bridge piers, it foamed whitishly like a crumpled wedding dress.

"Hey you!" the second lieutenant of the pioneers shouted after him. His distinctive Friesian voice easily pierced through the rattling of the tracks and engines. Engelmann turned to look at the officer, who was frantically flailing his arms and chasing after his tank.

"Can you take me over there?" he snorted.

"Sure, go ahead." Engelmann let his tank stop. Briefly, he wondered why no grumbling, no stupid comment made its way up into his copula from the driver's seat. Quasimodo halted, and Engelmann climbed out of his hatch to help the pioneer with a firm grip over the T-34's sloped flank onto the hull.

"Hang on tight," Engelmann grinned. The second lieutenant nodded, then they continued on their way. Bridges were hairy bottlenecks for tankers, which is why they liked to do them at high speed. Quasimodo roared across to the other side of the river, where Engelmann directed the tank off the road. He let the panzer stop next to a thick oak tree with a gnarled trunk.

"Thanks for the trip. It's better than riding a bike," the pioneer grinned and jumped off the hull, losing his balance when he hit the ground and falling down. Embarrassed, he jumped up. Among the trees, the pioneer grunts smiled in their foxholes. Engelmann noticed that the pioneers' positions almost took on a reserve slope position character due to the bump in the foreland.

"Well, I'll go and see what my landlubbers are up to..." the pioneer officer muttered into his non-existent beard. He grabbed his submachine gun, smoothed out his pants, and strode off in the direction of the foxholes north of the road, where he disappeared behind a man-high cover.

Engelmann gazed emotionlessly after the second lieutenant as Rita's lead tank rumbled past him. One by one, the 9th Company's panzers crossed the bridge.

"Not too far out on the field. Get off the road and form a hull-down skirmish line at the bump," Engelmann directed his vehicles.

"Rita understood," the sergeant's calm voice cracked over the radio. The platoon's tanks acted as instructed, fanning out and moving up behind the bump, presenting La Blanche only their turrets. The commanders looked down on mostly two-story stone houses covered with gable roofs.

Finally, Kranz's panzers rolled onto the bridge with the vehicle of the master sergeant leading the column. Kranz had stuck his upper body out of the copula and surveyed the surroundings with a serious expression on his face. Like a giant worm, his Panzer III slid over the stone of the bridge. The sturdy structure vibrated under the weight of the tank.

Suddenly, an insane bang echoed through the scenery. Two more followed a blink later. Engelmann ducked into his copula, not even realizing at first where the detonations were coming from. Kranz yelled something unintelligible. Engelmann peered over the edge of his hatch, focusing on Kranz's tank. The master sergeant swayed back and forth in his turret hatch, his whole tank swaying – the bridge was swaying! Kranz clung desperately to the edges of his hatch. Meanwhile the ground under his tank was crumbling away. All at once, the whole bridge collapsed. Kranz's panzer lost its footing under the tracks, tilted sideways, and plunged into the depths, where the steel monster slammed turret-first into the river. Water shot up like a blazing flame.

Engelmann had not yet grasped what was happening when enemy guns opened up, hidden among La Blanche's buildings. Huge bursts of fire rattled against the German panzers, ricocheted, howled away. Miraculously, none of the shells penetrated the armor. Machine guns clattered away. Tracer bullets hammered into the positions of the pioneers. They fired back in wild excitement, jumping about like startled deer. From the right of the road, the second lieutenant of the pioneers rushed out of the thicket with panic on his face.

At that moment, there was a bang in the south. The sound of the detonation roared thunderously over Engelmann. Still completely perplexed, he looked over to the other bridge. He was shocked to see that there, too, rust-red flames were eating through the pillars. A moment later, this crossing was shattered; one tank lay sideways in the river, another had wedged itself where the bridge had broken off. Quick as a flash, Engelmann turned to the pioneer second lieutenant, who crouched terrified behind Quasimodo, seeking shelter from the enemy fire from La Blanche. Anger, that unruly, evil beast, overwhelmed Engelmann's spirit all at once. He bared his teeth and roughly snapped at the pioneer, "No explosives?!" Engelmann roared like a wounded bear. "Just shut up, you blockhead!"

The pioneer no longer seemed to understand the world, but Engelmann had to turn his attention to other things.

" Rita, respond fire!" he yelled into the microphone of his headset. "Hit them with HE rounds!"

Rita's four tanks had come under heavy fire, as had the pioneers. A true barrage from umpteen barrels pounded the infantrymen's entrenchments, who barely dared to lift their weapons out of their foxholes. Meanwhile, Rita's tanks were being throbbed with shells. Detonations tore up the ground between the tanks, cascading earth.

"Hans!" Engelmann yelled into his tank. "Move forward! Get in front of Rita. This damn T-34 hull can take more than the IIIs!"

Wordlessly, Münster threw himself into the levers, engaged the gear. Quasimodo accelerated.

100

"Jahnke: load explosives! Ludwig: Fire on will! Ebbe: Anna is to start to recover Anna 1 immediately, then sitrep to Brunhilde! I'll be right back!" the lieutenant yelped. He tore the headphone from his ears and climbed out of his copula. At that very moment, his tank dashed over the bump at breakneck speed. Engelmann lost his balance, fell from the turret, and slammed down hard on the hull. Before he could have grabbed hold of anything, he slid backward. The rear slope of the hull offered no support for his body. Engelmann slid down, hitting the ground with a thud and a groan. But he had no time to give in to the stabbing pain in his shoulder and the nasty biting abrasion on the back of his right hand. Engelmann scrambled to his feet like a shot cow. Half staggering, half sprinting, he limped toward the collapsed bridge. Fountains of bullets spurted out of the ground to the tips of his boots. Engelmann threw himself down, hitting the earth. He hissed an angry sound. His hands became fists. Crawling, he pulled himself up to the river embankment until he had a clear view of the water. Kranz's tank was upside down, parts of the tracks sticking straight out of the foaming water. Pioneers and tankmen were already hurrying up from the other side of the river. They threw themselves into the water and swam toward the tank.

Engelmann bit his lower lip. He bit so hard that he tasted blood and felt pain. Kranz and his men had no chance of survival; he knew that. His right hand tensed. He slammed his fist hard against the ground. A painful sting went through his wrist. Engelmann pulled himself up. He stumbled after his tanks. One of Rita's panzers spewed black smoke. But all his vehicles were still up and running; they were all still firing.

La Blanche trembled under the high-explosive shells, where dozens of muzzle flashes twitched likewise. Snakes of fire flashed from between the buildings with each firing of one of the enemy guns. Earth and sod sprayed up next to the German tanks. A kind of veil of brown dust formed around the panzers. It threatened to swallow them. Engelmann ran for all his body was capable of. Suddenly the second lieutenant of the pioneers threw himself at him and stopped him abruptly. Grabbing Engelmann's shoulders with both hands, the man shouted, "We must form a combat formation and fight our way to the other river bank!" Engelmann wrenched himself from the pioneer's grasp. With fire in his eyes, he threw the man back with a mighty shove.

"See if you can get over there!" he snarled at the pioneer. "We, on the other hand, have an attack to lead!"

The pioneer stared at Engelmann in bewilderment, but the tank officer didn't care. Engelmann ignored his fellow officer, rushing after his tanks with powerful leaps. He saw that Quasimodo had moved in front of the other tanks. The half Soviet half German combat vehicle sat perched on the bump, mauled by long rosettes of fire. Sparks flew across the battered hull, but the Russian fabrication swallowed shell after shell. Ricochets hissed away, whirring in all directions.

From behind, Engelmann jumped onto the hull of the T-34. He almost slipped on the slope. He held on to the handle of the hatch, pulled himself up, and finally used that handle as a step. Groaning, he pushed himself up. A bazooka rocket howled past Quasimodo, detonating in a treetop farther back. Engelmann's heart hammered like a sewing machine. With both hands, he gripped the skirts of armoring that wrapped around the turret. He clawed at them as salvos from a machine gun knocked against the tank's steel skin. Glowing sparks extended their hot fingers toward Engelmann. He pulled himself up onto the turret and disappeared through the open hatch into its copula with lightning speed in a burst of strength. The tank shook terribly under the shelling.

"Man, get off the bump!" Engelmann yelled before he had even taken his seat. Enemy automatic fire thumped deafeningly against the hull of the tank. The acrid smell of gunpowder vapor mixed with the tank men's acidic sweat formed an aggressive mixture that crept up Engelmann's nose.

"Jawohl, Leutnant," Münster replied, backing up.

"Damn it, Hans...!" Engelmann was in a rage and felt further provoked by his driver. He grudgingly swallowed the anger; instead, he tried to get a picture of the situation.

At La Blanche, the enemy howitzers thundered. The shells dug up the bump, tore it apart, built up walls of earth. Engelmann's tanks drove back and forth to avoid the shelling.

Quasimodo backed up, seeking cover behind the bump, across which only the tank turret was in the enemy's field of vision.

The German panzers repeatedly spat out high-explosive rounds, smashing the tiny village in front to pieces. Just then, a farmhouse collapsed under the impact of several explosions. At that moment, Rita reported the failure of one bow MG.

In Engelmann's head, thoughts were racing. They had to get out of here! Behind the German combat vehicles, the pioneers ran away in a panic, hastily jumping into the river. Engelmann made a decision.

"Ebbe!"

"Jawohl!"

"Radio to Meier: we are sitting ducks here. My intention: move off to the South, unite with the I Abteilung parts that are on this side of the river. Then joint retreat, following the Vire, to finally meet with the Schwere 503 in the South. On our own, we are not worth a pfennig here! We have to make sure we get to the Tigers!"

"Understood! Move off to the South, unite with I Abteilung, then unite with the Schwere." Nitz got on the radio.

"Meier is to suggest that the rest of the regiment should follow us across the Vire, use the southern crossing, and join us. Without the regiment behind us, we'll soon close our eyes here!"

Nitz nodded, radioing Engelmann's demands to the battalion HQ. His forehead shone in the heat that wafted through the tank's interior. A fine, black film had settled over the radio operator's face, as well as over the faces of the other crew members. This was the smog whose fine particles irritated the men's lungs and clogged the pores of their skin.

"What about the sappers, Sepp?" Ludwig panted, staring intently through the periscope and just finding a new target.

"What about them?"

"We have to cover their retreat!" Jahnke interjected, snorting.

Engelmann exploded, "THEY SHALL COVER THEMSELVES!" He could feel his crew staring at him in bewilderment – except for Münster. He gazed stubbornly through his eye slit.

"We can't save the whole damned Wehrmacht," Engelmann explained himself, without thereby being able to wipe the confusion from the faces of his men. "Everybody's got to see for himself how he gets along."

Ludwig fired. The round went into the wall of a house at La Blanche, in front of which an American AT gun had taken up position. Quasimodo's breech ejected the cartridge case with a clang. Jahnke already held the next HE shell in his hands. He inserted it into the loading device and let the breech snap forward.

"Loaded!" he roared with a hoarse throat.

Ludwig adjusted the height setting of the barrel. He pressed the firing button. The round in the barrel ignited with a crash, darted out, and jetted off toward the enemy. An orange blaze ignited at the American gun.

Engelmann's words chased each other as he radioed Rita. With an iron-hard voice, he barked his instructions into the airwaves: "I'll take the lead, Rita will follow. Move off to the South. Out of enemy fire!"

Münster jerked the tank into action. Roaring, Quasimodo struggled through the butter-soft ground. The tracks dug into it, football-thick chunks of earth stuck between the track links.

500 hp pushed 30 tons of steel over the open area, always following the Vire flow. At that moment, Meier announced his agreement with Engelmann's proposal. The remnants of Anna, which had not made it across the bridge, would be

attached to the 10th for the period of separation, and Engelmann would take command of the parts of the I Abteilung that were on this side of the river. Six Panzer IVs in the variant H had made it across before the bridge collapsed.

"Ludwig Emil, this is Schnecke!" a master sergeant of the IVs called Engelmann over the radio only fractions of a second after Meier's voice had died away. The lieutenant's tanks rolled toward the cut off tank company code-named Schnecke. Their Panzer IVs were under fire too. Enemy AT guns now pounded both tank formations as the bump became more prominent to the South. Engelmann's tanks picked up full speed. At this point, the bump had expanded into a high dam that stood like an impassable wall between the German tanks and the U.S. guns. However, the enemy's artillery could still hit the panzers behind that natural wall. Earth splashed up as high as a house, covering the tanks, pelting down on them like hail as mortar and artillery shells rained down on them.

"Anna 1 here," Engelmann grunted into his throat microphone, "I'm taking command."

"Copy that."

"Schnecke! You keep command of your Abteilung's vehicles. I will continue to address you as Schnecke. My unit, codename Rita, is taking over the lead. My intention is to move us in unison to the Heavy Battalion 503 to the South. Fire on will, but our motto is breakthrough! We only fight when it is necessary."

"Understood. We breakthrough!"

"Break a leg, Schnecke!"

"You too!"

Münster threw himself into the steering levers, getting everything out of the Russian fabrication. The engine squeezed the last bit of power out of the creaking steel colossus howling. The tracks of the T-34 tore through the ground, which was becoming muddier and softer with every meter. Münster pushed Quasimodo forward.

The tank moved past Schnecke's panzers, which had moved up to a wedge formation, and took the lead. Rita's vehicles followed. The tanks of Schnecke took up the rear as ordered. In a long convoy, the German panzers moved along the riverbank, accompanied by the impacts of the enemy artillery shelling.

Over the commander's periscope, Engelmann observed that the regiment's tanks and trucks were also gathering on the opposite side of the Vire. Countless vehicles moved up to form a seemingly endless convoy that slowly inched its way south along the river, parallel to Engelmann's panzers. The crossing that the Tigers were supposed to use now probably had to serve the entire regiment.

Suddenly, amid the regiment's long line of vehicles, earth-brown balloons appeared on the opposite bank, inflating like lightning before bursting.

There was an oppressive atmosphere in Engelmann's tank, where the rattle of the engine, the clatter of the tracks, the clicking of the devices mingled with the stench of boiling oil, the sour smell of sweat, and the stuffy atmosphere of heated, thick air. Everyone was silent. Engelmann sensed that something was between him and his men – above all, he sensed that he himself was more agitated than usual. Inside he was seething, and it cost him strength to keep his emotions under control. Engelmann's tongue was swollen, his lips chapped. His body longed for a piece of chocolate – but the red box he was carrying was empty.

U.S. artillery mercilessly plowed up the banks of the Vire. Dripping wet bushes and bundles of dirt flew into the air between the tanks. Quasimodo was digging through the miry ground, mechanically groaning, as it grew boggier meter by meter.

"Can you get through here, Hans?" Engelmann panted.

"Let's see."

"You got to be kiddin' me! If we get stuck, we're history."

"I'll do my best, Herr Leutnant."

Münster did little to soothe Engelmann's upset temper. The lieutenant felt the resentment growing in his chest. He drummed his hands against the steel of the copula. Shell splinters knocked against the turret from outside.

106

Engelmann took the map from the turret's sheet metal compartment, on which he had drawn the swampy areas in pencil. They had to get away from the riverbank, that was for sure. They had to take a road. Otherwise, they would get stuck and perish in the artillery fire...

An angry shout rang through the airwaves. Engelmann heard from the voice, interspersed with technical noise, that it was the company sergeant major. The lieutenant jerked his head around, peering through the narrow glass block on the turret to the rear. The CSM's tank had caught fire. Thick smoke was pouring out of the engine compartment. Tongues of fire licked outward. The hatches popped open, but the flames had engulfed the ammunition store. A massive detonation prevented the crew from dismounting. The turret popped out of the swivel, revealing a fireball. It rose mushroom-shaped into the sky, while the tank disappeared entirely beneath it.

"Scheisse," Engelmann groaned. That was all he could utter at the sight of the destruction.

"This is Rita 3; I'm taking over!" That was Master Sergeant Bäumer's voice, sounding upset.

"Understood," Engelmann replied briefly.

Meanwhile, it went on; it had to go on. The tanks struggled through the boggy ground until one of Schnecke's Panzer IV suddenly got stuck. The tracks spun on the slippery ground so that the vehicle could neither move forward nor backward. A second Panzer IV came up, heading full on the stuck vehicle from behind. Meanwhile, the turret spun to turn the barrel away from the impending impact. There was a brute clang, and the on-rushing tank shoved its stuck colleague out of the trap.

"We've got to get out of this miserable swamp," Engelmann muttered to himself. He straightened his throat microphone, called his men. By now, there was a paved road running along the river on the large dam. After three kilometers, this road led to the runway that the Heavy Battalion 503 was trying to reach. Somewhere along this route, they would rendezvous. It was no use; Engelmann had to get up on the dam, out of its cover. He sighed.

With short, clipped words, he directed his tanks onto the road, and at last, the German artillery joined in the action. As the panzers struggled to get onto the road under Engelmann's command, a severe artillery beating hit La Blanche behind them. Seconds later, batteries of Nebelwerfers joined the concert of death. Howling, the seemingly burning shells sped up, roaring into the battered hamlet. The multiple explosions shattered buildings and tore bodies apart. A whirlwind of splinters swept through the streets of La Blanche. The whole village was enveloped in a gigantic cloud of dust.

All enemy fire from La Blanche had ceased, but the American long-range guns continued to hit Engelmann's panzers unabated.

Millions upon millions of fragments of dying shells struck Engelmann's tanks' steel skins. Besides the steady clattering of the splinters, a thick hummer thundered again and again against Quasimodo. Projectiles of all sizes hammered down against the Russian armoring, deafening the ears and causing the steel to heat up dangerously. Silently, the men in Engelmann's tank looked at their devices; silently, the lieutenant stared out at the terrain. The visibility was good; there was hardly any cover. If it weren't for these damned swamps, it would be the perfect tank terrain.

Suddenly, four tiny objects came rushing from the West. They drove at high speed over the fields, rolled over hedges.

"Four enemy tanks, 9 o'clock, 1,000!" the report crackled over the radio. The American tanks stopped abruptly in the cover of a hollow, only their turrets still peering above.

"All panzers halt!" Engelmann snarled. "Schnecke, fire a volley!"

The six Panzer IVs fired. The steel monsters staggered under the impact of the firings. Up ahead at the small U.S. tanks, the world flew apart. The so-called M3 Stuarts – light, fast tanks – were no match for a direct hit.

As the earthen curtain began to evaporate on the enemy, a blazing pile of scrap metal appeared, billowing black smoke into the air. Beside it, however, still, three intact Stuarts

108

were lurking. Lightning flashed across their turrets. Their small-caliber rounds thumped against the German tanks. Ricochets whirred away in all directions, hissing. At 37 millimeters, they had no chance of cracking the German panzers at this range.

But now the Stuarts got back into the action. Their drivers stepped on the gas and got their tanks out of the hollow. They turned sharply to the South and chased away. Schnecke's boys sent another package after them, their rounds detonating between the agile enemy tanks without hitting anything.

"Gosh, they are tired of living," Ludwig whispered. Engelmann, however, suddenly understood. Instinctively, he clung to the steel of his tank with both hands. He also instinctively put his body under tension before opening his mouth: "DRIVE, HANS!" he roared as loudly as he could. His voice resounded through the interior of Quasimodo, as the heavy shells of the Allied naval guns were already whistling. Giant cannons had opened fire on the German panzers. All hell broke loose over Engelmann's small combat formation.

The ground swayed under the panzers. Sinkholes so deep that a house could have disappeared in them were knocked into the earth. Cones of dirt rose hundreds of meters into the air. The ground broke away under the tanks; the road burst open.

"Drive! Get out of here!" Engelmann barked into the airwaves, but he didn't have to give the order at all. The tank drivers pushed their vehicles, straining gearboxes and engines to the limit. They rolled away at top speed - trying to escape the naval guns' hammer blows that fell upon them by the second. Not all of them made it.

One of Schnecke's tanks received a direct hit. The vehicle burst into pieces. When the explosion was over, the tank was also gone—just gone.

Another Panzer IV received no direct hit, but on its right flank, one of the killer projectiles drilled into the ground, where it unleashed kilograms of explosives. The blast smashed against the tank, braced against its side. As if struck by the thunder god, the tank whirled around and landed on its turret.

Engelmann saw the whole spectacle of cruelty through his periscope. The overturned tank disappeared in a wave of earth and dust. Incessantly the pounding went on. The tank men had no chance to do anything for the hit comrades – if there were any survivors at all. All they could do was flee – flee and pray that it didn't hit them, too.

Engelmann's tanks finally made it out of the infernal conflagration, out of the deadly field of fire of the enemy naval guns. Behind them, the landscape was still being dug up, earth by the ton was being shoveled into the river, and everything was drowning in a swirling cocktail of dirt and things shredded into tiny particles.

Engelmann's tanks, however, sped away. In the West, the Stuarts had disappeared, but now their bigger brothers appeared. Twenty, thirty, forty Shermans showed themselves on the horizon. Now there was only one thing left to do: speed!

Engelmann's combat formation rolled to the South. The Shermans' main armament muzzles flickered, then the first impacts lay close to the German tanks. Fountains sprayed up, tearing deep wounds in the ground. Schnecke's command tank took a hit, but the armor deflected the projectile, which fizzed into the ground as a ricochet.

Drops of sweat had formed on Engelmann's forehead, his hair soaked as if he had taken a bath.

"ATTENTION! ENEMY BOMBERS FROM THE NORTHEAST!" Bäumer's voice croaked through the radio. Engelmann peered on the outside and was startled: the sky in the German tanks' rear had darkened. Flying Fortresses of the Americans – colossal bombers – passed by the hundreds over the firmament.

Beyond the Vire, at the regiment, the enemy fighter bombers were already in action. Whole squadrons swooped down on the German column. Missiles hurtled into the ground, where they burst. Bombs fell among the tanks and troop vehicles. Machine guns roared. The German AA guns also fired. With each attack of the Allied aircraft, however, with each time the planes tilted, threw themselves at the German convoy, and fired their weapons, burning wrecks were left behind on the German side. The rest of the convoy, that seemingly endless iron snake that struggled across the road on the other side of the river, crept on unperturbed.

Half-tracks, trucks, and tanks were hit, drove wavy lines, stopped. The regiment left a trail of debris.

The enemy fighter bombers attacked relentlessly. Tracer bullets from machine guns ricocheted off the armored hulls of the Thunderbolts, sending sparks flying. A salvo from an anti-aircraft gun sawed through one of the approaching planes. The machine spat fire, looking for a moment like a dragon from ancient myths. Glowing, it thundered into the German convoy. Some of the fighter bombers had now also discovered Engelmann's combat formation. In a first approach, they chased over the tanks. Thick bullets hailed against the steel.

But real hell broke loose over at the regiment when the Flying Fortresses were above it. Bomb bays opened, long stalks fell to the ground. They ignited a fire of destruction. More and more German vehicles became melting scrap metal. Tanks came to a halt. Men shrieked, but no one heard them in this cacophony of horror, in which the roar of the fire blasts merged into a single, mighty thunder.

In Engelmann's tank, there was a baking heat. Each of the crew members concentrated silently on his task. Engelmann stared with dull eyes into the forefield. Quasimodo's tank engine rattled. The tracks were moving forward steadily.

German long-range weapons also continued to intervene in the battle, although they could not come close to outweighing the enemy storm of iron. Far in the hinterland, the Nebelwerfers howled once again. Rockets whooshed toward the formation of American Shermans that sank the U.S. tanks in a sea of detonations. Here and there, track links and road wheels were shattered – and briefly, the enemy tanks were blinded by the shelling. But when fire and smoke had cleared, when the curtain of hurled earth had settled, the majority of enemy tanks rumbled

111

inexorably toward Engelmann's combat formation. The Shermans soon unleashed another burst of fire. As if out of one cannon, they all fired at the same time so that one big bang swept across the landscape. Shells pelted the German combat vehicles. There was a terrible racket in Engelmann's tank when they received a hit that tore at the right side skirt like a whirlwind. But the Germans were lucky. Impacts all around them. Impacts again and again. In long tracks, ripped out earth rose to the sky. The panzers, however, pushed through the shelling. Splinters and large chunks drummed them. More shells were hurled at them. A tree standing on the embankment of the Vire was struck. The explosion tore a thick wound into the trunk. The wood cracked; then the whole tree buckled sideways. The top of it slid rustling into the water.

At that moment, the next formation of bombers roared in from the sea. More Flying Fortresses, these gigantic floating monsters, these dragons of iron, their bellies filled with pure death, packed in phallus-shaped boxes, were humming along. Combined with Liberator aircraft and massive fighter protection, the enemy planes slid between sky and earth like a black stencil. The fuselages of the aircraft opened, and the blessing started.

Once again, the regiment's convoy on the opposite river bank went into a bestial frenzy of destruction. Tankmen were cooked in their vehicles like lobsters in a saucepan. Human skin could not withstand the heat – the thousandfold heat of the fierce explosions -- for a second.

It began to bubble and seethe as the dying men roared their lungs out in their steel coffins. Their skin burst open, melting like cream in the midday sun. What remained were corpses, their flesh hanging from their bones.

Steel was bent in this conflagration. Steel was shattered, melted away in the seemingly endless round of the Allied bombardment. What remained were tanks whose barrels were deformed as if they were made of rubber. The regiment was brutally battered. But it rolled on – what was left rolled on, because, at Carentan, the decisive battle had to be fought no matter what. There the Germans had to break the enemy's backbone if they did not want to lose this war.

The Flying Fortresses and the Liberator bombers had not yet turned off when the next squadron of enemy bombers came rushing in from the Northwest. Incessantly they flew into Northern France. The Allies also knew what was at stake. And they wanted that beachhead; they wanted it so badly that they threw all the steel and blood they had into this meatgrinder.

The whole battle was just a battle of attrition. Who would be able to send more men, more material into this blood mill in the end? Which side would still be standing after hours of bombardment, after hours of the destructive fury of thousands of weapons of war?

The bombers roared in. The regiment's vehicles were speeding. The long line of destruction left behind looked like a burned snake. And the fighter bombers! Thunderbolts and P-38 Lightnings from all sides! Several twenty in number! They swooped down on the Germans like mighty eagles on their defenseless victims. Somewhere a German anti-aircraft gun was sputtering into the sky. It was like throwing pins into an angry swarm of hornets.

"JEEZ, WHERE'S THE FUCKING FIGHTER PROTECTION?" Engelmann shouted in a burst of desperate rage. Quasimodo shook under the impacts of the Shermans, which narrowly missed the tank.

From above, however, the Thunderbolts roared in. Bombs were released from under their fuselages, burrowing into the ground between Engelmann's tanks, digging up the road and the fields. One of Rita's panzers took a hit. The track burst and rippled open. Immediately the tank steered to the right in a screeching circular motion. The engine caught fire. Engelmann wanted to help them. He really wanted to. But what was he supposed to do? He could not sacrifice his remaining tanks - could not stand still in this hell. Not for two or three survivors. Finally, he reached for the microphone with one hand.

"Rita, come in!" he roared with a hoarse throat.

"YES?" Bäumer returned.

"Dismount! Dismount over the river!"

"We're trying!"

They didn't stand a chance. A variant of the American P-51 Mustang, specially designed for ground combat, zoomed in. Tongues of fire spurted from its wings and nose with its red propeller head. Those were the heavy machine guns bellowing. Simultaneously, some of the Shermans also had their machine guns pointed at the disembarking tankers. Engelmann was staring stubbornly straight ahead – had to think of his survival. Fear was omnipresent at that moment. The confinement of the tank was suddenly like a foretaste of a coffin to him. The sour smell of sweat clogged his nose.

Projectiles howled away as ricochets when they knocked against the armor of his tank. Jahnke crouched spellbound over the ammunition, condemned to inaction. Behind their panzer, Rita 3's tankmen were being blasted by bullets of all calibers. The iron slugs hissed through the soft bodies, tearing viscera, tissue, and bone in two.

The doomed victims sank to the ground screaming. Suddenly Engelmann saw rescue on the horizon. Dark, angular panzers crawled, like giant turtles, over a hump and disappeared into a hollow. Immediately they reappeared. Those were the Tigers! They stopped!

Engelmann was surprised. Smoke rose in front of the Tigers. The sound of firing first thundered over Engelmann's small combat formation as the armor-piercing rounds from the eight-eight tank guns went off between them. One of Schnecke's tanks immediately exploded in the friendly fire. The turret jammed, flames spurting from every opening.

"Smoke!" Engelmann gasped. Then he yelled into the radio, "SMOKE!"

The tanks of his combat formation stopped. Their smoke mortars fired — a ball of dense white fog formed around the German tanks. Inside the fog cover, the panzers instantly moved. AP rounds detonated between the tanks — impacts from all sides.

Engelmann swished the sweat from his forehead with fluttering hands.

114

"Give me Meier!" he ordered Nitz in a voice that was no more than a rasping scrape. But Nitz understood and immediately adjusted the radio. Engelmann called the battalion commander. Without waiting for a reply, he screamed into the airwaves, "Heavy 503 shoots at US! Cease fire immediately!"

There was no reply. Seconds passed. The Tigers appeared to cease fire. Engelmann breathed a sigh of relief – just a moment, a tiny moment. Around his tanks, there was clatter and thunder and crash. The world was on fire.

"Ebbe, get back on our frequency!"

"Jawohl! Already plugged!" Nitz's expression was a single, pain-distorted, silent scream. But he bore it.

"Transmit: THIS IS ANNA! SCHNECKE, DO YOU COPY? Turn in to the Northwest, form skirmish line! You take left flank! Get out of the smoke, up against the enemy!"

Nitz made a face like a whipped dog. He passed the message on. And he was also thinking, because Rita, of course, had to go to the right.

"We push forward in the center!" Engelmann croaked down to Münster. He carried out the order without a word.

Engelmann's combat formation struggled out of the artificial fog. The scene that presented itself to the lieutenant made his blood run cold. Shermans, Shermans... endless Shermans! There were a hundred of them appearing on the horizon. At least! Like a fat cork of steel, they clogged the way to Carentan with their sheer mass. Over by the Tigers, 35 of the steel feline predators had come up. Five were already on fire. Fighter bombers circled like vultures above the German tanks. But finally, the foremost vehicles of the regiment rolled up. They had taken the road south at a hellish pace, thundering across the bridge and rushing with all their might toward the battlefield. They were decimated, incredibly decimated. And the remaining tanks were ripped open, dented, damaged. But the engines were still working; the electronics had not yet failed, the guns were still able to hurl armor-piercing rounds at enemy tanks. And finally – finally – German fighter planes were approaching: 24 Bf 109... one group. A joke! Eventually, they would hold the enemy planes in check long enough for the German ground forces to dare an advance.

Behind the heavy battalion, more tanks rolled in, all armaments blazing. Tanks detonated. Above the steel monsters, planes turned into burning flares, falling from the sky. Their fuselages were drilled into the ground, where they unleashed scorching fireballs.

The Sherman units paid a gigantic blood toll. In the inferno, they were perforated by the dozens. The staccato of the fire blasts turned countless of the U.S. tanks into metal lumps. The battle-hardened Germans outgunned the inexperienced American tank crews; moreover, the Sherman, with its thin armor, was vulnerable to AP shelling, especially the Tigers. But the flow of enemy tanks did not stop. More and more Shermans poured out of the narrow aisle in front of Carentan onto the plain where the tank battle was raging. Thick exclamation marks of smoke stood in the air above the Americans. Tank wreck after tank wreck blazed in the fields. But the mass of enemy tank forces threatened to overwhelm the German advance. An endless stream of tanks rolled toward the Germans. The Tigers fired round after round. Nonstop they sent Shermans to hell. The Tigers' losses were moderate. But Panzer Regiment 2 was suffering.

More Shermans invaded the battlefield. The German fighter planes burst into pieces in the sky, falling to the ground like shooting stars, trailing long flame tails.

"This can't be done," Engelmann whispered. "That's not..." He flinched when, next to Quasimodo, Schnecke's panzer took a hit that rumbled brute-like. Only a millisecond later, the combat vehicle's stored ammunition exploded, and with it, the whole panzer. It shattered like a glass that had been thrown against a wall.

Ludwig fired ceaselessly. Engelmann assigned him target after target. Nitz repeatedly shot opened up with the machine gun, aiming it at disembarking tank men. Quasimodo's 5-centimeter gun could usually only scratch the Shermans. They had to be lucky.

More U.S. tanks were coming. And even more. A

hundred of them burned on the field. A hundred more drove up behind them. The open country outside Carentan, enclosed by swamps, had become a vast tank graveyard. But while the Germans were losing valuable tanks with every burst of fire, the Allies seemed to have limitless reserves.

Even now, the losses of the Sherman units were incomparably higher. But regardless of such numbers, regardless of the snarling Tiger tank guns, the advancing IVs of PzRgt 2; regardless of the Nebelwerfer rockets howling between the U.S. tanks – the enemy did not retreat. The Yanks wanted to close this bottleneck – and they closed it. More and more canons were firing on the Wehrmacht tanks so that the 16th Panzer Division's armored forces were crumbling away like old bread.

It was also of no use that now even the half-tracks were advancing that the infantry pushed forward. They hardly got the better of a single square meter in this armageddon out of the depths of hell. No, this battle was a pure tank battle – everything that didn't have a skin of steel around it was smashed, crushed, and shredded. No one knew how the attack on the other side of the marsh was proceeding at that moment. The Taute River, with its boggy, muddy banks, separated the two battlefields. Over on the other side of the river, the 5th Panzer Division was advancing against Carentan with reinforced troops from the Southeast. There, too, the guns thundered. There, too, the sky lit up under the impacts of the weapons of war.

Engelmann's panzer took a hit on the right track. The track links flew apart with a clang. Quasimodo stopped. Engelmann looked out through his periscope. The horizon was littered with enemy tanks, both destroyed and combat-ready. Lined up as if on a string of pearls, they occupied the line between heaven and earth. Engelmann considered giving the order to dismount. He hesitated. Just then, Ludwig pulled the trigger. The AP shell started on its journey. The shell case was ejected from the breech and landed in the catch tray embedded in the T-34. The round hit a Sherman between the two front hatches below the turret. Sparks flew, jumping over the armoring. The projectile failed to penetrate the tank.

A hundred Sherman guns fired. A hundred 75-millimeter rounds chased toward the German steel front. It seemed as if a thousand – ten thousand – explosive-laden hollow parts were slamming into them. Tree-high cones rose from the earth.

German tanks burst. They dropped like flies.

"We're not going to make it," Engelmann stated. Suddenly, he was gripped by a stoic composure.

However, all at once, a new force intervened in the action – a force that brought the decision. Sherman's detonated as the Japanese amphibious tanks with German 7.5-centimeter guns suddenly crossed the Taute River and emerged from the swamp just like alligators. They charged right into the back of the Shermans. The boat-like tanks from Panzer Schwimm Regiment 31 were attacking!

Two different types of these strange amphibious tanks arose out of what should have been an impassable marsh: one was small and maneuverable, the other large and lumbering. Nearly 100 of these tanks slid between the endless Shermans and Carentan. Now the Americans were trapped in a German tank pincer grip: Tigers and the Panzer Regiment 2 to the South, the amphibious tanks to the North. The battle turned into a massacre.

At the same time, the combat vehicles of the 5th Panzer Division entered Carentan. Some of the outer boroughs had already been captured. The enemy resistance collapsed.

Engelmann's hands were shaking. Sweat burned in his eyes. His men were silent. The strain of the battle pressed down on them like a concrete blanket, but they had survived.

East of Saint-Sauveur-le-Vicomte, France, June 11th, 1944

Private First Class Tom Roebuck pulled the trigger of his Browning M1919 machine gun. It appeared as if glowing filaments flew from the barrel toward the Germans charging out of the woods in the forefield. Some of the field-gray men staggered under the fire before falling. Many jumped for cover. Bullets also whirred around the ears of the Americans, who lay in hastily dug foxholes in an open area.

"Fuckin' Krauts!" Pizza roared, who had the next ammunition belt at the ready. A foxhole away, D'Amico, who had his right earlobe torn off by a bullet, fired his BAR machine gun, a handy MG with a bipod. Again and again, the Private First Class wiped his crimson hand over the lacerated ear, which would not stop bleeding.

Captain Morgan had hammered it into the men's heads that they weren't going up against recruits here. Opposite them was the 24th Panzer Division, a battle-hardened unit from the Eastern Front.

Roebuck had truly believed it would be a piece of cake. The Gunny had told them dozens of stories from the last war; he had narrated that the Krauts were nothing but cannon fodder. However, what Roebuck and his comrades had been up against since the invasion began was anything but cannon fodder. They were experienced, superbly trained, tough bastards, those Krauts. And worst of all, the Allied forces were outnumbered!

At the beginning of the landing, the Germans at Utah had actually been caught on the wrong foot. But now that everywhere else, the landing had failed, and all the enemy forces of Northern France were concentrated on the tiny Cotentin Peninsula. The U.S. Army and Navy troops saw no more land. The Germans pressed with tremendous might against the still narrow and fragile Allied beachhead – the enemy had already managed to make breakthroughs in some places, and the Americans were in retreat almost everywhere. Even the massive deployment of the Air Forces had not impressed the Krauts. The Germans suffered enormous losses under the constant bombardment from the air, but that did not stop them.

German shouts reached Roebuck's ears between the bursts of fire from his Browning. Each time he pulled the trigger, however, his gun cracked off so deafeningly that the roar drowned out all other sounds.

From the neighboring foxholes, semi-automatic M1 Garand rifles sounded, Grease Guns clattered, Tommy Guns clacked. Company L, which was to block the road between Saint-Sauveur-le-Vicomte and Saint-Côme-du-Mont in this section, threw all the fire it had at the Krauts. Behind the U.S. men's positions, on the opposite side of the road, was a large farmhouse. Over there, the typical "pop" of mortar fire could be heard. The shells roared into the dense forest near the Germans, throwing up earth and branches. Screams filled the air. Many field-grays were already lying in the open space between the American foxholes and the forest. Some were squirming back and forth; others were screaming for help. Roebuck's fists clutched his weapon tighter as he let his gun spit more bursts of fire toward the Krauts. Even in their death throes, their strangely choppy language sounded aggressive and robotic. It hadn't taken Roebuck many days in France to realize why the whole world was going to war against the German Reich. The Germans were poisonous warmongers, without humor, without feelings. They had to go!

And Roebuck, by now, was good at putting Krauts away. Again he pulled the trigger, and the last projectiles of the belt left the machine gun barrel. Immediately the Private First Class pulled back the MG, and Pizza began inserting the next belt.

Before Roebuck could have rejoined the firefight, the German assault died down. The enemy still lay at the edge of the woods, firing sporadically. But after a good 40 dead and wounded lying in the grass, the Krauts seemed to have realized that there was no getting through to the Marine Raiders.

Suddenly there was a terrible screeching sound, accompanied by the cracking of branches and logs. Roebuck remained frozen in his hole. His entire unit went into shock.

"German Panzers!" Pizza whispered. Then from the right flank, the Gunny roared, "German Panzers incoming! Lay low!"

Roebuck squinted over at the farmhouse in his back, where Juergens, aka Batman, lay in position with the bazooka fire teams. Juergens had been assigned to the Company's Weapons Platoon to make up for the heavy losses there. Constantin was also serving there in a bazooka fire team.

Suddenly, steel colossi painted in brown camouflage with white and black Balkenkreuze on their flanks burst out of the undergrowth. Roebuck's eyes grew wide, Saviano's mouth dropped open in the horror of the massive attackers. Five, ten, fifteen enemy tanks rattled into the open area. Clearly modeled on the T-34, these panzers were considered an exceedingly dangerous opponent by the Army's tankers. The Krauts called these things Panthers.

Those Panthers immediately let their barrels and machine guns speak. Monumental earth fountains rose between the foxholes of the company. MG burst impacts danced around the positions.

D'Amico's foxhole abruptly disappeared in an inferno of fire and dirt. When the brown curtain cleared, only his torn corpse was left.

Roebuck's breath caught in his throat.

"Shit!" he roared in a fit of sheer hatred that blazed in his chest and ignited a hell-hot fire within him.

"Friggin' Krauts!" he vented his anger. "The bastards killed D'Amico!"

Grief and rage mingled with Roebuck's pure hatred, and somewhere the issue with Marie also played into the wild mix of emotions Roebuck felt inside him, threatening to overwhelm him.

Saviano groaned, fumbling for the next belt out of the ammunition box.

"Let them pass! The bazooka boys will take care of that!"

the Gunny's raspy voice sounded over. The Panthers rolled inexorably toward the company positions.

"He's a real optimist," Pizza groaned, dropping back into the hole at the same time as Roebuck.

Roebuck grabbed his machine gun, pulling the weapon, and tripod down toward him.

Behind them, the bazookas banged. Detonations echoed across the battlefield. Engines rattled. Squealing tracks grinded their way through the ground.

"I want to see our boys fuck these tanks!" Roebuck exclaimed. He straightened up his torso.

"If you want to get killed," Pizza commented casually.

Roebuck peeked over the edge of his foxhole. The Panthers were pushing relentlessly across the fields, having almost reached Company L's positions. Under cover of the tanks, German infantrymen left the woods. But as long as the Panthers dominated the battlefield, none of the GIs had to think about opening fire. They had no choice but to let the tanks pass and finish off the Krauts in close combat.

"Fuck," Roebuck whispered.

Behind him, the bazookas banged once more. Solid-fueled rockets, trailing a tail of fire, hissed out of the farmhouse toward the Panthers. One tank took a hit on the front hull. It stopped. Thick smoke poured out of the palm-sized hole the Bazooka rocket had punched. Other rockets missed. A few Panthers stopped, firing at the building. The old country house shook terribly under the high-explosive shells. Roebuck held his breath. If the bazooka teams failed, the whole company could pack up.

Once again, he peered over at the farmhouse. An exploding tank round tossed rose bushes and small hedges around in the front yard. Suddenly, however, something hurtled out of the sky. Roebuck narrowed his eyes, squinting in the bright sunlight. A black, bean-shaped thing was racing through the air at tremendous speed, dashing toward the company's positions. A buzzing sound accompanied this "cigar with wings". The strange device touched the earth about thirty meters from the farmhouse. A disastrous, infernal explosion followed. A ball of flames shot high into the air, devouring everything in its vicinity. For a fraction of a second, the farmhouse disappeared behind the wall of fire. A massive shock wave swept in all directions, including over Roebuck's foxhole. For a moment, he felt as if he were standing in the middle of a tornado. As the ball of flames collapsed, it left a sizable crater, so large that several of these Panthers could easily have disappeared into it. Even the Germans – apparently as surprised as Roebuck's fellow Marines – paused, staring wide-eyed at the spectacle. The farmhouse, however, was still shaking, and suddenly the wall on the right broke away. Within the blink of an eye, the entire building collapsed. The gray cloud of dust became a mere wall of dust.

Not a single bazooka gunner was firing his AT weapon at the Panthers after that. The Krauts, however, quickly regained their composure – faster than the Americans. Under roaring fire, they continued to charge forward. The Panthers slammed into the Marines' positions with explosive munitions. German machine guns had taken up positions at the edge of the woods. A skirmish turned into a slaughter. After minutes of fighting, the first Marines scrambled out of their foxholes, trying to escape. Many fell in the enemy fire.

"Retreat, Marines! Back to Charlie position!" the gunny's voice struggled through the noise of battle. After that, all resistance from the U.S. troops died away. The Marines ran for their lives.

Outside Blosville, France, June 14th, 1944

After the capture of Carentan, the penny seemed to have dropped, and since then, the German advance has continued unabated. The destination of the day was Sainte-Mère-Église, and slowly the air in France became thin for the Allied invasion troops. The beachhead was already reduced to a few square kilometers. Only in the North the

Americans could still hold Valognes at this hour. In the South and West, however, they were virtually only on the run.

German reconnaissance had also concluded that the Western powers had realized their defeat. Instead of landing more troops, the remaining forces were now loaded and shipped back to England. This had to be prevented at all costs. The Allies were not allowed to evacuate their valuable troops in a second Dunkirk!

Engelmann snorted at this thought. In the last few days, he had gotten more and more furious. He no longer wanted to throw the Allies out of France – he wanted to destroy them, all of them! In his opinion, this is how it had to be because the gruesome murdering would continue forever if one side in this war would not be defeated clearly, distinctly, and devastatingly. For this reason, Engelmann longed for the final decisive battle so that finally he could go home and start to forget all this. His greatest wish was to lead a life as a teacher and family. But between him and that wish still lay countless dead Americans and Germans. Engelmann felt the hustle and bustle of the war tugging at his soul, threatening to swallow it up. But for a time he had to endure, he had to preserve his humanity in this terrible conflict. And since the way to peace apparently only led over the corpses of the German Reich's enemies, it probably had to end with a gruesome bloodbath. With this realization in mind, Engelmann was ready to apply once again the terrible art of killing that he had learned to perfection. If it should become necessary, he would then apply it once again in the East, where von Manstein's troops were currently fleeing from the onrushing Red Army. After that, however, it had to be over! After this war – Engelmann was sure of this – his country could never again demand anything from him.

Once again, the repair units had done a remarkable job. Moreover, the men from the regiment's replacements were now almost all in tanks of some kind. Barely 60 percent of the required strength was left of the regiment – after all the reinforcements of the last few days that had been activated to replace wounded or fallen men. But, as mentioned, the penny had dropped. The Allies fled.

Engelmann breathed lightly into the membrane of his throat microphone. The crackle in his headphones told him the intercom was working.

"Company march, thrust Sainte-Mère-Église!" he ordered the poor rest of his unit. In addition to his T-34 misfit, he had one other tank of this type left, plus three Panzer IIIs. The commanders reported combat readiness one after the other – Engelmann had finally disbanded his platoons and led the entire unit directly. They started to move.

The 9th Company, with its fast, light Panzer IIIs, actually had a reconnaissance mission to carry out for once. Von Burgsdorff had placed Engelmann's tanks as the regiment's vanguard. They were now to advance toward Sain-te-Mère-Église in the early morning hours of the invasion's eighth day. Off the main road, Engelmann's tanks were to push through the hedgerows and orchards of the surrounding countryside, approach the village, and make contact with the enemy there. The Americans had formed an anti-tank gun belt around the periphery of the village. It was necessary to reconnoiter their positions, determine the nature and number of the enemy, and possibly find a soft spot for a breakthrough into which the battalion's forces then would push. The division wanted to isolate Sainte-Mère-Église by surrounding it with the tanks of PzRgt 2 before the armored infantry would take the village building by building.

Engelmann looked out of the copula of the turret. Quasimodo had taken the lead of his small reconnaissance unit. The tracks were digging through the soft ground as the tank entered a hollow and rolled out the other side.

The company's panzers broke through endless lines of hedgerows on their way. They passed fields where barley glowed in the sun. They rolled over uncounted hills that dotted the entire landscape. Engelmann looked up into the sky. Not a single airplane was to be seen. That could change at any time.

They drove to several spots. Each time, Engelmann had

his company stop, got out, and scouted the forefield on foot. In many places, the American positions were superbly fortified. Sometimes the lieutenant even recognized infantrymen carrying those dreaded "stovepipes. " How did the enemy call that weapon? Bazooka?

Finally, they reached a light forest. The steel monsters advanced past old birch trees whose trunks shone whitish as if they were infested with mold.

"Company halt!" Engelmann ordered when they had almost reached the end of the forest. The tanks took cover behind tall brush or rolled into hollows so that, if possible, they would present only the turret to the enemy in the event of an attack.

Engelmann climbed out of his hatch, ran over the hull, and jumped onto the dry leaves that made the ground crackle. With submachine gun and binoculars in his fists, he stalked off. Ducking, he worked his way to the edge of the forest, behind which a wide-open space scattered with more hills opened up not far behind lay Sainte-Mère-Église.

Engelmann lay down in the undergrowth next to a sturdy birch tree and looked through his binoculars. He recognized three howitzers of the Yanks standing close together — distance 1 000 meters on the hills. The gunners were strolling like vacationers next to their guns. Some sat together, playing cards. Some had taken off their uniforms down to their undershirts. Two men stood far away, tossing a strangely shaped ball to each other.

Bunch of bunglers, Engelmann commented snidely on the scenery. Quickly, he scanned the hills to the right and left of the three guns with his binoculars.

Nothing!

Engelmann looked carefully into the sky and listened to the distance. No sign of airplanes.

The lieutenant's thoughts were racing. Did they really have the time to wait for the remnants of the regiment? Or should they take the opportunity? Did they not even be duty bound to take the opportunity? After all, they had to win this war!

If the German Reich could not score points by numerical

material superiority, well, were they not obliged to use every moment of the enemy's weakness mercilessly?

With a very definite idea in mind, Engelmann returned to his tank and squeezed through the turret hatch into the fighting compartment.

"Ebbe!" he gasped. "To Meier: Position Dora is suitable."

Nitz got behind the radio.

However, Engelmann put on his headphones and called his commanders, all of whom he addressed himself since the platoons were dissolved. He gave the order to attack.

"We're attacking?" Münster barked.

"Jawohl."

"Just us?"

"Yes."

"What about the Abteilung?"

"Will follow."

"We only have five tin cans!"

"I know."

"FIVE!"

"Got it."

"Who knows what else the Yanks have around!"

"Have you finished now, Hans?" Engelmann roared suddenly. Out of the corner of his eye, he saw his tanks starting to move to his left and right.

"No! WHAT'S THAT ALL ABOUT?"

"I hardly think I have to explain myself to a staff sergeant!"

"Of course! OF COURSE! Damn it, if my fucking life is on the line, Sepp, then..."

"SHUT THE FUCK UP, MÜNSTER!" Engelmann was losing his temper. His words echoed through the tank. Everyone froze in the face of the raving, snarling lieutenant.

Münster stared at his commander with a horrified expression. »...Sepp, you..." he whispered.

"I think a *Herr Leutnant* is more appropriate for you right now so that you can remember your place," Engelmann replied in a dry voice.

The opponents stared at each other like hungry sharks, as best as the improvised tank construction allowed them to

127

stare at each other at all. Seconds passed. Suddenly, a tremendous thunder started in the terrain in front of them as Engelmann's tanks broke out of the woods and opened fire. Two of the three enemy guns were smashed with the very first salvo of HE rounds. The Americans didn't know what was happening to them.

"Come on, step on it and attack the enemy!" Engelmann yelled.

"Jawohl, Leutnant," Münster breathed softly into his throat microphone.

"HERR Leutnant. Here in the Wehrmacht, the address still begins with a Herr!"

Engelmann's panzer rolled after the other tanks of the company. Without any losses on their part, they overran the enemy. They set up for defense by the battered guns. Soon, however, Sherman tanks rushed in. After a brief clash, they pushed the 9th Company back into the forest. Shortly after that, the battalion moved in, once again occupying the hillside. Engelmann's record was two tank men wounded with no tank losses.

Outside Picauville, France, June 14th, 1944

With the Russian-experienced Senior Lance Corporal Meinhard, fireteam commander of the MG nest, assistant gunner Private First Class Lucas Klopp felt safe. Meinhard was not a slave driver, nor one who thought he was better than anyone else just because he was an old front-line veteran whose chest was adorned by the Close Combat Clasp.

The blond Meinhard, with the gleaming reddish scar that stretched from the corner of his left mouth up to his ear, plucked a crumpled pack of cigarettes from his field blouse and fumbled out two butts. He put Klopp and himself one between each of their lips. The private first class pulled out his storm lighter and produced a long flame.

"Cover your lighter with your hand, kid," Meinhard instructed him before Klopp lit both cigarettes. "Even such a small flame can be made out by the enemy."

Meinhard was a real buddy who looked after the young guys, among whom, within the squadron, Klopp was undoubtedly one. Meinhard gave the inexperienced comrades numerous survival tips. Since he got along well with the company sergeant major, he was sometimes even able to save the men in his orbit from unpopular chores such as cleaning the latrines.

Klopp nodded gratefully at Meinhard's advice and put away his lighter. With relish, he blew the smoke out of his lungs, peering steadily over the edge of the narrow hole in the ground toward the aisle in the coniferous forest that opened up in front of their position. In the distance, a heavy thunderclap sounded again and again. It was said that the Wehrmacht was bombing the Americans with so-called winged bombs, about which the propaganda had been raving for some time already.

In the meantime, Klopp had been able to gain his first combat experience because of the invasion, and indeed, all the enthusiasm for the war that had been taught in him over the years by his training, his time in the organized youth, and the numerous newsreels had fizzled out after the first enemy contact. Here in Normandy, the war had nothing romantic, nothing honorable. Here the landsers lay most of the time in hastily dug foxholes in the ground. Here, the German "master race" clawed themselves in the ground like worms while they were exposed to the Allies' fighter bombers without any protection. Flying Fortresses poured out their bomb loads over the 24th Panzer Division, unhindered by German fighter planes. Fast Hawker Typhoons and Thunderbolts hammered the poor German infantrymen, often just 18 years old, into the soft ground like nails. Dead and buried bodies remained after each air raid. During the endless bombardments, in which the enemy steel birds appeared wave after wave above the squadron's positions, some men even went mad. Twice Klopp had to witness that in the middle of the attack suddenly laughing or shouting men, wildly flailing their arms, got out of their foxholes and ran around. It usually took several comrades to force such a madman back into a hole.

In Normandy, Klopp had experienced the hell of war – and if the stories Meinhard sometimes told about Russia over a cigarette or a bottle of gin were even partially true, the fight against the Yanks was still a Sunday morning walk in contrast to the bitter struggle in the Russian winter. Meinhard had been there when Stalingrad was evacuated. The senior lance corporal had participated in the entire long retreat from the city on the Volga River to Shakhty, not far from the Sea of Azov. At that time, the 24th Panzer Division had fought side by side with the 16th Panzer Division, just like these days. Reunited under the umbrella of the 6th Army, both divisions had been advancing from the South against the American beachhead during the last few days and had even managed to push it in. For 20 hours, however, the squadron men had been squatting in their foxholes northeast of the village of Picauville while enemy aircraft dropped bomb after bomb on their heads. These 20 hours had cost the squadron 26 dead and wounded – the casualties in the other units were partially many times higher. Unfounded rumors, so-called latrine paroles, circulated about the point in time when they could finally move on, but, as always, nothing was communicated to the ordinary landser. They were simply posted, sent into battle, transferred back. Why and for what reason they were never told.

"I wonder what the Hauptmann wants?" Klopp whispered. He was afraid that talking too loudly might draw the attention of the enemy planes again, which, of course, was nonsense. An hour ago, for whatever reason, all the Allied planes had disappeared from the sky. Since they had landed on the peninsula more than a week ago, this had never happened before; strong fighter bomber formations and heavy bombers had accompanied every twitch of the division. Perhaps it was related to the rumor that the Yanks had taken flight and were currently loading their soldiers back into the boats? Klopp could only guess.

"Rittmeister," Meinhard grumbled, taking a deep drag.

"Ah, yes," Klopp remembered. He would probably never get used to the fact that some ranks in the 24th Panzer Division were designated differently. The division wanted to express its roots as a cavalry unit by doing so.

"Just don't call him that when he's around. The old man can get furious," Meinhard warned. Klopp nodded obediently. He absorbed everything this experienced soldier said like a sponge anyway. Sometimes the senior lance corporal's advice was worth a mint, for example, that one should not take off one's boots after long marches, or that one should wash oneself and one's clothes at every opportunity because of pants, rabbits, and lice; just things from practice that the recruit did not learn in training.

"Yes, but what does the Rittmeister want?"

"Not a clue." Meinhard was always calm, even in the heaviest bombardment. Klopp admired him for that.

With wide leaps, the said captain, a man with a Hindenburg mustache on his face, rushed from foxhole to foxhole until he finally reached Meinhard and Klopp's position. The officer held a kind of scarf in his hands.

"Moin, sailors," the officer from Rendsburg greeted his soldiers.

"Good day, Herr Rittmeister," Klopp returned respectfully as if embarrassed that an officer had deigned to speak to him. Meinhard merely nodded as a greeting.

"What's the situation?" the Rittmeister asked.

"All quiet. Not one Ami to be seen, and not a bird in the sky."

"That's the way it has to be. But let's cut out the chatter. Every moment something unique might happen."

"Well, what is it?" Meinhard seemed to get curious.

"Herr Eisenhower himself will be coming down the aisle with his car in a moment."

"WHAT?" Meinhard whispered.

Klopp's eyes widened.

"It's authorized by our commander-in-chief. I'll receive him here and lead him into the rear area."

131

Meinhard and Klopp blinked their eyes in disbelief.

"So, keep your eyes peeled, but not so nervous index fingers today!"

"Jawohl," Klopp whispered. Then all eyes turned to the aisle. Meinhard passed the news right and left to the other foxholes. Then they waited...

Again and again, guns of all calibers thundered in the far distance. For almost four days, the sounds of exploding winged bombs mingled with the usual racket of fighting.

After a good forty minutes, a so-called Willy jeep actually appeared in the aisle. The vehicle, open on the flanks and covered with a tarpaulin, drove at walking pace toward the German positions. A white star sparkled on the olive-colored hood. Klopp spotted two men in the car. Something inside the private first class forced him to clutch his carbine tighter. The captain, on the other hand, jumped out of the hole and waved at the jeep. Slowly the officer and the vehicle approached each other. Now Klopp also saw that the driver was a German colonel. He could not know that he was Richard Schmidt, the former commander of Grenadier-Regiment 473. He also could not know that the noose had tightened around the Americans, that they were, in fact, already evacuating their troops.

Klopp watched as the two men got out of the vehicle. The captain shook hands with both of them. Eisenhower, who looked very serious and whose chest flashed with decorations and medals, had a narrow face and pronounced dark circles under his eyes. It also became apparent what the scarf was intended for: the captain blindfolded the American General with it before Schmidt helped him squeeze into the Willy jeep's back seat. The colonel got behind the wheel, while the captain joined the American General in the back seat. Thus the jeep drove past Meinhard and Klopp's foxhole and disappeared into the hinterland.

La Roche-Guyon, France, June 14th, 1944

The afternoon had broken when the three men in the U.S. Willy jeep reached the chateau at La Roche-Guyon. After passing several guards and following a long driveway, Schmidt parked immediately in front of the steep limestone wall against which one of the castle's buildings stood.

Major General Zimmermann was already waiting in front of a stone staircase that led into the building. Rommel's chief of staff took over the "guest" at this point, had him remove his blindfold, and led him up the stairs. Schmidt trailed behind, but the captain had to wait by the car.

Field Marshal Erwin Rommel was in a large hall together with an interpreter. Gigantic paintings, which reached from the floor to the high ceiling, adorned the bright walls. Not only the room but the entire palace bore witness to the class and wealth of the German-friendly owner. One of the white double doors opened, through which Zimmermann, Eisenhower, and Schmidt immediately stepped. The colonel saluted with a respectful expression at the sight of the Commander-in-Chief France-Benelux.

Rommel returned the salute with a brisk hand gesture, after which the men shook hands. Each remained friendly but reserved. Rommel pointed to a set table in the corner. The smell of coffee drifted into the room; subtle steam rose from a pot. Eisenhower waved it off. He merely wanted to negotiate and then return immediately to his troops. Rommel nodded.

"First of all, I thank you, Field Marshal, for agreeing to my request for a meeting," Eisenhower let him know through the interpreter. Rommel nodded again.

"I may tell you that your troops have fought extraordinarily bravely in the last few days. You have excellent men here in Normandy," Eisenhower continued.

"Herr General, I am sure you have not come to butter me up," Rommel countered.

Eisenhower's eyes narrowed.

"Certainly not. You will not have failed to notice that we

133

consider the invasion a failure. We cannot hold the beachhead."

Rommel nodded.

"I still have 100,000 men in Northern France. The men are worn out, overtired, done for. Many wounded, almost every second one. I think you also do acknowledge that these men fought bravely and honorably?"

"I don't deny that. But all the same, it's easier to be brave when you're not being bombarded from the air every second." Rommel's words had a sharp ring. The corners of Eisenhower's mouth twitched.

"At present, the evacuation of my men is taking place under the heaviest German artillery fire," Eisenhower continued, "Your batteries already firing down to the beaches, and by the minute these robots are rushing in as if from nowhere and inflicting terrible casualties on the already battered men."

A brief smile flickered across Rommel's face. Apparently, the enemy had not yet found the hell hounds' launch pads; otherwise, he would indeed have bombed them into nirvana by now.

"Therefore, I ask you, from a man of honor to a man of honor, for a ceasefire. My men are defeated. The invasion has failed. There is nothing to be done about it—Grant the weary remnant a safe passage home. Don't shoot the wounded and defeated men who have already been through hell in the days of the invasion. Be the decent soldier and officer reported in your newsreel. Stop this massacre – in the name of chivalry."

Rommel's features darkened. His forehead wrinkled.

Eisenhower continued: "As a sign of my goodwill, I ordered all aircraft back to the bases immediately after you agreed to this meeting. Make sure about that through your commanders. Not a single attack is taking place at this moment. Besides, I want to turn over to you Colonel Schmidt, the highest-ranking prisoner we captured during the operation."

Schmidt looked down at the ground, somewhat embarrassed.

134

"Once again, I appeal to the decent soldier and knight in you. Let my men go with their heads held high."

That was the end of Eisenhower's speech. He stretched his back, looking Rommel straight in the eye. The German field marshal instantly replied: "Don't be a fool to speak of chivalry in such a total war! There is no place for it in this." Rommel's hands turned into fists. "Don't expect us to be gentle, Herr General," the field marshal replied in an iron voice. "Every winged bomb and every fighter bomber at my disposal I will bring into action against your invasion troops. The bombardment will not stop until the last American of this attack force lies dead in the Cotentin Peninsula fields. Moreover, I have not asked you to stop the air attacks – nor do I expect you to do so."

Eisenhower's features stiffened.

"If you want to save your men, there is a way to do it," Rommel added. "It's called surrender."

Both stared at each other like predators.

"That's it," Eisenhower let the interpreter state.

"All right. I guarantee you'll be able to return to your men unharmed."

Pointe du Hoc, France, June 17th, 1943

Berning sat a little away from the buildings in the hinterland of the cliff. He was leaning against an apple tree, on whose branches small fruits were slowly turning reddish. The sergeant stared at some letters from his mother that she had written to him during the war.

He sat very still, and his head was strangely empty. A light breeze blew around his nose. Everywhere on the cliff, German landsers were walking around. Now and then, Berning blinked through the branches of a narrow hedge that blocked his view of the trenches. The Americans, however, were long gone.

Since the Russians had launched their large-scale

offensive in the East, there had been a lot of unrest among the soldiers. It was said that the Red onslaught was enormous - unstoppable. A catastrophe was brewing in the East, they heard. Whole army groups were fleeing in a panic! Tens of thousands dead! Hundreds of thousands wounded! Some were already whispering behind closed doors that the Russians could be at the Polish border in autumn. Ivan was running against the positions of the Army Group Center and Army Group South with unbroken power; moreover, he had used his naval supremacy in the Black Sea, which had always been a thorn in von Manstein's side, for his attack: Russian forces had landed in Karkinitska Bay northwest of the Crimea as well as on the peninsula itself and were mercilessly stabbing the retreating Wehrmacht in the back. Von Manstein had always expected such an action by the enemy, but nevertheless, he was not prepared for it.

For Berning, the bad news from the East primarily meant that soon he would be heading back there. The division had received its marching orders – in the middle of the Battle of Normandy. But what else could the Wehrmacht do when more divisions were so urgently needed in the East?

All other European theaters were already thinned out except for a few units, whose combat value was also questionable. Convalescent soldiers, footsore and older men formed the battalions in Norway, Denmark, and the Balkans these days. Meanwhile, the situation in France seemed to be under control. For several days the 253rd Infantry Division, which had suffered heavy losses due to the Allied landing, was no longer in combat. All members of the division who had been captured in the enemy airborne landing were freed. The battle for Normandy was undoubtedly drawing to a close, and while Germany was victorious in this theater, on the other side of Europe, it was once again struggling to survive.

So it is the Eastern Front again, Berning sighed to himself. The squadron was supposed to have moved the day before, but the marquis had blocked stations and signal towers all over the country in a large-scale operation.

So now the motto was: wait and see!

After the start of the Russian offensive, which had opened on June 9th, a battalion of paratroopers had appeared rather quickly on Pointe du Hoc to relieve the 253rd Infantry Division's men. At that point, the Americans were still cowering in their trenches – holding out resolutely without food, without ammunition supplies.

The massive use of flare ammunition by hastily brought mortars had permanently illuminated the cliff every night after the invasion. Flares after flares were fired into the air by the mortars – and when the Yanks tried to hide among the rocks, the German tanks mercilessly intervened with high-explosive munitions. There was no escape for the enemy.

When even the paratroopers arrived, the Americans surrendered in the face of the several hundred men of reinforcements. This made Hege the last victim of American gunfire on the cliff, and Berning was still waiting for a message from the master sergeant of the platoon, whom he had asked to inquire about Hege's condition. Berning hoped that his comrade would make it. Nevertheless, he knew that such a gut shot was no small matter.

The paratroopers were scurrying around on the cliff in front, expanding their positions, taking care of their equipment and weapons.

Berning put the letters away. He rose, turned the corner of the building, and found himself on the small field road that led away from the cliff into the hinterland. Several orchards bordered it, and a few more buildings lay to the right and left of the road. Berning was pleased to see that the rations had arrived. Dozens of men on horseback populated the area to the left of the road in the shadow of a building. The CSM of the 1st Reconnaissance Squadron took care of the barrels in which goulash soup was waiting to be served. The supply men had brought bread, sausage, jam, chocolate, water, and apples and lavish personal demand items, mainly tobacco and wine. The rations were indeed not that fantastic every day.

However, Berning was pleased for a completely different

137

reason about the picture of the soldiers and horses swarming around. While all over the cliff, the landsers pricked up their ears and waited eagerly to be called to eat, Berning moved straight toward "his" master sergeant, whom he had long since spotted in the tumult. The blond man in his early 30s was hoisting more metal containers from one of the carts. Now Berning would hopefully receive good news about Hege...

The paratroopers had settled on the other side of the road with their share of the rations. Berning had almost reached the master sergeant when a loud commotion broke out over at the paratroopers. A soldier with straw-blond hair, feminine lips, and deep googly eyes suddenly shouted as if stung by an adder. A lanky comrade with a mustache countered with a stammer.

"A NASTY MUCK! There is none at all!" the blond yelled in top volume. The bizarre scene attracted the attention of all present.

"Yes... yes, well, you do not have to eat..." the lanky one replied, shrugging his shoulders.

"What do you say, moron!?" The blond roared at the top of his lungs. His screaming echoed all over the cliff. As he did so, he stalked back and forth like a stork, circling the lanky man like a satellite.

"You don't have to eat it..." Once again, the lanky man shrugged his shoulders.

"WHAT DO YOU SAY?"

"Eat what you want!"

"You're worse than a... a... a... penitentiary, YOU ASSHOLE! You want to tell me what I get to eat? We'll see about that..." The blond bent over, wagging his index finger frantically before putting both arms on his hips like a defiant child.

"Same shit with him every day," a paratrooper near Berning whispered.

"... then you just don't get anything anymore..." the lanky one sheepishly interjected.

"... that... OCH!" Completely aghast, the blond turned to an Oberjäger, which was the sergeant's equivalent in the

138

paratroopers. "That's a lunatic!" he complained, pointing at the lanky one. "Hey, come on, Luckie, that's a lunatic. Get him out of here... this shit here!"

The paratrooper, who had just whispered, apparently interpreted Berning's horrified face correctly. He grinned and explained: "He thinks he's in the theater instead of the army. Making such a fuss when he's just a little Jäger."

Berning nodded in disbelief but then became aware of his intention again. While the bickering continued unabated across the street, Franz finally made his way to his master sergeant. Both spoke briefly to each other.

"A lunatic!" the blond in the background complained. "He says to me I don't get anything to eat. He's crazy, that idiot!"

All the while, the master sergeant confirmed the sad news with compressed lips and a silent shake of his head. Berning felt sick for a moment, his knees wobbly. At the last moment, he saved himself from falling over. Private Heinz-Gerd Bauer, called Hege, was dead.

Berning turned away with a dry throat and a sinking feeling in his stomach from the illustrious scene that the blond paratrooper was still performing. Raging and theatrically, he screamed at his lanky comrade: "... mad, man! You need to be shut up... you need to be locked up because you're not normal anymore!" The blond tapped his forehead with aggressive gestures, but Berning didn't care about all that. He had such an irrepressible rage in his stomach as he had never felt before. A fire of hatred blazed in his chest, tightening his muscles, turning his hands into fists. Shocks ran through his body like an earthquake. He had become a boiling volcano about to explode. The disgust against Pappendorf... this misanthrope... this asshole... burst out of all his pores. Hege was dead – died pointlessly during a pointless action. And that only because Pappendorf had to prove once more that he was the great master sergeant. But now, this bastard had finally gone too far! Berning would no longer put up with the harassment! He wanted... he had to confront Pappendorf! He wanted to make it unmistakably clear to him that he – Sergeant Franz Berning – and his men were no serfs. Pappendorf's manner

139

and methodology were inappropriate. Sergeant Berning would tell this to the scumbag's face; he would tell him that he would no longer put up with this treatment. Berning would tell his platoon leader that he would go to the company commander if necessary, or beyond that, he would use his right to complain. Berning was ready to fight back! The sergeant from Austria was fuming. Briefly, the face of the dead Rudi Bongartz appeared in his head. Finally, Berning wanted to start doing things right!

He trudged straight toward the building in which the platoon was housed and in which Pappendorf had also set up his HQ. Berning yanked the door open with such force that he briefly felt as if he had ripped the door panel off its hinges. He stomped into the large room with firm steps, which served two squads of the platoon as crew quarters. Numerous beds covered almost every inch of the wooden floorboards. Between them, the platoon's soldiers squatted and played cards, drank wine, nibbled brown bread, or were engrossed in letters. It stank of sweat and aftershave. Berning made his way through the field-gray crowd – all the platoon's soldiers were, of course, dressed in neat uniforms. Berning almost stormed through the door into Pappendorf's room, but then he forced himself to knock. He was not allowed to offer this swine an attack surface because of trifles. Berning knocked. And waited.

"Come in!" Pappendorf's voice pierced through the door only after minutes. The long wait had caused Berning's anger to build up even more in his chest, to almost burst with rage. With cramped limbs and clenched teeth, he pushed the door open. He had to be careful not to smash the door when he opened it, he thought... but Berning restrained himself – for now. He stood to attention and saluted. Pappendorf returned the salute. He sat behind a narrow desk and brooded over some army regulations. On the wall to the right was a comfortable wooden bed with thick pillows and soft-looking wool blankets. Above it on the wall hung a portrait of Adolf Hitler and Pappendorf's membership certificate in the NSDAP.

"Make it short, Unteroffizier," Pappendorf snarled, having

already turned back to his regulations.

"Gefreiter Bauer is dead!" Berning thundered.

Pappendorf looked up, focused on the sergeant with his small eyes, nodded, and returned to his reading. "Too bad," he muttered. "Good man."

The gorilla had not made a face at this, and the Lance Corporal had been an old and honored soldier in the unit. But Pappendorf had taken note of the news, just as he took in reports on ammunition consumption or training levels.

"Herr Feldwebel, I must vehemently complain about your behavior toward me and my squad!" Berning said firmly. He almost shouted. Pappendorf's gaze, however, continued to linger over his reading.

"No," Pappendorf replied calmly. "There is nothing wrong with my behavior."

Briefly, the master sergeant looked up, staring directly at Berning. Pappendorf's eyes narrowed. He pressed his lips together so fiercely that they turned white. A threatening look met Berning's eyes, frightening him. Heat and sweat overcame the sergeant. His armpits were moistening.

"I... I...," Berning stammered. He struggled for words with which he wanted to show Pappendorf. Those words had flooded his mind on the way here, had made him inwardly deliver powerful speeches against which Pappendorf would have nothing to say. Now everything was gone.

"I...," he started again, but his mind went blank.

"Herr Unteroffizier," Pappendorf hissed, "I have no time for such nonsense now. Get out!"

Berning stared at Pappendorf for a moment longer, but the latter had spoken his final word. The master sergeant once again turned his attention to his regulations. Finally, after long seconds, Berning turned on his heel and left the room.

Northwest of Saint-Marcouf, France, June 17th, 1944

Company L's foxholes stretched along a low stone wall that separated several gardens. Apple trees had been planted in long rows. Green-yellow fruit hung from the slender branches.

Tom Roebuck had positioned his machine gun at a hole in the wall. He peered over the gun's iron sight into the forefield, but because of the fruit trees, the view was not good. If the Germans came, the Marine Raiders would probably be very late in spotting them. Still, Shapley, the regiment's commander, refused permission to withdraw the 4th Marine Raider Battalion -- and for a good reason: the Allied-held section was only a few miles deep, and then the sea was already there. And with each passing day, the Germans pushed in the beachhead further. Despite the massive use of fighter bombers and naval artillery, the Krauts could not be stopped. As a result, the battalion, which was supposed to act as a barricade to prevent the Germans from reaching Saint-Marcouf, could hardly be withdrawn any farther.

"Nothing," Roebuck stated with a searching glance at the forefield and slumped back behind the cover of the wall. His buddy Pizza nodded mutely.

The oppressive mood that had settled like a heavy cloak over most Marine Raiders hung almost tangibly in the air. Batman was dead, as was Constantin. Captain Morgan was severely wounded.

The battalion had shrunk to half its original strength, and in many emplacements, wounded men squatted, barely able to hold a weapon.

Given the heavy losses... given good soldiers and friends' death, it was almost unimportant that the battle as a whole was lost. Now it was just a matter of somehow getting out of France alive, while the Germans' flying cigars hissed again and again into the American positions, causing havoc. These things had to be packed from bottom to top with explosives, given the infernal sea of flames each one set off. Some of the Marines called them robots, but the term buzz bomb had also come into use because of the rattling sound they made when incoming.

The Marines used to victory and always able to outmaneuver the Japs despite some heavy losses in the Pacific, had to swallow hard because the Jerrys had finally defeated them. Now the battalion lay in hiding, having been overrun by the Krauts again only during the night and having had to surrender nearly a mile of terrain.

During the day, however, as now, when the clouds did not hang too low, and the weather was not too stormy, nothing could be seen of the Krauts. During the day, the Royal Air Force, Army Air Forces, and Navy aviators formed a protective shield around the beachhead. Even now, the engines of Thunderbolts and Vought fighters of the Corps roared over the Krauts' suspected positions. The German cowards, of course, were hiding.

"The assholes are merely strong when they're in the majority," Roebuck muttered, looking again into the orchards where the no man's land began. "When they pull a Jewish family out of their store with a whole company, the sons of bitches are strong. But as soon as there's a plane in the sky, the bastards crawl into their holes with their knees shaking. At least they're getting their asses kicked in fuckin' Russia right now!"

"What are you talking about?" Pizza asked casually, seeming more preoccupied with his own thoughts.

Roebuck sighed. "I was thinking we'd get to Paris, you know? A little partying, some drinks... banging French girls."

Now Pizza looked up. "Boy," he replied, putting a hand on Roebuck's shoulder. "Don't worry about your wife. You don't have anything to prove over here."

Roebuck sighed again, deep and long. Then suddenly, his eyes became glassy. How much longer could he keep up the facade of the strong and cold-hearted Marine? No, he had to open up to someone! And Pizza was one of the few survivors of his unit whom he would call a friend.

143

"It's just unfair," he complained in a broken voice. "Marie is home – and can do whatever she wants. And I'm sitting here in the shit!"

"Do you think she has a new guy?"

"No fuckin' idea." Roebuck turned his head away, putting his hands to his face. He didn't want to think about the possibility that Marie was at home sleeping with a strange man. Not Marie, his little Marie...

"Isn't that forbidden?" Pizza continued to think. "Isn't there a law that you have to consent if she has someone else?"

"Oh, who cares about laws?" Roebuck hissed. "That's just unfair! She's not giving me a chance at all, presenting me with an accomplished fact!" Roebuck hadn't given up hope yet. Anger, hate, love, sadness, despair accompanied him in turns when he thought of her. And he couldn't stop thinking about her.

"Hey, Lads! You guys want a few more minutes to yourselves, or what?" A voice that clearly belonged to a Brit brought them both back to reality. They startled and looked up into the face of a British soldier smeared with black camouflage paint. The guy had snuck up on them like a predatory cat.

"What do you want?" Saviano asked.

"Relief. It's your Yanks' turn to board the ships."

About time, Roebuck stated in his mind.

*

The Gunny, who had taken the reins after captain Morgan's dropout, had his men assemble in the rear of the front line. The last few days had caused the gunnery sergeant to age significantly. He wiped his hand over his stubble-covered scalp, glanced at the faces of the men lined up. Twenty-four soldiers were left of Company L, not a single officer among them.

"Okay, men, listen up," he said in a weary voice, in which there was none of the confidence with which he had still inspired the Marine Raiders on the way to Normandy.

144

"Parts of the 51st Highland Division of the British are taking over position here, along with a unit of the Frogs so that we can get out of here."

"It's about damn time the French took some responsibility over here. It's not like this is our country..." Roebuck mumbled.

"Shut up, PFC Roebuck! We're going to move east as fast as we can now. The regiment has its staging area in the dunes above Saint-Marcouf."

The Gunny dug a neckerchief, on which was printed a map of the Utah section, including the hinterland, out of the pocket on his belt. Several of the GIs did the same. The Marines had copied the trick with the cloths from the Airborne boys. The Gunny pointed out the staging area on his cloth, then gave the coordinates.

"From there, we'll get assigned a ship and a time by Navy briefers. So let's go. Let's make sure we get out of here! Double time!"

At a run, the company set off, with the Gunny charging ahead. Regardless of the haggard and exhausted bodies, the confidence of getting out of the fighting soon activated the last reserves of strength in the U.S. soldiers.

They reached the white-sand dune terrain around noon, which was dotted with primarily dark, gnarled bushes. Again and again, the sun pushed its way between the cloud cover in the sky. A fresh wind blew, making the sweaty Roebuck shiver as he sat on the sand, watching the activity on the beach. Pieces of the Allied fleet still rested in the Channel, seemingly lying on the horizon line. Small barges – landing craft, troopships, and amphibious vehicles – floated back and forth in a constant shuttle between the ships in the background and the beach. Gigantic craters in the dunes indicated the impacts of the German "cigars." Wrecked vehicles lined the areas that had come under robot fire. Bomb craters had chopped up the beach.

But no matter how many of these things the Krauts deployed against the remaining buildup of Allied forces in Northern France, no matter how many casualties the Western powers suffered, the Allies would still be able to

145

rescue enough soldiers and materiel across the Channel. These robots were simply too inaccurate for that, descending seemingly aimlessly over the Utah section. On the day of the Panther attack, Roebuck had even witnessed one of the "cigars" crash into the middle of a formation of Germans, killing dozens of the Krauts.

Roebuck looked at the bustle of activity down on the beach. All around him, his fellow Marines were lying in the sand, some having dozed off. The Gunny, meanwhile, had gone off to look for the orderly. Allied fighters patrolled the air in large numbers. The Air Forces had quickly discovered that the Germans' flying bombs could be shot down in flight if an experienced pilot was behind the stick.

In the shallow waters of the shore lay a lot of landing craft, as well as two alligator tanks. Men climbed into the watercraft. Officers wandered across the beach directing waiting units. For several days, the Germans had moved close enough to Utah Beach to disrupt Allied loading efforts with massive artillery poundings. But every time new shells fell in the coastal area, Air Forces dive bombers instantly roared into action, putting an abrupt end to the German batteries' activities. As mentioned, as long as the Krauts attacked only with artillery and these unguided robots, too few of which reached the Allied section, the loading of the invasion troops was not seriously threatened, the Germans could not muster enough firepower, and the withdrawing troops of the Western powers were too numerous for that.

A strange sound in the distance, like the rattling of an old diesel engine, filled the air as if on cue. Already someone was yelling, "Buzz bombs!"

The Americans jumped wildly, clawing at the sand of the dunes. Roebuck pressed his body against the ground, at the same time squinting between some bushes at the waterline, where everyone was also running all over the place. The buzzing sound was coming closer rapidly. Roebuck spotted three of the winged bombs hurtling in at breakneck speed. One flew far too short. It crashed into the sea a hundred yards off the beach. No explosion followed. Anyway, word got around that this new German weapon had many flaws.

146

Some detonated in mid-air, others not at all. Many missed their target by miles, then crashed somewhere in the sea. One is even said to have hit Calais, killing several civilians there.

The other two buzz bombs rushing in, however, found their target. Hissing, they headed for the beach. One jetted into a cluster of landing craft. The device exploded, releasing a massive burst of flame that engulfed several boats and many men. The detonation whipped the water; waves were unleashed that ran out to sea. There they clashed against the natural waves of the Channel, and both currents broke against each other. When the cloud of flames had passed, there was nothing left of the soldiers in the blast radius. A deep hole that had been torn in the beach along the Channel's edge filled with water. The landing craft lay scattered in the silt, partly tossed on their sides, partly broken and bent. Immediately, soldiers rushed in from all sides.

The third flying bomb, however, seemed to be destined for the hinterland. It rattled over the heads of the Marines. Immediately, several fighters got behind the "cigar." The wings of a Spitfire spat fire. Roebuck clearly saw sparks fly over the buzz bombs skin. Suddenly, there was a terrible bang – and the German bomb exploded in the air, forming a colossal gulf of fire in the firmament. Splinters flew off in all directions. The Spitfire was caught in a real rain of small and smallest metal fragments. Its engine spewed jet-black smoke. The plane went into a spin, losing altitude. Before the pilot could bail out, his plane crashed to the ground, itself becoming a pillar of fire that rose into the sky.

"Thank God the Nazis don't have planes," Roebuck whispered.

*

"All wings report in!" Squadron commander Captain Voss, a first lieutenant, demanded.

"Red 10 standing by."

"Red 7 standing by."

147

"Red 3 standing by."

"Red 6 standing by."

"Red 9 standing by."

"Red 2 standing by."

"Red 11 standing by."

"Red 5 standing by."

"Hold formation. Target assignment by me," Voss ordered.

Now that Jap apparatus can show what it's really made of, he added in his mind. He gently pushed the control stick a bit forward, thereby lowering the nose of his Fi S2 minimally. The Japanese called this single-engine torpedo-dive bomber with the distinctive upward-curved wings and the extended glass canopy on the fuselage, under which two crew members could sit, the Aichi B7A Ryūsei, but who would remember such a name?

For this reason, the Oberkommando der Luftwaffe – the High Command of the German Air Force or OKL in short – had decided to name licensed productions such as the Japanese torpedo-dive bomber after the corresponding German production facilities, in this case, the Fieseler plant in Kassel.

First Lieutenant Voss had already noticed during the long testing phase that the "Pacific Bird," as the landsers called it, was an outstanding piece of engineering. The Fi S2 was fast as lightning, extremely maneuverable, and stable in the air. Moreover, it was superior to all current German models in terms of speed and operational range – and thus finally silenced the critics of von Witzleben's technology transfer project.

Many voices had been raised in recent years demanding that German soldiers deserved German technology. The project to exchange technologies within the axis powers had been running since the end of 1942. Skeptical officers first had to learn that high-quality products were not only manufactured in Germany. For example, the Japanese were strong in the field of air and naval warfare, and the Germans still had a lot to learn. In addition to amphibious tanks, the Fi S2 torpedo-dive bomber was an exceptional development from the Empire of the Rising Sun, for which there was no comparison in the Wehrmacht repertoire. However, in Voss's eyes, the most crucial aspect of the transfer project was not the provision of blueprints. Much more important, in his opinion, was the real exchange of leading scientists, whereby the participating nations' strengths interlocked. In the end, the entire alliance profited from it. Not even the Allies maintained such close cooperation.

With the Aichi, for example, the Japanese had some problems with the built-in Homare engine, which threatened to delay series production by several years. With the help of engineers from Valtion lentokonetehdas, the Finnish state aircraft manufacturing company, the problems were solved. From the spring of 1944, pre-production started in Germany, Japan, Italy, and Finland.

And Voss was pleased that production was up and running. His squadron was still the only one to be equipped with this great aircraft. If the Japanese torpedo-dive bomber performed well in the upcoming combat mission, the OKL would determine that it was ready for series production – and give the corresponding order to Fieseler. The long-term goal was to build up a support air force for the German Navy with the Fi S2 as its backbone. Meanwhile, in the Luftwaffe, its commander-in-chief, Erhard Milch, was pursuing a radical type reduction to a few models to increase the overall mass production of combat aircraft. Also, considerable resources should be rapidly diverted to jet engine technology.

Voss looked over the rattling propeller engine at the scenery that loomed before him many miles away. Even from up here, the black dots were visible – the immense craters left by the hell hounds, littering the beach where all manner of enemy troops were moving about. Voss also clearly saw the tiny barges heading for the coast or departing from there, fully loaded. Following the small boats, the squadron captain's gaze was fixed on the enemy's gigantic fleet, which still lay menacingly in the calm water. More enemy warships had gathered on the English Channel than the German Reich, the German Empire, and the Holy Roman Empire of German Nations together had ever possessed.

However, the sight of the overwhelming enemy fleet did not inspire awe or even fear in Voss. There was enough Pervitin in his bloodstream to cause him to be overcome by a euphoric feeling at the sight of the enemy. He finally wanted to sink ships!

The big vessels lay quietly on the water, their anti-aircraft guns silent. Voss made out small black powder clouds in the sky. That meant enemy fighters were in the air. It would have been too good to be true, and the pilots did not even need to indulge in the illusion that the German attack would remain undetected until the very end, given the superior British radar technology.

Voss's gloved hands clenched around the control stick. The ensuing battle would be a massacre. And it would only be the beginning, for the Luftwaffe had decided not to let any more Allies escape from France. No matter what the cost. This was how Rommel had expressed it in an unknown rage. There could be no second Dunkirk. Therefore, this fight would only end when either the last Allied soldier and the last Allied ship had been swept off the French coast or when the last German aircraft in the command area of the CiC France-Benelux had been destroyed. Rommel's directive, personally approved by the chancellor, was very clear in this regard.

A massive air force – 800 planes – accordingly floated toward the Allied beachhead. Huge for the German Reich, yes, but a joke by the standards of the Western powers, who dominated the skies over Northern France at all hours of the day and night with 4,000 aircraft of all types.

Voss's eight squadron aircraft formed a long wedge with his plane as the lead. Behind them, the other squadrons of the groups joined in a wedge shape. Above, below, in front of, and beside them, hundreds of engines hummed a concert of steady roar. Stukas, Henschel 129, Focke Wulf 190, Messerschmitt Bf 109, Heinkel 162, Dornier 217, and others; virtually every available bird in the Luftwaffe was in the air. At that moment, Voss's group commander in his Japanese Zero, which had not made it into series production, passed the 2nd Squadron and moved in front of the wedge formation. He briefly waggled his wings up and down. Immediately Voss returned the salute, then all the squadron's airmen waggled their wings and finally those of the squadrons behind them. This was the old ritual of the group. This was how the pilots wished each other "Good Hunting!"

The group commander pulled up his Zero, a sleek aircraft with a Balkenkreuz instead of Japan's red sun on the fuselage, and dropped back behind the squadrons.

A blink of an eye later, an entire squadron of Messerschmitt's new jet aircraft chased past the cluster of German fighters and roared toward the enemy ships. The arrow-shaped planes with the thick turbines on their wings were intended to clear the ground fighters' way. The Me 262 was twice as fast as the Luftwaffe's fastest other aircraft, so no Allied fighter could match it. Unfortunately, just under 70 aircraft, this one squadron was all the Reich currently had to offer in jet aircraft. And there were plenty of Allied fighters in the sky, thanks to radar.

Already the Messerschmitt dashed into a formation of British Spitfire fighters. Lightning shot across the gray-clouded sky, flames burst forth. Seconds later, smoke and fire-spewing Spitfires plunged into the sea. Operation "Germanenhimmel" – Teuton Sky – had started.

A hellish dogfight broke out, but Voss concentrated entirely on the enemy ships.

"Pelican ahead," he shouted into his microphone. "Red 9, you and your wingmen follow my lead. Red 5, you stay on top and watch for Indians."

"Viktor," the speakers blared several times in confirmation. Voss steered his plane to the right, breaking out of the group's formation. His two wingmen followed him. Red 9 also swung out to the right along with his two wingmen.

Enemy Spitfires and Mustang fighter planes roared in from everywhere. They swooped out of the clouds, whizzed into the crowds of German warplanes, and fired from all guns.

"Indians! Indians!" the radio calls went wildly through the airwaves.

Red 5's bird made its way through the enemy fighters. The second man in the cockpit was already clinging to the machine gun, sending glowing sheaves whirring through the air. Sparks leaped across the steel skins of the enemy planes. Red 6 suddenly trailed a light, gray plume of smoke. The pilot turned away while his co-pilot fired like mad with the tail MG in all directions. Several Spitfires threw themselves down on the Fi S2 from above. Glowing salvos cut through the plane. It caught fire, got a hefty spin all at once, and rapidly lost altitude. Seconds later, the plane smacked into the sea.

Over the East Coast of the Cotentin Peninsula, above the heads of thousands of American soldiers, a tremendous air battle had erupted. At first, the GIs looked up at the sky in bewilderment. Fighter planes turned into flares rained to the ground, rockets and tracer bullets swirled through the air. Hissing and humming and snarling, the fighter planes of various types fought each other, drew tight circles around each other, and performed insane maneuvers.

When the Stukas then tilted over their wings, when they howled like Satan turned into metal and rushed towards the coast, the Americans on the ground only ran. Bombs fell on landing craft, tanks, and vehicles. Splinters hailed across the beach. Men collapsed. From all sides, German planes shelled and bombed the enemy's ground forces. The soldiers on the beach and in the dunes swarmed through each other like cattle gone wild. But the Spitfires, Mustangs, Warhawks, and Hurricanes were also rushing in from all sides. They mercilessly shot out dozens of aircraft from the formations of swooping German warplanes. In addition to bombs, rockets, and MG fire, the burning wrecks of dive bombers also smacked into the French sand in no time. German fighters were outnumbered one to ten by their Allied counterparts. Nevertheless, they did not shy away from confrontation. The lightning-fast Me 262 darted into

152

the enemy formations, torching Allied fighters. A German pilot had underestimated the speed. When the Spitfire was directly in front of him, he jerked the stick, but it was too late. The fighters crashed into each other, shattering as if they were made of glass. Man-sized pieces and torn wings plopped to the ground, killing several British.

The pilots of both sides blew each other out of the sky. It was a spectacle beyond compare. The clouds flashed and sparkled, twitched, and flickered. Balls of flame danced across the firmament. Down on the ground, bombs and bullets from machine guns and autocannons extinguished life by the second. The Americans, Canadians, British, French, Polish, and soldiers of other nations, who had no chance to fight back on the beaches and in the dunes, ran for their lives. The world was ending around them. No one down there suspected that the Germans had a far nastier surprise in store for them.

Next to the onslaught of German units pressing against the Allied beachhead from all sides, next to artillery fire, next to the infernal hell hounds, and now the deadly hail of fire from the ground attack airplanes, another cruel danger was slowly and leisurely roaring towards them. Bombers! More than 200 of the sleek, twin-engine Heinkel He 177, with their distinctive glass canopies in the ball-round nose, buzzed toward the Allied-held stretch of beach. They were accompanied by a handful of converted Focke-Wulf Fw 200 and Ju 52. In their rage and desire for retribution, the Germans had filled every available aircraft with bombs and sent them into action against the narrow Eastern beach of the Cotentin Peninsula. Immediately the fighters of the Americans and British formed up for the attack. It was an unfamiliar role for them to rush into enemy bomber formations and engage the flying whales in close combat. Usually, they discouraged German fighters from such ventures. Even if a Ju 52 burst under the first defense fire that hit the German bomber formation, because a bomb in its belly exploded, even if one of the Focke-Wulf planes lost both engines of its right wing and went down in a spin, the Allies were unable to prevent hundreds of bomb bays from opening up at that very moment. Thick eels with tails empennages were tumbling towards the earth. Within moments, the beach was transformed into a wall of fire. Landing craft and trucks were tossed about like toys. The invading forces suffered horrific losses, but the Germans also paid a heavy toll. Already, more Heinkel bombers were shaking under enemy fire. Airmen jumped out of side-slipping planes. Flames were lashing out after them.

As the sky was burning, while the beaches turned into a deadly inferno, Lieutenant Voss's squadron threw itself at the enemy fleet. He stared at the millions of gross register tonnage the Allies had brought into the Channel in awe. There were more warships off the coast of France than there were Luftwaffe planes in the sky!

"Fire at will. Watch our bees!" Several "Viktors" blared to Voss from the loudspeakers. His planes roared apart. The squadron's "bees" were their fighter protection, several Bf 109 that were already fending off attacks by enemy aircraft from all sides.

Voss headed directly for an American liner, about 150 meters long, which had been converted to military service. The vessel's hull was painted in various shades of black and gray, creating a large-scale camouflage pattern. It was the USS Ancon. The pilots had been instructed to concentrate on the enemy's troopships because they just could not sink enough Allied battleships to establish a balance of power with the German navy. So the philosophy was: better to go straight for the troopships. This approach offered the chance to crush as many of the enemy's invasion forces on board as possible.

Everywhere the German airmen in their Fi S2s and other planes dove into the deep, speeding death-defyingly towards the ships. Bombs and torpedoes were released from under the fuselages before the pilots turned around. Now there was a movement in the hitherto silent fleet. The huge ship engines awoke from their sleep. The colossal vessels slowly began to turn or picked up speed to somehow escape the attacks.

Voss had gone into a steep descent. The AA crews on the

154

USS Ancon were losing their nerve. Antiaircraft guns went off all over the deck. Twenty-millimeter shells raced toward Voss. The gunners kept on, thus setting up a carpet of bullets directly in front of Voss – and Voss had to get through it! He pulled the plane up even as he flew only a few tens of meters above the water's surface. On a straightforward approach, he headed for that troopship. Sparks sprayed across his plane. The wings became punctured. The side window of the cockpit clanked and showed a long crack. Voss approached the Ancon at an insane speed. Everything around him blurred into a blue-gray haze. Only the ship, growing larger and larger, lay before him, while flashes of rust-red fire leaped across the deck—glowing steel shot toward him. With the push of a button, Voss unleashed the air torpedo mounted beneath his plane. The long, slender steely eel, half as long as the plane itself, smacked into the water. Immediately, its tiny engine switched on. The torpedo plowed through the sea, swimming inexorably toward the USS Ancon. Voss looked over his shoulder, saw the back of his second man's head, then peered out through the glass. Down there in the water, the torpedo they had long since overtaken was tracing a long course. Voss had aimed excellently: The steely eel was on a collision course with the USS Ancon. The Japanese air torpedoes were much better than the German ones and could be launched at higher speeds.

Suddenly, a jolt went through Voss' plane as another projectile bored into the fuselage. Voss looked forward, his fingers clutching the control stick with all his might. A violent vibration rippled through his Fi S2. The plane began to buck and spin. Voss sped right into a carpet of AA rounds. He pulled up, his plane jerking forward. Bullets pounded the wings, thundered against the fuselage, digging deep into the steel. They damaged the vital mechanics of the engine, causing it to cough before spewing thick smoke. The instruments went berserk. The engine died. The aircraft tilted slightly forward before beginning to lose altitude. Voss saw the deck of the Ancon in front of him. In his back, the second man screamed out as the anti-

155

aircraft rounds cut through his legs and lower body. Voss didn't even realize at first that he, too, had been hit. Only when he saw the blood on his leather jacket, he realized what had happened. Voss looked out over the propeller of his plane at what appeared to be the approaching American ship. A blink of an eye later, he crashed into it.

Saint-Marcouf, France, June 20th, 1944

The scenery was spooky. Dozens of wrecked landing craft lined the water's edge. Shell holes and huge craters littered the beach and the dunes. The steel carcasses of destroyed American trucks, shot-up tanks, and wrecked planes dominated the scene. In some places, the white dunes were scorched black by the flames of war. Burnt bushes moved eerily in the wind. Near the coast, the bridge and chimneys of the 100-yard destroyer USS McCook rose out of the water. For three days, the Krauts had been attacking incessantly with their air force, as if to sink every single landing craft that dared to leave France. In suicidal commando operations, the German pilots had gone on the attack, again and again, relentlessly throwing themselves into the tumult of Allied fighter planes.

Despite immense losses, the Germans deployed every available aircraft against the evacuation site of the invasion forces. Wave after wave of Wehrmacht aircraft roared in, some of them faster than lightning, so fast that no Allied plane could keep up with them. Wave after wave, the British and American fighter pilots thinned out the formations of the Luftwaffe. Wave after wave, they fought the attackers. But the Krauts did not tire of trying. They kept coming and coming. More of them crashed into the Channel or slammed down on the Cotentin Peninsula ground with each raid. Still, the survivors flew back to their bases, refueled and reloaded ammunition, and appeared back in the continuous air battle over Utah Beach. It was said that the German chancellor was pulling all available air forces from every theater in Europe – except the Eastern Front and Italy – and throwing them into the air war over Northern France. And so with each wave, new planes arrived. Day and night, their engines roared over the Allied ships. They shot at fleeing landing craft and troopships, attacked the fleet, and the invasion troops lying in the sand. Apparently, the Krauts were pissed off that someone had dared to enter their France. And they succeeded, even if this success was bought with the loss of half of the German Air Force. The Germans sank ships; they destroyed landing craft, they thinned out the exhausted invasion forces. With each sinking ship, countless soldiers who had boarded that very vessel and thought they were safe were dragged to their deaths. The USS McCook was also carrying 400 soldiers of the 29th U.S. Infantry Division, in addition to her 275 crew members, when German torpedo bombers targeted her. The ship's captain lost his nerve under the bombardment and suddenly headed for the coast, where the destroyer received several hits and sank.

Initially, the German Luftwaffe had fought the Allied beachhead with over 800 planes. After days of continuous fighting, the Germans had a little less than 300 aircraft in action, but they did not stop attacking the beach. For days, already, it was almost impossible to think of shipping troops. The Krauts may have lost a large part of their air forces from Northern Europe on Utah Beach, but the Allies lost tens of thousands of soldiers in the hail of bombs, in the storm of splinters, in the chaos of shattering hulls. The initially almost smooth shipment of the invasion troops turned into a slaughter.

Meanwhile, on the mainland, the Allies continued to lose ground. The haggard forces that tried to hold a perimeter around the evacuation site were no longer able to withstand the Jerrys' pressure. Since the beachhead had shrunk to a diameter of a few kilometers, the enemy's flying bombs failed to appear. Instead, the Krauts' artillery batteries and Nebelwerfers now fired uninterruptedly into the tiny area that the Allies still held. The remaining invasion forces of

157

the Western powers were on the verge of collapse. Heavily wounded men squatted in hastily dug foxholes. Ammunition was scarce; rations were not available anymore. Not much longer, and German panzers would be firing on the landing craft.

With anger and hatred for these inhuman Krauts in their bellies, the last units bravely continued to defend a few miles of dune country. The Allies had almost nothing left but wounded to ship, but even that the Germans refused to allow. They would probably not rest until the last Allied soldier had been killed and beaten into the sand. Almost 20,000 Allies, mostly Americans, still had their feet on French soil. They had their backs to the sea.

Another bad weather front was on the horizon. Thick, gray-black clouds wafted across the sky. Regardless of the weather conditions, the battle raged on. Glowing tracer bullets flashed across the firmament. Planes went up against each other, engaged in dogfights. Smoking aircraft fell like stones from the sky. On the ground, they became flaming balloons. The battle also raged above the fleet fanning out on the Channel. Ships that had been hit poured thick clouds of smoke. Antiaircraft guns shot into the sky. Tangles of rust-red fireworks flashed across the gray cloud-covered sky like bright strings.

And every now and then, those strange, superfast planes of the Germans appeared, which were very successful in giving fighter protection to the bombers. Fortunately, the Germans had few of these jet fighters.

The dunes around Tom Roebuck and Tony Saviano were virtually thrown into the air. The Krauts were on the move. Field-gray uniforms leaped between the bumps in the ground. The enemy advance was supported by three of those tanks the Germans called assault guns. Constantly firing explosive shells between the American positions, these things successfully held down the GIs.

Twelve men of Company L were still fit for action, and the battalion numbered less than a hundred soldiers. Up to that day, the 1st Marine Raider Regiment had failed to ship out. Nearly no troops had been able to evacuate at all in the last few days. With a stubbornness that bordered on insanity, the Kraut pilots threw themselves incessantly between the Allied fleet, the Allied fighter planes and the coast. Roebuck hated the Germans for their fanaticism.

"Can't the fuckin' Jerrys just accept that the U.S. is in charge of the world?" he yelled, furious with rage, as he fired his Thompson in an untargeted burst of fire toward the gray figures that were closing in on the Marines with each leap. An explosion shredded the dune against which Roebuck and Pizza's position leaned. Sand and bushes and dirt rained down on the two Americans, who pressed their hands protectively over their helmets.

"They're fucking Germans!" Pizza shouted, with thick chunks of dirt pelting down on him. "Look at history! Apparently, they need to be punched in the face all the time! Probably the fucking Germans wouldn't be able to handle it at all if there was suddenly peace!"

Roebuck emptied his magazine; in the forefield, one of the Germans was staggering. An MG 42 sounded. Impacts splattered across the sand just ahead of Roebuck. Fine particles flew into his eye.

He slid down into his foxhole, yanking the staggered magazine out of the weapon.

"My last one!" he gasped, reloading his weapon. He had lost the MG the day before.

Roebuck stuck his upper body out of the hole and fired.

"These scumbags ought to be wiped out!" he raged. Already he had to drop back into his hole. German shelling of all caliber pelted the battalion's line.

"Otherwise, we'll have to fight two more world wars because the English and the Frogs are too stupid to sweep in front of their front door!"

In the forefield, the assault guns fired again. A German four-barreled anti-aircraft gun joined in the concert of death. Fountains of all sizes shot from the ground. Marines were hit, screaming out. The anti-aircraft shells tore off one man's arm.

The entire Company L foxhole line was plowed up; the Marine Raiders pinned to the bottom of their holes like insects. It looked as if the dunes would turn into boiling water; the sand was shaking so much.

"The assholes are fucking us from behind!" the Gunny roared as he stuck his bloody head out of one of the foxholes. "Willis, Teller! Covering fire! We're retreating!" One of those addressed, a bald man with a casual expression, nodded in agreement. But there was no more covering fire. A threatening hiss filled the air, then the shells of the German rocket artillery, the Nebelwerfers, rushed in from all directions. Countless of the screaming rockets hit the 4th Battalion. Burning splinters cut through the air, penetrating tissue and organs, disfiguring and killing people. Not only did fragments fly off in all directions from the impacting rockets, but a dense wall of artificial fog quickly formed.

Seconds passed; Roebuck could barely see his hand in front of his eyes, while Pizza, only a meter away from him, had disappeared entirely in the white mist. The aggressive, artificial smoke invaded Roebuck's mouth and nose, entering his lungs. He had to cough violently. Somewhere the Gunny was barking orders. German voices rang out, then the Krauts, who had pulled gas masks over their faces, burst out of the wall of fog. They looked like monsters. Pizza hurried out of the foxhole and ran away. He bumped into a Kraut. Both dropped their weapons in fright and now used their hands. In an instant, they clawed at each other, threw themselves to the ground, wrestling for life and death. More Germans approached, dragged the bravely fighting Saviano away from his opponent, hurled him into the sand. Boots hit the American against his body and head. All he could do was curl up like a baby, cover his face with his hands, and hope that these brutes would let him live.

Roebuck aimed, pulled the trigger. The sand around him turned red. He then jumped out of his foxhole, rushing off. He had to help Pizza! He reloaded his gun. Krauts everywhere! They were coming out of the fog! From all sides! Men rolled across the ground in close combat. An explosion in Roebuck's back took him off his feet. He tasted blood. He tasted sand. When he opened his eyes again, he was lying backward in a hollow, looking into the strange grimace of a German gas mask and the cold barrel of a German machine carbine.

South of Carentan, France, June 21st, 1944

The shining moon was over Normandy, June 21st was nearing its end. The Allied invasion had been defeated. Several tens of thousands of dead Americans, British, French, Polish, Luxembourgers, Belgians, Dutch, Canadians, South Africans, New Zealanders, Australians, Czechs, Greeks, and Norwegians lay on the shore, even more, had become prisoners of war. For them, a life of labor in the war service of the German Reich would now begin.

The III Abteilung soldiers of Panzer Regiment 2 had found shelter at some farmhouses, where a friendly Frenchman had offered the tankers a warm place to sleep in a large barn lined with straw.

Engelmann hoped that the second victory on French soil over the Western powers would lead to a rethinking among the French. The underground Résistance movement was a painful thorn in the side of the occupying forces. The invasion operation had finally proven that organized and coordinated attacks from the underground could have a high military value. A population that cooperated could deprive the underground movement, which was so damaging and dangerous, of any breeding ground.

Engelmann had distanced himself from his men, who drank wine to celebrate the victory while singing folk songs. Once again, he longed for a bit of privacy, but he also could not stand the exuberant mood of his comrades. A bruising battle for moral values raged in Engelmann's chest.

Hadn't he always thought he had integrity enough to survive a war without losing face? Had he even made himself a criminal against humanity? Was he simply too soft for these hard times? Were Christian values and faith in

161

a good power out of place in times when people were at each other's throats?

Engelmann painfully remembered his first conversation with Kranz. Now Kranz was dead. So many were dead. Engelmann sighed. He wanted to use the minutes of solitude to say some intercessions.

The night was silent. A dog barked in the distance. A cool breeze blew around Engelmann's ears. The light birch grove in which he was standing offered no protection from the wind. In his mind, Engelmann struggled for words that he could address to the Lord. Desperately he thought of a formulation, a beginning... but he could not. He could not pray. He felt so false and dishonest as a Christian. He could not even ask for protection for his family. He sighed, turned on his heel, and marched back to the hamlet where his unit was accommodated. Halfway there, he met Nitz leaning forlornly against a fence post, drinking a bottle of strong alcohol.

"Oberfeldwebel?" he addressed his old comrade in a depressed voice.

"Oh, Herr Leutnant?" Nitz raised the hand holding the bottle in salute. His movements seemed awkward, and his voice was a little flat.

"Did something happen?"

"Nope, nope." Nitz waved it off vigorously. "I just sit here and drink until my fucking pain goes away."

"I told you you should have stayed in the hospital."

"Oh, it's the age. The blue nitwits can't do anything about that. Want a sip?" Nitz held the bottle under Engelmann's nose.

"Me? No, I... oh, why not." The lieutenant took a hearty swig and lowered himself to the ground beside Nitz. He handed the bottle back to the master sergeant, who immediately started sucking on it again.

"What do you think of the Russian offensive?" Engelmann asked after a while. It was one of those topics that bothered him. The Wehrmacht had had to retreat behind the Dnieper in the areas of Army Group South and Army Group Center or tried to reach the crossings in time in a race with their pursuers. Orel, Kursk, Kharkiv... all again in Soviet hands. So many men had miserably died to conquer these cities – and now?

"What I think of that?" Nitz snorted in his Leipzig dialect. "Crap! It's crap! Let's face it, Leutnant, we know the Eastern Front. Ivan is unstoppable sooner or later."

"Then why are we still fighting at all?"

Nitz shook himself. "Because it's ordered."

The silence that followed lasted only a short time, for Nitz soon brought up another subject after again coercing Engelmann to take a sip from the bottle.

"You've changed, Herr Leutnant. The boys have noticed that, too."

"Doesn't this war change us all?"

Nitz laughed out loud. "All of us? No! Not me! The Great War already destroyed my mind and soul; there's not much left for this one."

"Why do they call the last war the Great War?" Engelmann snatched the bottle from Nitz and continued. "Isn't this one the greater war?"

"Maybe. Let others judge."

"You know, Oberfeld, after my studies, I volunteered when it came to the Sudetenland, and Hitler was also preparing to solve the painful Polish question. Of course, I wanted to become a teacher sometime later, but before that, I felt it was my duty to serve my fatherland. I wanted to protect my homeland, my family – I was not married at that time, you know? Everything had sounded so noble... but reality catches up with you, I guess."

Nitz laughed again. "What are you talking about?" he mocked Engelmann. "You haven't experienced anything yet. We sit in a tin can like herrings all the time and don't get to see anything of the gruesome dying around us. In the Great War, I experienced horror. This war here is a walk in the park compared to that." Nitz spread his arms.

The master sergeant's words hit Engelmann where it hurt.

"But you see some things," the lieutenant muttered all at once, "terrible things that shake you so deeply you never thought it was possible."

163

"You're talking about the incident with the Frenchman?"

"You know about it?"

"Are you kidding? The whole damn company knows about it."

"And you don't care about such things?"

Nitz wiped his stubble-covered chin. "There's a war going on, Herr Leutnant. Terrible things are happening. And those Marquis fighters are quite bad sons of bitches. We should just be glad that our comrades could be freed. Who knows what the partisans would have done to them."

Pointe du Hoc, France, June 23rd, 1944

Second Lieutenant Beppo Klauser of the Propaganda Platoon of Propaganda Company 649, a scrawny little man with filigree limbs, looked in his uniform as if it were two sizes too big. Nevertheless, he gave his speech to the soldiers with a fiery passion. The words virtually gushed out of him, accompanied by changing images, which a staff sergeant threw onto a screen set up in front of the men at the push of a button. All the defenders of Pointe du Hoc, except for a few alarm posts, were present for the demonstration. The propaganda company's men worked extra shifts throughout the army divisions since the Eastern Front events began to unfold.

It had long since dawned; the sun had disappeared behind the horizon. In the flickering twilight of the projector, the second lieutenant had something almost threatening about him. But what he told the soldiers was anything but threatening. The men listened attentively to the officer, and their enthusiasm grew with every syllable Klauser uttered. The audience of the spectacle had leaned forward with interest, whispering among themselves. Was what the second lieutenant was saying the beginning of the end of the war? Had the German Reich really landed the political coup of the century? A tension that could almost

164

have been grasped lay over the present landsers.

Berning blinked continuously. The glare reflecting off the screen against the soldiers stung his eyes unpleasantly in the twilight. Still, he did not dare to move. Pappendorf, standing aside from the platoon, kept a watchful eye on his men. While the comrades of the other units were more or less loafing around, the 2nd Platoon of the 1st Reconnaissance Squadron stood at attention. Berning's feet ached, which began to affect his concentration. Basically, he liked the troops' propaganda events. The officers of the propaganda units knew their business; every time after such an event, Berning felt much better, was generally more confident.

This time, however, Klauser's euphoric words rolled off Berning like raindrops on a windowpane. Evil thoughts overcame the sergeant, for this evening would be his last in France – France, which after the repelled invasion had once again become a paradise for the soldiers. At that point, it didn't matter how much Pappendorf had maltreated the platoon. The next morning, the men of the division would board the train and make their way toward the Eastern Front, where all hell seemed to be breaking loose at the moment. Most of the division was already on its way.

Berning did not want to go back to Russia.

"Two days ago," Klauser finally got down to the facts after a lengthy speech drenched in ideological phrases, "on June 21st, the Imperial Japanese Army joined Chinese and Manchurian forces in the fight against the Bolsheviks."

The projector threw a map of East Asia on the wall. Visible was the Japanese puppet state of Manchukuo, whose southern border extended to the Japanese-occupied part of China. To the west, Manchukuo touched Mongolia, and to the north, it was bordered by Soviet territory.

"Fifty-eight divisions and division-like formations participate in the Japanese attack, which is directed in two wings of attack against the territory of Russia as well as Mongolia. A strong thrust in the North against the Russian lines along the Manchukuo-Soviet border," Klauser said, indicating with a pointing stick the areas referred to, "is to

165

tie up the majority of Russian forces. At the same time, the Southern wing of the offensive advanced directly into Mongolia."

One landser whistled through his teeth; others murmured in excitement. However, Berning was not particularly interested in the details of a Japanese offensive – and indeed, so were many here. The only interesting thing was the impact of that on the Eastern Front. After all, Germany was no longer utterly alone against Russia since allies like Italy or Finland did not count in most German soldiers' minds anyway. Many landsers had the feeling that the war in the East was only a German fight. However, the Japanese Empire was a real force to be reckoned with, even if it was increasingly being troubled by the Americans.

Klauser let what he had said take effect for a moment. Joy, relief, and confidence spread abruptly through the audience. Finally, the Reich had a real ally in the fight against the gigantic Red Army! No one present was aware of the intense internal struggles within the Japanese Empire that had preceded this very offensive. The Kwantung Army, which had always been very stubborn and had been discredited by the Japanese-Soviet border conflict in Tokyo in 1939, had been considerably strengthened and expanded to be allowed to lead this attack, much to the displeasure of other armies and the navy. For a German, the situation in Japan was difficult to comprehend – including the fact that military formations acted almost independently. Before Pearl Harbor, a war had almost broken out between the Japanese Navy and the Japanese Army – a scenario unthinkable for Germany.

"Two goals of war go hand in hand with the Japanese offensive," Klauser continued. "First, the capture and occupation of Mongolia to provide a strong base for attacks against the center of Russia. Second, the advance into Siberia to gain access to resources there that Japan desperately needs in the fight against the United States."

"No way they'll succeed against the Ivans," a master sergeant from the front row groaned. Klauser blinked kindly at the interrupter.

166

"Maybe," the second lieutenant admitted after a brief pause for effect. "But the decisive factor is that the Japanese, with their attack, absorb strong forces of the enemy. It allows us to force the decision in this conflict with an offensive against Moscow. Once Russia is defeated, Japan will have the raw materials necessary to fight back against the Anglo-Americans."

"With all due respect, what do we care about the Japs?" the same master sergeant asked. In other armed forces, troop support events would indeed have been conducted with the draconian hand of an unteachable doctrinal master. In the German Wehrmacht, however, a particular culture of discussion had been established that even allowed criticism to be expressed. This was by no means a weakness of Germany, but a tremendous strength that had made the Wehrmacht what it was then. Klauser cleared his throat, then smoothed out the sleeves of his uniform.

"Believe me, Herr Oberfeldwebel, the fate of Japan should concern us all. If Japan falls, the second half of the Allied forces will be freed to intervene in Europe. To fight such power would demand terrible losses from our fatherland. So as long as Japan holds out, it draws upon itself crucial forces that would otherwise work against us."

"They won't last long anyway. With this offensive, they're running straight to their deaths."

"No, I can't agree with that. The Japanese are losing island after island in the Pacific, that may be. But this is only because they have ordered their naval and air forces back home. The Japanese have realized that they are no match for the Allied fleets, so they are entrenching themselves on every little island, defending it to the last. They have already inflicted terrible losses on the Americans because the Japanese have proved themselves as an extraordinarily defensible and sacrificial people. At the same time, they are making their main islands defensible, assembling strong forces there. We currently assume that the Americans will have reached the Japanese islands in the winter of 1945/1946. But if they want to storm them, they will face a bloodbath. Believe me, I was allowed to speak with a liaison

167

officer who recently visited Japan. He was extremely impressed with the actions the Japanese are currently taking." Klauser smiled confidently. "It will take a miracle for the Anglo-Americans to get Japan to surrender." The propaganda officer clapped his hands vigorously. "But the seizure of Mongolia – to come back to this once more – is indispensable if we want to defeat the Bolsheviks. After our preemptive strike in 1941, Russia made great efforts to move its gigantic armaments industry behind the Ural Mountains, inaccessible even to our great Luftwaffe. Undisturbed, the Russians can produce tanks and cannons there. The axis powers have set themselves the goal to disturb the armament of the Bolshevists severely. The starting point for this must be Mongolia. Our steadily increasing assortment of special weapons, developed in the German-Japanese alliance, will also be used against the enemy armament industries from Mongolia. The Höllenhunde have already been used successfully against the Americans right here in France, as has our excellent Messerschmitt's jet fighter. The Japanese have used the hell hounds to test bomb Chongqing, which these days is on the verge of surrender." Klauser showed Chongqing, the provisional capital of all the Chinese opposing forces that had formed a shaky alliance against Japan. In a surprise raid in the first quarter of this year, Japan had advanced far to the West. Following the Yangtze River, the Imperial Japanese Army had advanced as far as Sichuan Province, where it had surrounded Chongqing and besieged it ever since. Simultaneously, it had succeeded in conquering the Hunan, Jiangxi, and Fujian regions, finally creating a land bridge to the occupied territories on the Southeast coast of China.

"Soon, the enemy will also feel the power of the brand-new Höllenhund II, although details are still secret, of course," Klauser concluded with a cheeky smile on his lips.

"Yes, it's always secret... we're not stupid after all!" a voice with a Berlin dialect nagged from the middle of the formation. Klauser batted his eyelids, then asked, "What do you mean?"

168

"Well, it is always said, it is secret, it is secret. You can say that about everything! Only rumors are spread, but there is no proof for these allegedly war-deciding special weapons."

Klauser smiled again. "Wait and see," he demanded. "The hell hounds we've been reporting on since the beginning of the year are now in action. And they work! So do our jet fighters. Have faith in our leadership that Hellhound II is no feint either. Hellhound II is far superior to its predecessor in range, speed, accuracy, and striking power. It will be the deciding factor in this war."

That would be too good, Berning pleaded inwardly, because the end of the war would mean that he could finally free himself from Pappendorf's clutches.

Klauser looked around for a moment, then smoothed out the sleeves of his uniform again. Afterward, he continued, "But that should not be the topic today."

Klauser nodded to the staff sergeant at the projector. The latter pressed a button, and the next image appeared on the screen.

A single murmur went through the rows of soldiers. The whispering began anew. The screen showed a close-up of a Tiger tank pushing through tall grass. Foreign-looking soldiers with repeating rifles and tufts of grass in their helmets charged forward under cover of that tank. However, the side of the Tiger pictured here was not adorned with a Balkenkreuz, but the vehicle was painted with a strangely intertwined camouflage pattern.

"Let's be real," Klauser said, raising his arms. He visibly enjoyed the reactions of the auditorium. "Rumors had been buzzing through the bush radio for a long time, but yesterday our dear Herr Reichskanzler made an announcement concerning German-Japanese cooperation in a call to the troops. We propaganda units have been instructed to inform you as soon as possible about the developments. We want you all to know that our Asian allies will not attack Ivan with sticks and stones. Rely on the fact that the Japanese have combat-ready, highly motivated, and well-trained divisions. In the technology transfer project, we have started at the end of 1942, Japan has always played a decisive role. Under Walther Nehring's leadership, who was promoted to Generalfeldmarschall last month, a Wehrmacht delegation plays a significant role in strengthening the Japanese armored forces, and motorizing the Japanese army, and introducing it to the principles of Blitzkrieg warfare. One element of this plan was the release of crucial German armament licenses, namely the Panzer IV, Tiger, Panther, Sturmgeschütz III, Ferdinand, and, for the aviation sector, the Messerschmitt jet fighter, among others.

Besides, however, under the German military's influence, some outdated elements of the Japanese concept of firefighting could at least be broken up. Thus we managed to make Japan finally rely more on firepower than merely on the individual soldier's prime motivation. However, the Japanese did not allow us to interfere with all of it, as the German and Japanese understanding of warfare is worlds apart.

Nevertheless, under the command of General Itagaki Seishirō, the Japanese delegation for the Reich could be valuable to the Wehrmacht. Especially in terms of close combat and laying ambushes, the Japanese are providing first-class training in Germany; moreover, their experience in naval warfare, in particular, has been worth its weight in gold for our great Kriegsmarine. Perhaps some of you have already had the pleasure of being trained by Japanese instructors?

The Japanese, I can also tell you, have turned out to be excellent tank men. A Japanese crew in a German Tiger is the most deadly little fighting team you will find east of the Ural Mountains.

An uneasy feeling formed in Berning's stomach.

They gave our tanks to these monkeys? he groaned in his mind. Images of him fighting against Tiger tanks under Japanese command materialized in his mind's eye.

In the audience, the overall mood was mixed. Many seemed to share Berning's fears; others seemed downright enthusiastic. Quiet discussions broke out again. Only the 2nd Platoon of the 1st Reconnaissance Squadron remained silent.

Pappendorf watched the activity of the other units with a lurking look.

"In the short time, we have now been able to equip two Japanese divisions entirely with our panzers, including forming two heavy battalions." Klauser deliberately allowed the emerging discussions to continue. At least he did nothing to stop them. Instead, he smiled victoriously. Finally, the propaganda officer raised his voice to drown out the murmurs. As he did so, he pointed to the photo on the screen, "This shot is certainly not from the offensive that was recently unleashed. Even we aren't that fast." Klauser grinned as if he had cracked a joke. "This shot was taken in late March during an attack on the Lingling-Liuzhou railroad line. The offensive at that time and the raid against Chongqing was the ordeal by fire for Nehring's Pacific tanks – and they passed with flying colors!

It should be noted now, of course, that the Japanese entry into the war is already having its effect on our Eastern Front. Ivan has fallen into rigidity. His offensive against us is at a standstill. I say..." Klauser fell silent as over on the cliff, the newly brought in four-barreled anti-aircraft gun suddenly started barking. The next moment, two fighter bombers dove down from the gloomy evening clouds. Machine guns roared. Then an explosion occurred at the anti-aircraft gun. The planes turned away. The AA gun had been silenced. The metal fuselages and wings of more planes flashed in the sky.

"Air raid warning!" the soldiers yelled in confusion before scattering in panic. Berning was hit in the shoulder as soldiers whizzed past him. Many threw themselves to the ground, for it was too late to reach any foxhole. Already the enemy steel birds were above the landsers. In a dive, they roared towards the earth. Their autocannons boomed. Men screamed. Those who were hit staggered. Projectiles as thick as children's arms shredded fleshy lumps from the bodies of German soldiers. Occasionally, rifles were heard. Berning pressed against the earthy floor with all his might. Instinctively he opened his mouth. He saw Pappendorf throw himself to the ground and put both hands over his

171

head. Sometimes even the master sergeant acted like a normal human being.

A blink of an eye later, the swooping steel birds released their bombs. Berning squinted under his field cap into the crowd of comrades. He wished he had a helmet on his head. Men ran for their lives; others pressed their bodies against the ground like worms. Berning saw Weiss and Reuben running away in panic.

Lie down, you fools, he yelled at them in his mind.

But Weiss and Reuben ran, fleeing in the direction of the buildings. All at once, a bomb rattled in between them. A ball of flame, clouded with earth and dust, bulged up between the two, swallowed them, engulfed them. The deafening noise of the explosion burned itself into Berning's hearing. He yelled out in despair. When the wall of earth and fire settled, there was nothing left of Weiss and Reuben. It had taken only a heartbeat, and the war had taken two very good comrades from Berning. In a fit of desperation, Berning jumped up. He wanted to get to the site of the detonation, wanted to help his men – his friends who had literally dissolved in the flames of that bomb. High up among the clouds, another wave of enemy fighter bombers descended. Their projectiles dug tunnels through the soft bodies of German soldiers; others hit the soil. Then more bombs fell. Berning stood in the open. Around him, the world broke apart. Razor-sharp splinters hailed down on him. A tiny metal plate hissed through his right uniform sleeve and burned into his arm. Berning felt nothing of it at that moment. He stormed off, wanting to find Weiss and Reuben. Somewhere deep in his brain, he already knew that they were gone. But he didn't want to admit it. Without Weiss and Reuben, Berning had no one left in this damn squadron!

The sergeant ran and ran. Around him, perfect chaos. Soldiers were jumping around, wounded men were screaming. The ground was bloody red, littered with body parts. Suddenly, a bomb crashed into the ground just in front of Berning. The sergeant stumbled and threw his arms in front of his face. He almost hit the phallus-shaped metal object, the tip of which had disappeared in the ground. Berning remained in a state of shock, staring at the bomb stuck in the soil in front of him. The small propeller in the empennage was still spinning.

Dud! Berning hissed in his mind. He could not take his eyes off the bomb. His heart was pounding, thumping, hammering, hammering all the way into his head. A heat as hot as hell overcame him. Berning did not dare to move. The rotation of the small propeller on the empennage slowly died away. Then the bomb was stuck in the ground in complete stillness. The sharp smell of urine filled the air. Berning's pants were wet, but he was unaware of his mishap at that moment.

Moudon, Switzerland, June 24th, 1944

Federal Councillor Karl Kobelt, head of the Military Department, threw a last glance into the hospital room where a single patient lay: that patient, guarded by two soldiers, was hooked up to an IV bag and covered all over with bandages. The doctor in charge of the ward, an elderly man with narrow nickel glasses on his nose, closed the door and looked expectantly at the two gentlemen waiting in the hallway: in addition to Kobelt, there was the deputy commander of the Bern police, Martin Durant.

"There's a good chance he'll make a full recovery," the doctor remarked as if casually.

"It's outrageous." Kobelt shook his head decisively. "Simply outrageous, the way the warring parties are fighting their battles on our territory as if we had nothing to say about it! And now the Americans have also expressed interest in this prisoner as if the Swiss people's need for justice didn't exist!"

"At least we now have the option to show that such actions do not remain without consequences," Durant returned with fire in his eyes.

"And we must do that! The Americans are invading our airspace as they please. The Russians have set up a spy network in Bern, and the Germans are roaming our cities, shooting like maniacs." Kobelt shook his head again. "I thought things would get better under this von Witzleben. After all, he has loosened the sanctions. Unfortunately, severity seems to me to be the order of the day, instead of reconciliation. Regardless of the German power to bully us once again, we must not tolerate such behavior!" Kobelt cleared his throat. "In any case, I am glad that the German could finally be transported because he is best off in the internment camp."

Because of Switzerland and the German Reich's political back-and-forth, it was unclear for a long time how the Swiss should deal with their aggressive neighbor from the North – and political forces in the country were still at odds over the issue. Nevertheless, after Hitler's death, the neutral country's situation had improved considerably because von Witzleben had adopted a course of understanding. Still, there were interned Germans, including some fighter pilots who had crashed over Switzerland, in Swiss custody. At least von Witzleben had ensured that a large collective camp could be set up for the internees with money from Germany at the cost of economic concessions. In the meantime, the Reich was also financing the German inmates' feeding, while negotiations for releases were going on behind the scenes.

Durant and the doctor nodded. In Moudon, a village in the French-speaking part of the country, the camp for German prisoners had been set up on a fast-track basis.

"I'm glad he's here for a completely different reason," Durant finally hissed, licking his lips.

Kobelt motioned the policeman to continue. Durant added in a sharp voice, "The only thing our justice can do is put him in jail." The deputy police commander glanced angrily at the door of the hospital room. "The military justice, however, will sentence this Swabian to death."

Kobelt and the doctor agreed.

"And all the better that he will recover fully. He should be awake to witness when he receives his sentence – and even more so when it is carried out!" Durant jeered, apparently forgetting that he was facing a federal councilor.

"Please remain factual, Herr Durant," Kobelt remarked dryly.

"Excuse me, Herr Bundesrat, but in the face of three dead, including a comrade from Lucerne, as well as two severely injured, it's hard for me to remain factual. And I think Herr von Steiger sees things the same way."

"That may be." Kobelt got lost in his own words. Thousands of thoughts flooded his mind. For years the small but defensible Switzerland had endured in the stranglehold of the German National Socialists, had not yielded to countless demands of the axis, and had paid the bitter price of economic isolation for it. Bread, sugar, butter, fuel – virtually all vital resources were scarce at times and had to be rationed. Besides, the active service of the army had deprived all economic sectors of men.

Finally, political decisions had to be taken, which a democracy can only take in extreme emergency times: The authorities told the farmers where they had to grow how much of what; soccer pitches and parks became fields. The ingredients of bread were regulated by law so that nothing would be wasted. Everywhere in the country, passive air protection was practiced, training was given on how to smother flames with fire blankets and help the seriously injured.

However, since this von Witzleben was in power in Germany, things were noticeably better for the Swiss. Von Witzleben, in contrast to the insane Hitler, had realized that, given the problematic war situation, the German Reich had to start making friends in the world again for a change. After all, the German chancellor had reduced the pressure that was weighing on Switzerland. Wehrmacht troops had retreated from the Swiss border – and German planes no longer provoked Switzerland with bold overflights. Lately, it was instead the British and Americans who did not respect Swiss neutrality and dropped bombs on Swiss cities.

It was evident that the Swabians wouldn't leave us alone for long, Kobelt thought inwardly, with flaring anger in his chest.

Bénouville, France, June 25th, 1944

Schneider knocked on the doorframe to the room where the crazy captain had set up his command post.

The British airborne troops that had landed in the region had been defeated along with the other invasion forces. Only the day before, the last pockets of enemy paratroopers east of the Orne had surrendered. After the destruction of the beachhead near Caen, they ran out of options. It was assumed that individual soldiers and special equipment and weapons had found shelter with the Résistance, but the danger had been averted for the moment.

On Schneider's field blouse, the Iron Cross was shining, which had recently been awarded to him for his bold pursuit against the retreating English on the night of the invasion.

The crazy captain, who was sitting behind a desk with his feet propped up on the tabletop and stuffing a pipe, looked up as Schneider entered the room. The officer grinned like a Cheshire cat.

"Ah, Feldwebel!" he beamed. The captain jumped up, smoothing his uniform pants.

"Nice of you to come to visit me in my little domicile," he said, pushing a chair toward Schneider. The master sergeant sat down. "And I heard the writers from the press were here yesterday and took a picture of your bunch?"

"Yes." Schneider grinned. "The heroes on the Orne!" he quoted the headline of the article that appeared that day in an affected voice.

"I think that guy from the VB didn't even know who we were. Maybe it's better that way. It's stupid enough that the division allowed this press event to happen in the first place."

"Ah, yes! Yes, yes, yes... biscuits?" The captain held a torn open package from a British rations kit under Schneider's nose. Gratefully, the master sergeant took one. In this war, he had learned that you didn't turn down food if you had a chance to get your hands on some. Munching, he followed the captain with his gaze as he lit his pipe and puffed the tobacco with relish. Steel-blue smoke filled the room.

"So, what can I do for you?" the officer inquired about Schneider's reason for appearing, expressing himself like a salesman addressing a customer.

"I wanted to say goodbye."

"Oha. You're leaving?"

"Yes. We have our marching orders."

"So, where will you be headed?"

"You know I can't talk about that..."

"Probably to Russia, eh? All hell is breaking loose there at the moment..." The captain thoughtfully sucked on his pipe. However, Schneider was caught up for a brief moment by what he had heard from time to time about the situation in the East. Von Manstein had had to give up massive numbers of troops to the Western Front at the beginning of the year. Now the Russians had broken through from Orel to Kharkiv at full width. The Russians had only come to a halt when the Japanese had intervened in the war; von Manstein nevertheless allowed his troops to fall back further in order to reach more advantageous terrain. Army Group South Süd rescued itself with bag and baggage across the Dnieper. The thinning of the Eastern Front in favor of France theatre had been necessary, but perhaps a too high price to pay to avoid another land front in the West. Schneider, at least, was optimistic about the situation. The Wehrmacht had dealt with other problems in the past. Moreover, the captain was wrong – Schneider and his men would not be going to Russia; their comrades over there would have to see for themselves how they got along.

Therefore he just smiled in response to the captain's question as he gulped down the last of the British hardtack. They weren't too delicious, but they were better than an empty stomach.

"Ah!" the captain gloated, wagging his index finger. "So it is! Russia! I read you like a book!"

"Whatever you say," Schneider murmured, before changing the subject. He sensed the captain eyeing him from head to toe.

"You know... someone like you would suit me just fine."

"What do you mean, Herr Hauptmann?"

The officer smacked his lips with relish, pulling his pipe out of his mouth along with a thread of saliva.

"I'm making a bold move. Ready, Feldwebel?"

"Ready... for what?" Schneider folded his arms.

"As is common knowledge, I learned the profession of herring tamer before the war. You know what that is?"

Schneider shook his head.

"What do they teach you in school these days?"

"Mainly that we're the master race. Well, not me, I'm Greek or something, but the others are."

"Ah yes." The captain squinted his right eye briefly, giving him the appearance of a pirate captain. "It's important, after all," he decided after a moment's consideration, nodding with satisfaction. "So, they don't tell you about the herring tamer at school?"

"Nope."

"Then pay attention and listen up, kid: you know about a grocery clerk?"

"Jawohl."

"Well, you see! Herring tamer is what we call it. And I've got an idea in the back of my mind. Now... now it's getting exciting, dear Feldwebel!"

Only now? Schneider grinned.

"You know Nordsee?"

"Nordsee – the North Sea?"

"Yes, Nordsee."

"The sea?"

"No, the shop!"

"I see."

"They sell fish."

"Uh-huh."

"From the North Sea."

178

"All right... all right... I got the concept."

Abruptly, the captain paused, rubbing his chin. "But I think from other waters too," he murmured. Schneider wondered how sane this man, who after all held command of dozens of soldiers, really was.

"The point is: Nordsee is taking a completely new approach that the Americans have been practicing for years: Many businesses under one leadership. This idea... just imagine a merchant store of this kind... it's been thriving in me since I was in the trenches of Belgium during the Fourth Battle of Flanders." The captain's eyes became glassy. "Did I ever tell you about the Fourth Battle of Flanders, Herr Feldwebel?"

"Yes, you did."

"When?"

"Well, um... back then... on the day of the invasion."

"Ha! Right as rain! I don't want to repeat myself either. Anyway, I've had this idea since then. And now I have enough money together. When the war is over, I'll open my stores."

Suddenly Schneider understood.

"You're aiming for discounts because you're buying in larger quantities than all the little shops, which will allow you to get the goods to the people at lower prices, right?"

At first, the captain paused, seeming to think about what Schneider had said. Then his countenance changed to a single, broad grin.

"Yes, yes, yes! That's right, Feldwebel! I knew you were smart!"

"All right," Schneider laughed, tugging at his uniform sleeves. "Well then, Herr Hauptmann, I think I must leave."

"I can understand that, my boy. I'm Dieter, by the way."

Schneider stared at the hand the captain suddenly held out to him. Incredulous, he grasped the old, wrinkled hand and shook it.

"Pantelis. Pantelis Schneider."

"Pantelis?"

"Yes, Pantelis."

"What kind of name is that?"

"Greek."

"Oh, right, you mentioned that. Yeah, whatever. You know what? I could use someone like you for my stores. Someone with brains and all that stuff."

"Uh-huh."

"Give me your address. I'll get in touch with you after the war. Probably next year. Ah... if the Russian resists a bit more, the year after next." The officer grinned with his features disappearing under a mountain of friendly wrinkles. Schneider got out his report pad and pen, scribbled his address on the top sheet, tore it off, and handed it to the captain. Then they said goodbye. Schneider left the building in the firm conviction that he would never hear from crazy Dieter again.

Dnepropetrovsk, Soviet Union, July 9th, 1944

Dnepropetrovsk had suffered great destruction in 1941. Buildings had become ruins; many people had fled. Among those who had stayed, the Nazi henchmen had wreaked havoc. Accordingly, when the Soviets entered the Eastern half of the city a week ago, they were hailed as liberators by the ragged and starving population after similarly welcoming the Germans three years earlier.

After the large-scale Russian offensive, with which the Soviets had overrun the entire Southern half of the Eastern Front from Tula to Rostov, had been aborted due to the Japanese's attack, the Germans had retreated behind the Dnieper. Von Manstein was unable to counter the enemy attack. It had been quiet on the Eastern Front for one year – for a whole year, the Ivan had assembled his units behind the front, refreshed them, and formed new ones. In that one year, the enemy had produced nearly 26,000 tanks and 37,000 aircraft, all exclusive of the enormous Lend-Lease Act deliveries.

These figures contrasted with almost 13,000 panzers and

slightly more than 30,000 aircraft on the German side; war material, however, could not be supplied exclusively to the Eastern Front but had to be distributed to all theatres of war. Accordingly, the Russians had a brute superiority of men and material at the beginning of their offensive. 17,345 tanks, 4,200,000 men, and 21,480 aircraft, supported by over 38,000 cannons, had pushed against the German lines; that were 263 divisions. They had simply flooded the German positions, crushing all resistance into the ground. Companies were extinguished within minutes; regiments became platoons, divisions disappeared in the Russian fire. For one day, the Germans' deeply staggered defense system, which they had painstakingly dug and built up over the course of the last year, withstood the onslaught before the Russians were able to achieve several breakthroughs. Even the most robust bunkers and the most expansive trench systems were doomed to ineffectiveness when enemy divisions were thrown against sections of German companies or platoons. When the first break-ins into the Wehrmacht lines had succeeded, the Russians threatened to roll up the entire front sideways simply. From then on, it was a matter of bare survival for von Manstein's Eastern troops. The Germans fled, running for their lives. They left behind equipment, weapons, sometimes even vehicles and tanks. The Red Army truly had put all the resources at its disposal into this one offensive and had dangerously thinned out the North of the Eastern Front and also the border to the Japanese-occupied territories. There was no more room for von Manstein's backhand strikes in view of the enormous enemy superiority; instead, already in the first week of the Soviet offensive, it was exclusively a matter of somehow keeping the Army Groups Center and South from disintegrating and of getting order into the chaotic withdrawals. Kursk fell, Tula as well; Orel, Belgorod, Kharkiv followed.

Von Manstein reacted immediately, building a precautionary defense line along the Western bank of the Dnieper, called the Moltke Line. Up to this line, an orderly withdrawal should take place. The retreating units were to take the crossings over the river, take on defense positions, and from there finally fend off Ivan. The Commander-in-chief East did not want to take any chances because the Russians already started a race to the said river, letting their motorized forces advance far ahead. If the Soviets had taken the few crossings over the Dnieper before the retreating Wehrmacht units had reached the river, millions of German soldiers would have been trapped along with their tanks and guns. It would have been the catastrophe of the war, which would have sealed the German defeat.

For this reason, von Manstein did not want to take any risks. Thus he had ordered the majority of his Eastern troops to retreat behind the Dnieper. He would rather lose 400 kilometers of land than half of his men.

Due to heroism, self-sacrifice, and ultimately the clever tactics of thousands of German military leaders, the Russian attack did not turn into a German catastrophe. The military leaders managed to calm down the men who were fleeing in panic, reorganize them, and get them to retreat in an orderly fashion. This was the only way to save millions of soldiers from death or captivity and the only way to prevent the Russians at the very last moment from tearing enormous holes in the Wehrmacht's lines.

When the Japanese attack against the Soviet Union started, the Russians were already halfway to the Dnieper, still mercilessly chasing the Wehrmacht in front of them. But the unexpected attack by the Japanese, which had been kept entirely secret, shocked Ivan. His offensive ceased. He began to move troops to *his* new Eastern Front, where the Japanese could achieve some initial successes with their unexpectedly powerful armored forces.

Von Manstein, however, who had always been an officer whose deepest concern was avoiding unnecessary risk, did not want to take advantage of the moment of Russian confusion, even continuing with the German retreat behind the Dnieper, which eventually lasted until early July. The Russians were following the Germans only hesitantly.

Von Manstein would undoubtedly have preferred to fight back, but he lacked the strength to do so alone. Only slowly, the divisions from the invasion front streamed back to the East.

And once again, von Manstein wanted to play it safe, wanted to first survey the situation from the safe positions behind the Dnieper and assemble his forces before he would proceed to attack. Once again, both sides began to dig in.

*

The sun beat down mercilessly on the dusty walls of the large industrial city of Dnipropetrovsk, a place divided in two by the course of the Dnieper River. Sergeant Berning heard the rushing of the water from his position. Together with his 2nd Squad, he had taken up position in a shot-up factory building that lay directly on the banks of the Dnieper. Berning squatted on a metal gangway that led past some war-related openings on the outer wall. He had to lean forward only slightly to overlook the other bank of the river from his position, where the Russians had taken up positions. The new uniforms handed out when his unit arrived in Russia felt a little more comfortable against his skin in the current heat. The field blouses and pants, printed with the so-called Leibermuster, were supposed to do wonders in terms of camouflage if the Wochenschau was to be believed. Especially in the woods and high grass, the soldier in the black-green-brown uniform was supposed to blend in with his surroundings immediately. Infantry Division 253 was one of the very first units to be equipped with the new uniforms. Gradually, they were to replace the classic field-gray throughout the Wehrmacht. In any case, Berning was delighted with the new clothes, which were not as felty and scratchy as the old stuff; now, the brass only had to provide proper semi-automatic carbines.

Berning looked up at the blue ceiling of the hall. A few of his comrades' voices echoed through the shattered factory building, telling stories from home. Two lance corporals were playing cards.

By now, Berning was very confident that Germany would

183

win this war. For example, the new uniforms were even interspersed with carbon fibers to resist reconnaissance by so-called infrared, whatever that was. For Berning, this again showed the technical and intellectual superiority of the German Reich, and therefore they simply had to achieve the final victory... a simple calculation. But how long this would take, how long Berning would be in this shit, he could not guess... he did not dare to guess.

He sighed. He leaned against the heated stone wall of the factory. Further down the passage, two soldiers had taken up an alarm post with their K98s, looking out of a large opening onto the gigantic river, which was several hundred meters wide at this point. The machine gun had been taken away from Berning's squad and placed instead in the newly formed MG squadron. But that almost didn't matter because nothing would happen so quickly. The Japanese had advanced far into Russian territory, and the Soviet Union moved men and material from its Western Front to its Eastern Front in a panic. Berning's hopes now lay in another long period of a standstill at the front, just as before the enemy's great offensive. Of course, even in positional warfare, death lurked around every corner: mortars delivered the daily blessing to the enemy, which the Russians gladly answered in kind. Machine guns shot, spoiling fire across the river. But, life in positional warfare – most of all if one was lucky enough to live in halfway intact buildings – was a comparatively good life. How modest Berning had become!

Once upon a time, he had dreamed of a life as a civil servant in Burgenland, with a wife and a flock of children waiting for him when he came home from work. In the meantime, however, it was quite enough for him to hope for quiet days on the Eastern Front to be something like happy. Like almost all his comrades, Berning had also lowered the expectations of his life.

With shaky fingers, he took a cigarette out of his breast pocket, a so-called active, because he didn't have to roll it himself. He put it between his lips and lit it. He sucked the smoke into his lungs with relish, then blew it out in long puffs. He had become a smoker after all – but why not? He expected nothing more from life, so he could quietly succumb to all the vices that the moment offered him. Surviving the day, getting something in his stomach, sleeping a few hours at night without backache and nightmares; and sometimes, when the opportunity presented itself, sleeping with a girl again, whether it was Gretel or someone else – such banalities had become Berning's goals in life. That was all he needed.

"Franz!" a voice sounded from the ground of the hall. Berning rose and looked down over the edge of the gangway into the large hall where parts of streetcars had once been produced with tired eyes. All that remained of the production were large, dusty machines and idle assembly lines, which the soldiers of the squadron used as benches.

Berning recognized Private First Class Schwarz as the source of the call, one of the countless newcomers. The sergeant felt as if his old unit had vanished into thin air and been replaced by a new one. And he was almost right. Apart from Pappendorf and Balduin, there were not many left who had already been with the squadron in Kursk.

War turned soldiers into short-lived creatures. Berning had understood this – and internalized it. Why waste thoughts and feelings on anything else when he could be killed any day anyway?

"You are to see Balduin." Private First Class Schwarz looked up at the gangway with a pinched expression.

Berning struggled to pull himself up. What did the company commander want from him? The sergeant reached for his K98 carbine before walking down the gangway to the narrow ladder that led down into the hall. While Schwarz had already disappeared between the machines again, Berning climbed down the stairs with silent curses on his lips. He had to walk quite a distance to reach the commander's command post.

What an ordeal in the heat!

Indeed, an oppressive sweltering heat wafted through the ruins of Dnepropetrovsk. Berning was sweating, his clothes stuck to his skin. But it was no use. If the commander wanted to see him, the commander wanted to see him.

Finally, the sergeant reached a heavy metal door that led to a large factory complex's small annex. Berning knocked, and Balduin's voice was heard on the other side.

Cautiously, Berning pushed the door open a crack and squeezed through. In the room beyond, which had once been a recreation room for the factory workers, were tables with maps on them. A knapsack radio lay on the floor. Amid the maps, papers, writing utensils, and tinware with dried-on food leftovers, First Lieutenant Balduin looked somewhat crestfallen when he saw Berning. Wordlessly, he pointed with a weak hand gesture to a wooden door that was ajar and led into a tiny room that served as a storeroom.

Berning paused for a moment, looked questioningly at his commander, but his eyes flickered threateningly. Finally, the sergeant bowed his head, marched to the door, and pushed it open.

In the next room, two sinister figures sat behind a table on which a large briefcase lay. A dim ceiling light barely managed to illuminate the room. It cast grotesque shadows on the faces of the strange men.

"Close the door, Herr Unteroffizier," a raspy voice demanded. Berning did as he was told. With a loud clack, the door panel fell into the lock.

"I am Oberst Trzewik, on my left sits Hauptmann Doktor Kirsch," the raspy voice continued in the most bitter intonation. "We are from the Secret Field Police, special unit War Crimes."

Berning did not understand a word, but suddenly he felt quite uncomfortable. The colonel's stern voice said tinny, "Do you know a Viktor Mintz?"

Slowly Berning shook his head, clueless as to what this appearance was about.

"Well, no?" the one whom Trzewik had introduced as Captain Kirsch suddenly murmured.

"No, I don't know any Viktor Mintz," Berning stuttered in a brittle voice.

The captain, a broad-shouldered fellow whose face was hidden by the darkness, nodded thoughtfully, then slowly pushed his right hand, which rested on the tabletop, into the light. His thick, small fingers clutched a blue fountain pen.

Kirsch opened the folder, pulled out a sheet of paper, and began to take notes. He wrote a single sentence with curved lines, after which the fountain pen and hand disappeared again into the darkness. Berning thought he recognized the statement he had just made in abbreviated form on the paper. Sweat broke out of all his pores.

"We almost thought so," Trzewik stated, leaning forward. His voice suddenly had something dark, something threatening. Now, a hellish heat swept Berning's body. Beads of sweat formed on his skin. Berning wanted to get out of here because he sensed that nothing good came from the two figures.

Trezwik threw his head back, then half rose and stretched his face forward into the dim light of the ceiling lamp. Berning recognized the colonel's protruding googly eyes.

"Then I'll give you a hint, Herr Unteroffizier," Trezwik muttered before pushing his lips apart. Yellowish teeth flashed. Trezwik licked his upper lip, glaring at Berning with his googly eyes. It was as if there was tremendous pressure on the colonel's eyeballs, trying with all its might to squeeze them out of his skull.

"Unteroffizier Franz Berning..." Trzewik puffed up like a rooster. »... I hereby inform you that we are investigating you. You are accused of having shot the prisoner of war Viktor Mintz on February 10th of this year at Velikiye Luki in a treacherous manner and without reason or order."

Trezwik let his words work on the accused for a moment – and how the words worked!

Berning's whole body trembled all at once. A sickening feeling dug into his stomach. His lips quivered, his eyes became glassy. Berning was unable to say anything back at that moment except to shake his head. This he did vehemently while pressing his lips together.

"On February 10th, 1943, at about 5:10 p.m., your platoon

leader, Feldwebel Pappendorf, transferred the Soviet prisoner of war Viktor Mintz into your custody. Is that correct?" Trzewik yelled at Berning in an agitated voice.

"I... I..."

"IS THAT CORRECT!?"

"I..." Berning's hand wiped across his forehead. It fluttered like a thin leaf in a storm. "I don't know his name, but..."

"Of course," Kirsch grumbled, shaking his head as he diligently took notes. "What does a murderer care about his victims, hey?"

"But... Pappendorf... Herr Feldwebel Pappendorf... he ordered me to shoot the man!"

"Oh?" Trzewik paused long for effect. "Is that right?"

"Jawohl, Herr Oberst."

"Herr Pappendorf's statement reads somewhat differently."

Trzewik pulled a document from the folder and placed it on the tabletop before tapping it several times with his index finger.

"Read it!" he commanded.

Berning did as he was told. The header of the document was marked with some of Pappendorf's data; rank, place of birth, marital status. Below that, in printed letters, was the master sergeant's statement. Berning read:

(Kirsch: Herr Pappendorf, please describe to us the events of the day in question).

I, Feldwebel Pappendorf, hereby describe to you, to the best of my knowledge and belief, the events of February 10th, 1943, which led to the prisoner of war being shot. On the day in question, I had the mission to lead a group of prisoners of war to a place West of Velikiye Luki, where a feint had been arranged. The man Viktor Mintz was with this group. I was accompanied by the then Grenadier Bailzer and Gefreiter Lenz. About a little before 10 o'clock, I noticed that the said Mintz had noticed our trick. There was no officer on the spot, so I had to make a decision myself. I assumed that the operation was of such importance that it could not be endangered under any circumstances. Before the prisoner could inform his comrades about the feint, I isolated him from the group and led him away to give the impression to the others that I wanted to shoot him. After the prisoners had believed our trick and left, I took Mintz back with me.

(Kirsch: Why did you take the prisoner back to your company?)

I couldn't let him go, after all. So I took him with me to talk to Oberleutnant Balduin about how to proceed with him. I assumed that Mintz would be returned to a prison camp or a work unit. Then we returned to our area of responsibility, where I had the prisoner wait away from my company's bivouac places.

(Kirsch: Why did you move Herrn Mintz to a place away from your unit?)

My assignment was top secret. Under no circumstances was the feint to be leaked to the Russians. Therefore, I did not want the prisoner to be seen unnecessarily. When I had found a right place far away, I went to get Herr Unteroffizier Berning.

(Trzewik: Although you had two soldiers on the spot to guard him? Why?)

Herr Unteroffizier Franz Berning always proved to me to be a very loyal and exemplary NCO. He alone lacked experience. I considered it right to let him in on the assignment. He had proved to me often enough that I could rely on him. Since he is still young and inexperienced and has only dealt with prisoners of war once, I decided to entrust him with this prisoner's guarding until Herr Oberleutnant Balduin had decided on him.

(Kirsch: Mintz is said to have been taken prisoner of war in the battle for Olkhovatka in May 1943. Your unit was also involved in that fighting. Did you see Mintz there?)

That may be, but I don't remember any such encounter.

(Trzewik: Why did you send the landsers away? Why should Berning guard the prisoner alone?)

For one thing, because the two soldiers were tired and had fulfilled the assignment with extraordinary dedication. In my eyes, they had earned a rest. On the other hand, because I thought that if Herr Unteroffizier Berning had to guard the prisoner alone, this experience would exceptionally shape his mind.

(Kirsch: What happened when you reached the prisoner together with Herr Berning?)

First, I sent my soldiers away. After that, everything happened very quickly. As soon as my men had disappeared, Berning raised his carbine and fired at the prisoner. He immediately fired a second shot at the poor man lying on the ground.

(Trzewik: Did you give an order to shoot?)

No, I did not.

The report went on, but Berning stopped abruptly. He looked up with watery eyes. The two officers were sitting like black stones in the darkness. Berning was shaking all over.

"That... that... is not true. Pappendorf gave me the order to shoot."

"Herr Pappendorf says something different."

"Did... did you question Bailzer?"

"Of course." Trzewik tugged at the folder again. "Do you want to read his statement? Herr Bailzer confirms Pappendorf's version. According to it, he didn't hear anything about a shooting order either, although he was still within earshot. And... well... unfortunately we can no longer question Herr Lenz. So the air is getting pretty thin for you, Herr Berning."

Trzewik put the document containing Bailzer's statement on the table and smoothed it out with his hands. However, Berning did not move, merely staring at the written statement in his hands, which Feldwebel Adolf Pappendorf signed. Next to the signature was the date: June 1st, 1944.

Silently, Berning looked up. So many different emotions were coursing through his body. He was petrified.

"I don't understand all this excitement," he finally said, entirely composed, "after all, he's just a Slav."

Kirsch sighed long and emphatically while Trzewik kneaded his fingers so that they cracked. The two took their time answering. At some point, the colonel explained, "According to the Beck Doctrine of December 13th, 1942, with the additional protocol of April 23rd, 1943, you are threatened directly by court-martial." Trzewik recited his text with relish, clicking his tongue from time to time.

Berning could hardly bring a syllable past his lips.

"Beck Doctrine?" Of course, Berning knew about the Beck Doctrines, but they were old rules wrapped up in new directives in his eyes. During Hitler's reign, nobody had been interested in the existence of these rules. And these days, too, hardly anyone seemed to care about them... except for those two assholes of the Secret Field Police.

"You don't know the Beck Doctrine?" Trzewik crossed his arms. "Must have spent so much time slaughtering defenseless people that you've let the policy change in the Reich slip through your fingers, huh?" the colonel snapped, baring his yellow teeth.

Berning's gaze flickered. His hands balled into fists. He opened his mouth – and blurted out, "Are you kidding me!? Slaughter people? SLAUGHTER PEOPLE?! You two clowns! I didn't want all this shit! I didn't want to slaughter anybody! And I keep getting my ass handed to me because I don't want to shoot at them! So I start shooting at them. Because the fucking Wehrmacht wants it that way! AND NOW THAT'S SUPPOSED TO BE WRONG, TOO? What the hell is wrong with this world?"

Berning's shouting left the two officers completely unimpressed. Instead, they matter-of-factly continued the questioning; they simply ignored the "clowns."

After 40 minutes of sharp questioning and constant scrutiny of every word Berning uttered, Trzewik finally leaned back. His teeth glowed yellowish in the light of the room.

"Very well, Herr Berning," he told the sergeant, who was standing there with his fists twitching, "things will now take their course as follows: Until the completion of our investigation, you will lose all privileges and rights of a military superior. The epaulets will be left to you for the sake of your honor – for the time being. But you will no longer give orders, lead a squad, etcetera. For the next time, your status is comparable to that of a recruit. Your

191

commander is already informed about it. Furthermore: Within the next two weeks, you will receive the typed protocol of this questioning for countersignature. In the course of the next nine months, you will receive a summons to appear before the Special Court of Berlin for Serious Crimes against Humanity, or – improbably – a decision to drop the case." Trzewik shook his head with a grin on his face. "No, my dear fellow, don't get your hopes up too high. You're in for a big one."

Berning was burning inside.

"In the event of a conviction, the Beck Doctrine under paragraph 31 requires a minimum sentence of eight years in the penitentiary. But, since your case is particularly devious... Mhm..." Trzewik made a skeptical motion with his hand. »... I'll put it this way: the shot in the neck of the lying, wounded man will probably break your neck, too – literally. Don't think the Wehrmacht will let swines like you get away with it."

Berning did not say another word. He was too speechless, too angry, too hateful. He turned on his heel and marched out of the little chamber. Pure, sheer hatred flooded his mind.

West of Cairon, July 9th, 1944

The III Abteilung of PzRgt 2 had finally returned to its original staging area West of Cairon. The unit was one of few to remain in France for some time to replenish personnel and materiel. In addition, rumors were spreading about the damned Panzer IIIs. The obsolete combat vehicle was finally to be withdrawn from the strike forces, and the battalion was to be equipped with another panzer type instead. The new tanks were already on their way.

The entire division was lined up in a large meadow, away from the tanks. Light woods surrounded the area, on which the small companies, each of which had assembled as rectangles, formed a U-shape. At the head of the formation was Major Meier as well as Major General Sieckenius, divisional commander of the 16th Panzer Division, who never missed the awarding procedure within his command. Therefore, he was busy with nothing else than driving from unit to unit and handing out awards.

What happened in the following was a single mass awarding of almost all soldiers of the division. Reich Chancellor von Witzleben had issued the "Defensive battle of Normandy 1944" medal for the successful defense against the invasion. The award criteria were so broad that virtually every German soldier stationed in Northern France during the Allied invasion attempt was awarded the medal. The High Command called this the motivation of the troops. Also, dozens of other medals were awarded, mainly to honor deeds and soldiers of the invasion front, but also for events that occurred long ago. Sometimes, the bureaucratic apparatus of the Wehrmacht took its time with the processing of applications.

Iron Crosses, German Crosses, War Merit Crosses, and Panzer Badges of all classes were cheerfully distributed among the soldiers of the division. Engelmann received the Panzer Badge level 4, as did Nitz, Münster, and Ludwig.

In the grand finale of the awards marathon, the division commander awarded two Knight's Crosses. The first was awarded to a senior lance corporal of the 10th Company for destroying no less than eleven enemy tanks in close combat. Captain Stollwerk was the recipient of the second Knight's Cross. The officer received the high decoration on the one hand for his action at Mont Fleury, and on the other hand for tracking down the sergeants abducted by the French underground. Lieutenant Engelmann could only shake his head at this, but what could he do? If the chancellor thought that Stollwerk deserved the Knight's Cross, he probably deserved the Knight's Cross.

When the division commander finally said goodbye and put the event back into Meier's hands, an hour and a half had passed. The soldiers had long been restless, having had to stand still the entire time. But it was not over yet, because promotions were on the agenda. Several enlisted men and NCOs were promoted in rank.

Afterward, Meier called Stollwerk and Engelmann to the front once again. Without much ado, he read out the promotions of both soldiers. The division commander explained to the puzzled looking soldiers that with immediate effect, the 9th of July had been made the "Day of the Battle of Normandy" by the chancellor himself. So this day was added to the few other fixed dates on which officers were allowed to be promoted at all. The division commander stepped in front of Engelmann, whom he shook hands with, beaming with joy.

"Herr Engelmann," Meier said, "this was more than overdue. No, really, I'm very happy for you."

Engelmann became a little embarrassed and thanked him meekly. Meier then took off his epaulets and fastened the rank insignia of a first lieutenant on him instead.

"I might add that you will, of course, soon be given your own company," Meier rejoiced. He retook Engelmann's hand. A broad, honorable smile stretched across the face of the newly minted first lieutenant. Engelmann was genuinely pleased. The more responsibility he had, the better he could serve his fatherland. In general, everything was going like clockwork at the moment: The invasion had been defeated, hopefully depriving the Western powers of their desire for Central Europe forever. In Southern Italy, the enemy was stuck not far from its beachheads. Moreover, the Japanese attack against the Soviet Union had enough power to deliver the decision in the East. The end of the war was virtually in sight. Engelmann felt the confidence that dominated his mind. Hard to believe, but the German Reich was on the verge of winning this war. A year ago, Engelmann had almost refused to believe in a German victory. Now, of course, it was essential that the Americans and the British would engage in negotiations instead of conducting a constant sitting down and aerial war. Engelmann, however, could not imagine that the Allies were interested in a continuous state of war. At some point, this tiresome slaughter had to come to an end... Engelmann considered the Western powers sensible enough to see it the same way. Josef simply wanted to be allowed to believe that the war would end soon. He also felt that he had to say goodbye to the front and the fighting as long as he still had a last shred of soul in him worth saving. However, he still held the opinion that no one should try any tricks to escape military service. Only the end of the war or death could free Engelmann of his obligations. While the freshly minted first lieutenant was wallowing in happiness, Meier had decorated Stollwerk's shoulders with the epaulets of the rank of Major.

Following up on the promotions, the battalion commander addressed the troops, "I would like to take this opportunity to announce that Herr Stollwerk will be my successor for my post as Abteilung commander. Beginning on August 1st."

A murmur went through the soldiers. Indeed, rumors about this had been spread over the bush radio for some time, and the officers of the unit had at least been informed of Major Meier's redeployment. But Stollwerk was to be his successor? This surprised Engelmann – not necessarily in a positive way. His exuberant confidence had already begun to crumble. Stollwerk would have no problem continuing his hard-line as commander – the man had enough supporters within the battalion. Engelmann sighed. In any case, he could hardly wait for the end of this event. Moments before, Nitz had put a package from Elly into his hands, and Engelmann wanted to read her letter finally. Above all, he wanted to answer her quickly. He wanted to explain to her the new political situation, wanted to express his happiness. And he felt an urgent desire to write to Elly how important she and Gudrun were to him. However, he would keep to himself the bad, the biting feelings that were bothering him more these days than ever before.

My Sepp!

Thank you for your words, even if they are short and factual. I can understand that in the days of the invasion you hardly have time to write to your wife and indeed everything is secret again that you are not allowed to say a thing anyway. But every sign of life from you is an enormous relief to me! Whenever I receive a letter that seems to be from the Wehrmacht, my legs feel shaky, and I can hardly hold on. I just hope you don't want to become a hero! Don't give up your life carelessly for a piece of land, my Sepp! Always remember that your family in Bremen needs you, and Gudrun needs a father who will watch her grow up and later keep her admirers at bay! Please write again soon, if you can. The Wochenschau says we were victorious in France, so are you out of danger or already on the road somewhere else? You must have quite a journey behind you if you come home sometime! I hope it will be soon. We can't just have war all our lives!

Gudrun already says a few things, and sometimes even daddy. She misses you very much. I hope you both get time to get to know each other soon!

With love

Elly

Perham Down, Great Britain, July 10th, 1944

Winston Churchill, a short, chubby man with a crumpled face and a white fringe of light hair on his head, waited in front of a large folding table on which all manner of handguns were laid out. M1 Carbine, M1 Garand, M1917 Enfield, Lee-Enfield, Thompson Gun, De Lisle special carbines, and other handguns had been brought in for the distinguished visitor. Churchill was joined by the Supreme Allied Commander in Europe, General Dwight David Eisenhower, and his deputy, General Montgomery. There was also a crowd of high officers of the Allied armies in the background, but nobody dared to disturb the three men. Everyone was waiting for the high-ranking guests to make a move.

The sun was shining strongly that day. The sky was cloudless, and visibility was good. The handgun firing range covered a vast area, bordered by mixed forests and barbed wire. The general mood seemed to settle over the scene like a stifling blanket.

Since the failed invasion, morale among the Allied Expeditionary Force had been low. As the High Command deliberated on how to proceed, the past few weeks' events drove noticeable wedges between the various nations involved in the anti-German pact. Among the surviving men of the invasion force, the feeling spread that they had been sent to a meat grinder on the beaches of Northern France – had been made to run into German fire despite knowing better. The American soldiers, in particular, began to wonder what they were doing in England since the old world was none of their business. The fact that there was hardly an Allied soldier in England who had not lost a good friend or acquaintance in Normandy also had a negative effect on the troops. The general mood had reached rock bottom. For this very reason, the top leadership, above all Eisenhower, who Roosevelt had given all liberties regarding Europe, and Churchill had launched an exceptional charm offensive.

The senior politicians and military officers wanted to show presence – wanted to show the men that they were there to listen to the soldiers' concerns and needs. Still, dark clouds also hovered over Churchill's, Eisenhower's, and Montgomery's heads. The three disagreed on future strategy. The political situation was exceedingly tricky these days, and the nations involved in the alliance were suspicious of each other.

First and foremost, Russia seemed to have lost all

confidence in its Western partners. Stalin raged over the failed invasion, feeling betrayed by the West. The Soviet leader seemed to think that the Americans and the British were deliberately playing for time until Germany and Russia had torn each other apart. But the British were also at loggerheads with the Americans.

Eisenhower had abandoned the British sector of Gold Beach in the invasion but had tried to evacuate Omaha and Pointe du Hoc with heavy losses. Roosevelt left Eisenhower in office even though the U.S. general had offered his resignation. All this rubbed off on the British-American relationship.

Churchill finally grabbed an M1 Carbine, a small, semi-automatic weapon. The British prime minister, a professed gun enthusiast, turned to his companions: "Ike, Monty. What do you say about letting an old Englishman show you how to shoot properly?"

Eisenhower grinned. His American pride ordered him to respond to the challenge. Montgomery remained more restrained, there were more important things to do that day, but he also agreed. A wave of Eisenhower's hand was enough, and the British and U.S. American officers in the background began to move. Three carbines with ammunition were brought in; the target area was cleared in a flash, targets carted in and set up. Churchill, Eisenhower, and Montgomery each grabbed a carbine and lined up next to each other so that the distance to the targets was 25 yards. Churchill had already finished loading his weapon. The British prime minister aimed – and fired. The recoil jerked into his massive body with each shot while he fired the bullets into the target in rapid succession. After a few seconds, a metallic click sounded instead of a shot.

Now Eisenhower and Montgomery also aimed at the targets. While Eisenhower used up his ammunition just as quickly as Churchill, Montgomery took more time in aiming, retargeting after each shot. The two gentlemen had to wait almost a minute until the British general had also fired his ammunition. As ordered, the officers in the background applauded when the last shot was fired.

"My friends, as much as I appreciate shooting with you, I'm afraid there are urgent matters whose discussion will not tolerate further delay," Montgomery urged gently.

The three men moved a little closer together, for no one needed to hear what they had to discuss. Montgomery's face was darkened. Churchill nodded silently and furrowed his brow.

"Ike," Churchill began, his eyes fixed on Eisenhower. The American's expression hardened increasingly. "I have had extensive discussions with my military officers. I have had long conversations with King George." No other words were needed. Eisenhower seemed to understand. He cast a questioning glance at Montgomery. The newly minted field marshal, with his lean face and thin upper lip beard, nodded affirmatively.

"I also support that idea," he confirmed Churchill's point.

Now it was Eisenhower who nodded decisively.

"All right," the U.S. general began. "You are aware that you are on your own in this matter? My Commander-in-Chief has been clear about that. I cannot support this operation."

"We are used to that," Montgomery commented sourly.

Eisenhower overheard the remark.

In the background, British crewmen were removing the targets. The general in charge was on his toes because any analysis of the shooting results was not desired for political reasons.

"We deeply regret that," Churchill admitted, "but the Empire is prepared to carry on this fight alone if necessary."

"You are not fighting alone!" Eisenhower clarified emphatically. "We Americans will stand by your side to the end. We follow exactly the directives prepared for the case of failure of the invasion: the total destruction of the German Reich from the air, further the tight encirclement of Germany, and the cutting off of resources and supplies from Norway, Denmark, Finland. We will gradually take away the Northern European area from the axis and finally cut off supplies from Sweden too. Besides, we strengthen our efforts in Italy. Everywhere else, the Germans are too

199

strong. The American public would not tolerate another invasion attempt with thousands of dead."

Montgomery grinned. He seemed to suspect that the upcoming election in November had become the driving force behind Roosevelt's actions after the failed invasion had not been kind to the president's popularity.

"That won't be enough," Churchill interjected grumpily.

Montgomery nodded.

"We've been bombing them for years with no significant effects. Berlin has been destroyed 70 percent, Cologne 65 percent, Hamburg 60 percent. Yet the damned Germans just keep on going." Churchill became audibly agitated. "And we don't want to wait until December until you Americans are sort of capable of making decisions again."

At this statement, Eisenhower's face grimaced, but he did not protest. Instead, the American replied, "We must show staying power in this conflict. Once we have the German Reich in our grip, the Germans will go down to their knees."

"You Americans can talk!" Churchill sneered, getting so loud that bystanders pulled faces in embarrassment. "Your cities, your families are not within the range of their bombers. And now these new robot weapons! What if the Germans turn them against my homeland?"

"Our experts can't imagine that the range of these things is sufficient for that..."

"Yes, yes! Not to mention the situation in Russia," the English premier continued to rage. "Nobody foresaw the attack of the damned Japanese. Our intelligence has failed miserably! Now the Russian summer offensive has already stopped at the Dnieper. At the bloody Dnieper! What happened to Stalin's pompous speeches? He wanted to be in Warsaw by October! Ha! The Germans have defeated our invasion, and now they are moving everything that can hold a weapon to the East. They'll counterattack soon, and then they'll be standing in Moscow in October, that's what it looks like!"

Eisenhower remained silent for almost a full minute before giving a thoughtful reply, "The Japanese have lost all touch with reality. They are falling more and more behind against us, and now they have brought another enemy of war down on themselves."

"No, my friend, you misjudge the Japs. They are acting extremely cleverly. Their land forces may not be sufficient to defeat the Russians. No one seriously expects them to march through to Moscow. But they are taking the pressure off the Germans so that the Germans can crush the Communists once and for all. Our enemies are trying to take the Russians out of the game; with German tanks, mind you!"

"Even if. The Japanese can't win this war anymore."

"It's all about time, Dwight! On the Eastern Front, 12 million German soldiers would be freed – and millions of Japanese. The Germans can't get across the Channel; their navy is too weak for that. A stalemate is developing in Europe, so the Germans will engage in Asia, where the Japanese have at least potentially strong naval forces. They will attack us together. German soldiers shipped in by the Japanese. Japanese planes in the sky, German tanks on the ground."

Now the U.S. general laughed. "Dear Winston, that's quite a stretch."

"We British see this differently. Germany, in its present shape, is a powerful thorn in our side. A permanent danger for the Empire and Europe! That is why Germany must be destroyed – completely destroyed! Once and for all, we must smash this nation to pieces! But by the planned encirclement, we run the risk of merely isolating Germany. Then the bastards will be wounded, limited in their possibilities, but not eliminated. We will not bring down the Reich by bombing raids alone."

"But we can bomb them so far back to the Stone Age that they'll never be a threat again."

"What about that technology transfer? The Japanese are building Tiger tanks and German machine guns! According to reconnaissance, Japanese officers are training German soldiers in Bavaria. You Americans shouldn't feel too secure in your skin. Maybe soon the Japanese will be aiming robots against your shores?"

201

Suddenly Eisenhower's face darkened, but then he shook his head resolutely. "It's not that we're technologically inferior. You know we're working on a new kind of weapon that I can't even find in your account yet. So I don't share your views regarding possible future scenarios, but I'll raise your point again with the Commander-in-Chief."

"No need. I'll talk to him myself." Churchill sounded grumpy.

"Whatever you say. In the meantime, at any rate, you can count on all the support you can get from us: Material, planes, ships. I could also imagine the Army taking on more responsibility in Italy to relieve you. But: No Boots on the Ground! No American soldier will set foot on Yugoslav soil."

"No Boots on the Ground? You were talking big about Scandinavia just now, my friend!"

"After the election, Winston. After the election."

Aftermath

The men classified by the von Witzleben government as "special prisoners" had been distributed among many prisons in Berlin and the surrounding area. This way, it should be ensured that no unfortunate Anglo-American bombing raid or a targeted attack by Nazi loyalists against a single institution would release the Reich's entire former leaders. They were guarded exclusively by the Wehrmacht, which otherwise had nothing to do with the penal system, but the chancellor did not seem to trust the Order Police enough in this matter; and the SS – well, it no longer existed in that way.

The ashen light of the moon refracted in the narrow barred windows and fell as a strangely ribbed glow into the corridor of old masonry. To the right and left were heavy metal doors that led into tiny individual cells, like dark dungeons from times past. Under all circumstances, any contact among the inmates was to be avoided so that the only persons the inmates had contact with were the Wehrmacht guards.

202

Private First Class Max Sträuber, a 19-year-old soldier from the Cologne area, served in one of the four order battalions explicitly created to guard the special prisoners. Sträuber's blond hair was cut short at the sides, but his bangs were long and streaked with pomade to the back of his head. He wore his uniform correctly down to the last detail and was eager to finally get to the front and experience a real combat operation. However, his company commander had turned down a transfer request. Sträuber, who had been assigned to guard duty that evening, crept up the eerie corridor. Two dark figures in long coats followed him. The young soldier reached the last cell door on the right, and his followers closed in on him. A bunch of keys jingled. In the distance, the Allied bombers, again in action over the capital, boomed. The detonations of high-explosive and incendiary bombs, many of which ignited and tore apart civilian targets, rumbled as well.

"If anyone gets a whiff of this, they'll have me shot," Sträuber remarked in a shaky voice as he fingered the matching key from the waistband. The two men had had to put forth great effort – and some money – to get this far.

"Believe me; we gratefully acknowledge the great risk you are taking for our cause. You will not be forgotten when the time comes."

Sträuber nodded and inserted the appropriate key into the lock. A metallic click sounded. Slowly, Sträuber opened the door.

A dirty toilet bowl and a bunk came into view. It was pitch dark in the room. There was no window. The shabby light bulb was switched off. Only the moonlight from the corridor reflected very faintly from the masonry, cast its barely visible glow into the open cell.

A lean man sat at the head of the bunk. As he rose, his features became visible. A trapezoidal beard adorned the area between his upper lip and the tip of his nose, and a pair of glasses with circular lenses sat in front of his eyes. His dark hair was kept short and neatly combed on his head, wholly shorn off at the sides and on the back of his head. Due to the high forehead, it almost looked like the prisoner was wearing a kippah made of hair. It seemed that despite the unfavorable circumstances of his imprisonment, the man attached great importance to his appearance. Slowly, the prisoner, who had something of a schoolmaster about him, trotted toward the open cell door.

"Go ahead, Oberführer," Sträuber demanded. *The boy tensed all his muscles in anticipation of the blow and squinted at the same time. One of the figures brought his fist forward eruptively and thundered it into the private first class' face. Blood shot out of the young soldier's nose; he immediately fell to the ground.*

With a tear-dimmed look, he watched the former prisoner, and his companions run down the corridor.

*

That same night, the conspirators gathered in a dark cellar. They greeted the newly freed man and assured him of their loyalty. The freed man, however, looked around with a frown.

For almost a minute, those present were silent, after which the "schoolmaster" hissed in a sharp voice: "Comrades, it makes me immensely happy to see that there are still loyal German comrades-in-arms of our cause who have not conspired with the enemy in our own country. It honors our cause further that others besides us are also concerned about the welfare of our fatherland. Germans of all ranks, of all factions, have pledged themselves to our cause!"

He nodded to a man in his early 60s who wore a senior officer's uniform in the Wehrmacht. The golden shoulder epaulets of the field marshal gleamed in the darkness. An Iron Cross with a silver border and a swastika on a black background sparkled between the collar patches. The man wore a wispy upper lip beard. His old eyes and his facial features, which were crossed with deep wrinkles, gave the appearance of great kindness.

"Comrades, fellow warriors!" the freed man adjusted his circular glasses, "soon we will no longer have to hide in dark cellars. We will lead Germania into a golden age – and we will free the Germanic people from the filth that this Witzleben has allowed to breathe again! Let's see what you've got." The freed man looked demandingly at the field marshal. He handed him a file filled with documents.

"Operation Valkyrie," the officer explained briefly, "a plan created in the case the chancellor dies. Should something happen to von Witzleben, we could execute this contingency plan with access to the reserve army. Fromm is the key figure in this enterprise. We know the man is an opportunist. When it comes

down to it, it's hard to say if he's going to be on our side."

"The coward will always be where he thinks the stronger divisions are," the freed man interjected.

"However, influential friends of our cause are sitting in the Army Personnel Office. Within a few months, we can elevate one of our own to Fromm's post. Valkyrie would then be a piece of cake. We eliminate von Witzleben, pass the whole thing off as an attempted coup by the Jews, and have all the important posts in Berlin secured via the Reserve Army. Before the Wehrmacht..." The high officer suddenly paused, trying to read his counterpart's face. The freed man seemed less than enthusiastic. He casually leafed through the file. Then he threw the whole stuff on the floor. "This is something for dilettantes," he scoffed. "No, comrades! That doesn't do our cause justice! We are strong, and we have our comrades-in-arms everywhere. We are Teutons pure in heart. We don't need to hide behind plans. No, we will show ourselves openly and fight for our cause. We will bear witness before the world that not every German has yet fallen prey to the effeminate American Jewishness!

Do you have Feedback?

We love to hear from you!!
info@ek2-publishing.com

Glossary

76-millimeters divisional gun M1942: Soviet field gun that produced a unique sound while firing, which consisted of some kind of hissing, followed by the detonation boom. Therefore the Germans Wehrmacht soldiers called it "Ratsch Bumm".

Abwehr: German Military Intelligence Service

Acht-Acht: German infamous 8.8 centimeter Flak anti-aircraft and anti-tank gun. Acht-Acht is German meaning nothing less than eight-eight.

Afrika Korps: German expeditionary force in North Africa; it was sent to Libya to support the Italian Armed Forces in 1941, since the Italians were not able to defend what they had conquered from the British and desperately needed some backing. Hitler's favorite general Rommel was the Afrika Korps' commander. Over the years he gained some remarkable victories over the British, but after two years of fierce fighting ... two years, in which the Axis' capabilities to move supplies and reinforcements over the Mediterranean Sea constantly decreased due to an allied air superiority that grew stronger by the day, Rommel no longer stood a chance against his opponents. Finally the U.S.A. entered the war and invaded North Africa in November 1942. Hitler prohibited the Afrika Korps to retreat back to Europe or even to shorten the front line by conducting tactical retreats. Because of that nearly 300 000 Axis' soldiers became POWs, with thousands of tons of important war supplies and weapons getting lost as well when the Afrika Korps surrendered in May 1943, just months after the 6th Army had surrendered in Stalingrad.

In the PANZERS series von Witzleben allows the Afrika Korps to retreat just in time. Axis' forces abandon North Africa by the end of 1942, saving hundreds of thousands of soldiers and important war material.

Aichi B7A Ryūsei: Japanese torpedo-dive bomber

Ami: German word for US-Americans (short form for Amerikaner = American; plural Amis). It is not always meant as a derogatory term, but can also be meant in a neutral or even positive way. It very much depends on who uses this term in which context.

AOK: Short for Armeeoberkommando, meaning Army Higher Command. In this case army stands for the formation of an army, not the military branch

Arabic numerals vs. Roman numerals in German military formation names: I decided to keep Arabic as well as Roman numerals in the translation, therefore you will find a 1st Squad, but an II Abteilung. Normally all battalions and corpses have Roman numerals, the rest Arabic ones.

Armee Abteilung: More or less equivalent to an army. The Germans of WW2 really had confusing manners to organize and name their military formations.

Assault Gun: Fighting Vehicle intended to accompany and support infantry formations. Assault guns were equipped with a tank-like main gun in order to combat enemy strongholds or fortified positions to clear the way for the infantry. An assault gun had no rotatable turret, but a casemate. This made them very interesting especially for Germany, because they could be produced faster and at lower material costs than proper combat tanks.

Assistant machine gunner: In the Wehrmacht you usually had three soldiers to handle one MG: a gunner and two assistants. The first assistant carried the spare barrel as well as some small tools for cleaning and maintaining the weapon plus extra belted ammunition in boxes. The second assistant carried even more ammunition around. In German the three guys are called: MG-1, MG-2 and MG-3.

Ausführung: German word for variant. Panzer IV Ausführung F means that it is the F variant of that very tank. The Wehrmacht improved their tanks continuously, and gave each major improvement a new letter.

Avanti: German slur name for Italians.

Babushka: Russian word for "grandmother" or "elderly woman"

Balkenkreuz: Well-known black cross on white background that has been used by every all-German armed force ever since and also before the first German unification by the Prussian military.

Battle of Stalingrad: The battle of Stalingrad is often seen as the crucial turning point of the war between the Third Reich and the Soviet Union. For the first time the Wehrmacht suffered an overwhelming defeat, when the 6th Army was encircled in the city of Stalingrad and had to surrender after it had withstood numerous Soviet attacks, a bitterly cold Russian winter and a lack of supplies and food due to the encirclement. Hitler was obsessed with the desire to conquer the city with the name of his opponent on it – Stalin – and thus didn't listen to his generals, who thought of Stalingrad as a place without great strategic use.

In reality the battle took place between August 1942 and February 1943. The encirclement of the Axis' forces was completed by the end of November 1942. The Axis' powers lost around 300 000 men. After surrendering 108 000

members of the 6th Army became POWs, of which only 6
000 survivors returned to Germany after the war.

In the PANZERS series von Witzleben listens to his
generals and withdraws all troops from the city of
Stalingrad in time. Thus the encirclement never happens.

Beck Doctrines: A set of orders issued by President of the
Reich Ludwig Beck that demands a human treatment of
POWs and civilians in occupied territories. The doctrines
are an invention of me, neither did they exist in reality, nor
was Beck ever President of the Reich (but the main
protagonists of the 20 July plot, of whom Beck was one,
wanted him for that very position).

Bohemian Private: In German it is "Böhmischer
Gefreiter", a mocking nickname for Hitler, which was used
by German officers to highlight that Hitler never got
promoted beyond the rank of private in World War I.
Besides basic training Hitler never attended any kind of
military education. It is said that president Hindenburg first
came up with this nickname. He did not like Hitler and
wrongfully believed he was from the Braunau district in
Bohemia, not Braunau am Inn in Austria.

Brandenburgers: German military special force (first
assigned to Abwehr, on 1st April 1943 alleged to the
Wehrmacht) that consists of many foreign soldiers in order
to conduct covert operations behind enemy lines. The name
"Brandenburgers" refers to their garrison in Brandenburg an
der Havel (near Berlin).

Büchsenlicht: Büchse = tin can (also archaic for a rifle);
Licht = light; having Büchsenlicht means that there is
enough daylight for aiming and shooting.

Churchill tank: Heavy British infantry tank, with about
40 tons it was one of the heaviest allied tanks of the war.
Through the Lend-Lease policy it saw action on the Russian

side, too. Its full name is Tank, Infantry, Mk IV (A22) Churchill.

Close Combat Clasp: German military award for participating in hand-to-hand combat

Clubfoot: Refers to Joseph Goebbels, a high-ranking Nazi politician, one of Hitler's most important companions and Reich Minister of Propaganda (Secretary of Propaganda). He coined names like "Vergeltungswaffe" (= weapon of revenge) for the A4 ballistic missile and glorified a total war, meaning all Germans – men, women, elderly and children alike – had to contribute to "final victory". He is one of the reasons why German children, wounded and old men had to fight at the front lines during the last years of the Third Reich. "Clubfoot" refers to the fact that Goebbels suffered from a deformed right foot.

Commissar Order: An order issued by the Wehrmacht's high command before the start of the invasion of the USSR that demanded to shoot any Soviet political commissar, who had been captured. In May 1942 the order was canceled after multiple complaints from officers, many of them pointing out that it made the enemy fight until last man standing instead of surrendering to German troops. In the Nuremberg Trials the Commissar Order was used as evidence for the barbaric nature of the German war campaign.

Comrade: This was a hard one for us. In the German military the term "Kamerad" is commonly used to address fellow soldiers, at the same time communists and social democrats call themselves "Genosse" in German. In English there only is this one word "comrade", and it often has a communistic touch. I guess an US-soldier would not call his fellow soldiers "comrade"? Since the word "Kamerad" is very, very common in the German military we decided to translate it with "comrade", but do not intend a communistic meaning in a German military context.

210

Comrade Lace-up: A nickname German soldiers invented for Austrian soldiers during World War 1 ("Kamerad Schnürrschuh")

Danke: Thank you in German

Deutsche Allgemeine Zeitung: German newspaper that was de jure independent but de facto had to apply the standards defined by the Reich Ministry of Public Enlightenment and Propaganda

East-Battalions: Units that consisted of voluntaries from German-occupied regions of the Soviet Union and soviet POWs

Eastern Front Medal: Awarded to all axis soldiers who served in the winter campaign of 1941/1942.

Edi: Eduard Born's nickname

Einheits-PKW: A family of 3 types of military vehicles (light, medium and heavy) that featured all-wheel drive and were supposed to replace civilian cars the Reichswehr had procured before. The name translates to Standard Passenger Car.

Eiserner Gustav: German nickname for Iljushin Il-2 "Shturmovik" (= iron Gustav). Gustav is a German male first name.

EK 1: See Iron Cross

Elfriede: Nickname, Engelmann gave his Panzer IV. Elfriede was a common German female given name during that time.

Endsieg: Refers to the final victory over all enemies.

Éxgüsee: Swiss German for "sorry". By the way German dialects can be very peculiar. Bavarian, Austrian, Low German or other variations of German are hard to understand even for Germans, who are not from that particular region. Especially Swiss German is one not easy to understand variation of German, so often when a Swiss is interviewed on German TV subtitles are added. For interregional communication matters most Germans stick to High German, which is understood in all German-speaking areas.

E-series tanks: Series of German tank designs, which should replace the tanks in use. Among those concepts was yet another super heavy tank (E-100) that was developed parallelly to the Maus tank.

Fat Pig: Refers to Hermann Göring, one of Nazi Germany's most influential party members. As the commander of the Luftwaffe he was responsible for a series of failures. He also was infamous for being drug-addicted and generally out of touch with reality. Moreover he coveted military decorations and therefore made sure that he was awarded with every medal available despite the fact that he did not do anything to earn it. Göring was the highest-ranking Nazi leader living long enough to testify in the Nuremberg Trials. He committed suicide to avoid being executed by the Allies.

Faustpatrone ordnance device: See Knocker

Federal Councillor: Member of the Swiss federal government

Ferdinand: Massive German tank destroyer that later was improved and renamed to "Elefant" (= Elephant, while Ferdinand is a German given name – to be precise, it is Ferdinand Porsches given name, founder of Porsche and one of the design engineers of this steely monster). Today the Porsche AG is known for building sports cars.

Like many other very progressive German weaponry developed during the war, the Ferdinand suffered from Hitler personally intervening to alter design and production details. Hitler always thought to be cleverer than his engineers and experts. E.g. he forced the Aircraft constructor Messerschmitt to equip its jet-powered fighter aircraft Me 262 as a dive bomber, while it was constructed to be a fighter and while the Luftwaffe already had lost air superiority at all theaters of war (so you need fighters to regain air superiority before you can even think about bombers). Same story with the Ferdinand: Hitler desperately wanted the Ferdinand to take part in the battle of Kursk, so he demanded its mass production on the basis of prototypes that hadn't been tested at all. German soldiers had to catch up on those tests during live action! Despite its enormous fire power, the Ferdinand proofed to be full of mechanical flaws, which led to lots of total losses. Due to a lack of any secondary weapon and its nearly non-movable main gun the Ferdinand was a death trap for its crew in close combat. Another problem was the Ferdinand's weight of around 65 tons. A lot of bridges and streets were to weak or narrow to survive one of these monsters passing by, let alone a whole battalion if them.

Nevertheless the heavy tank destroyer proofed to be a proper defense weapon that could kill a T-34 frontally at a distance of more than two miles.

Its full name is Panzerjäger Tiger (P) "Ferdinand" (or "Elefant") Sd.Kfz. 184. Sd.Kfz stands for "Sonderkraftfahrzeug" meaning "special purpose vehicle".

Ferdinand II: In the Panzers universe the German Elefant (= Elephant) is designated Ferdinand II. It is an enhanced Ferdinand with a better powertrain, a MG 34 as second armament, wider tracks and more detailed improvements.

Flak: German for AA-gun

Frau: Mrs.

Front: May refer to a Soviet military formation equal to an army squad

Führer: Do I really have to lose any word about the most infamous German Austrian? (By the way, it is "Führer", not "Fuhrer". If you cannot find the "ü" on your keyboard, you can use "ue" as replacement).

Gestapo: Acronym for "Geheime Staatspolizei" (= Secret State Police), a police force that mainly pursued political enemies of the state.

Gröfaz: Mocking nickname for Adolf Hitler. It is an acronym for "greatest commander of all times" (= größter Feldherr aller Zeiten) and was involuntarily coined by Field Marshal Keitel. During the battle of France Keitel, who was known for being servile towards Hitler, hailed him by saying: "My Führer, you are the greatest commander of all times!" It quickly became a winged word among German soldiers – and finally the acronym was born.

Grüessech: Swiss salute

Grüss Gott: Salute that one often hears in southern Germany and Austria. It literally means "Greetings to the Lord".

Guten Abend: Good evening

Heeresgruppe: Army squad. The Wehrmacht wasn't very consistent in naming their army squads. Sometime letters were used, sometimes names of locations or cardinal directions. To continue the madness high command frequently renamed their army squads. In this book "Heeresgruppe Mitte" refers to the center of the Eastern Front (= Army Squad Center), "Heeresgruppe Süd" refers to the southern section (= Army Squad South).

Heimat: A less patriotic, more dreamy word than Vaterland (= fatherland) to address one's home country.

Heinkel He 177 Greif: German long-range heavy bomber. "Greif" means griffin. The Germans soon coined the nickname "Fliegendes Reichsfeuerzeug" (= flying Reich lighter) due to the fact that the He 177's engines tended to catch fire while the bomber was in the air.

Hell Hound: See Höllenhund

Hell Hound 2: See Höllenhund 2

Henschel Hs 127: German ground-attack aircraft designed and produced mainly by Henschel. Due to its capabilities to destroy tanks German soldiers coined the nickname "can opener".

Herein: German word for "come in". Hey, by the end of this book you will be a real German expert!

Herr: Mister (German soldiers address sex AND rank, meaning they would say "Mister sergeant" instead of "sergeant")

Herr General: In the German military, it does not matter which of the general ranks a general inhabits, he is always addressed by "Herr General". It is the same in the US military I guess.

Himmel, Arsch und Zwirn: German curse. Literally it means: Sky, ass and yarn.

Hiwi: Abbreviation of the German word "Hilfswilliger", which literally means "someone who is willing to help". The term describes (mostly) Russian volunteers who served as auxiliary forces for the Third Reich. As many military terms from the two world wars also "Hiwi" has deeply embedded itself into the German language. A lot of Germans use this word today to describe unskilled workers without even knowing anything about its origin.

Höllenhund: This weapon is known as the V-1 flying bomb is a German cruise missile. Since Goebbels coined its name it is designated Höllenhund (= hell hound) in the Panzers universe. Höllenhund was an early working title in development.

Höllenhund 2: Guided long-range ballistic missile known as V-2 rocket in reality. It is the first weapon of its kind ever developed and deployed.

HQ platoon leader: In German "Kompanietruppführer" refers to a special NCO, who exists in every company. The HQ platoon leader is best described as being the company commander's right hand.

IIs, IIIs, IVs: In German you sometimes would say "Zweier" (= a twoer), when talking about a Panzer II for example. We tried our best to transfer this mannerism into English.

Iljushin Il-2 "Shturmovik": Very effective Russian dive bomber, high in numbers on the Eastern Front and a very dangerous tank hunter. There are reports of squads of Shturmoviks having destroyed numerous panzers within minutes. Stalin loved this very aircraft and personally supervised its production. The German nickname is "Eiserner Gustav" (= iron Gustav). Gustav is a German male given name.

Iron Cross: German war decoration restored by Hitler in 1939. It had been issued by Prussia during earlier military conflicts but in WW2 it was available to all German soldiers. There were three different tiers: Iron Cross (= Eisernes Kreuz) – 2nd class and 1st class –, Knight's Cross of the Iron Cross (= Ritterkreuz des Eisernen Kreuzes) – Knight's Cross without any features, Knight's Cross with Oak Leaves,

Knight's Cross with Oak Leaves and Swords, Knight's Cross with Oak Leaves, Swords and Diamond and Knight's Cross with Golden Oak Leaves, Swords and Diamond –, and Grand Cross of the Iron Cross (= Großkreuz des Eisernen Kreuzes) – one without additional features and one called Star of the Grand Cross. By the way the German abbreviation for the Iron Cross 2nd class is EK2, alright?

Island monkeys: German slur for the British (= Inselaffen)

Itaka: German slur word for Italian soldier. It is an abbreviation for "Italienischer Kamerad" meaning Italian comrade.

Ivan: As English people give us Germans nicknames like "Fritz", "Kraut" or "Jerry", we also come up with nicknames for most nationalities. Ivan (actually it is "Iwan" in German) was a commonly used nickname for Russians during both World Wars.

Jawohl: A submissive substitute for "yes" (= "ja"), which is widely used in the German military, but also in daily life

Jäger: German military term that historically refers to light infantry but is of much boarder usage today. In the Bundeswehr for example the term Jäger has more or less replaced the term infantry. Jäger is also a rank in some military specializations.

K98k: Also Mauser 98k or Gewehr 98k (Gewehr = rifle). The K98k was the German standard infantry weapon during World War 2. The second k stands for "kurz", meaning it is a shorter version of the original rifle that already had been used in World War 1. Since it is a short version, it is correctly called carbine instead of rifle – the first k stands for "Karabiner", which is the German word for carbine.

Kama: Refers to the Kama tank school, a secret training facility for German tank crews in the Soviet Union. After World War 1 the German Armed Forces (then called "Reichswehr") were restricted to 100 000 men because of the treaty of Versailles. Also no tanks and other heavy weaponry was permitted. The Germans sought for other ways to build up an own tank force, so they came to an agreement with the Soviet Union over secretly training German tankers at Kama. The German-Soviet cooperation ended with the rise of the Nazis to power in Germany.

Kampfgruppe: Combat formation that often was set up temporarily. Kampfgruppen had no defined size, some were of the size of a company, others were as big as a corps.

Kaputt: German word for "broken"; at one Point in the story Pappendorf uses this word describing a dead soldier. This means that he reduces the dead man to an object, since "kaputt" is only used for objects.

Katyusha: Soviet multiple rocket launcher. The Katyushas were feared by all German soldiers for its highly destructive salvos. Because of the piercing firing sound, the Germans coined the nickname "Stalin's organ" (= Stalinorgel).

Kinon glas: Special bulletproof glass produced by German manufacturer Glas- und Spiegelmanufaktur N. Kinon that was used for German panzer's eye slits. The well-known Tiger scene in the movie Saving Private Ryan would not have happened this way in reality, because one could not just stick one's firearm into the eye slit of a German panzer in order to kill its crew.

Knight's Cross: See Iron Cross

Knocker: German nickname for the Faustpatrone ordance device, the ancestor of the well-known Panzerfaust. German soldiers coined the nickname due to the bad penetrating power of this weapon. Often it just knocked at an enemy tank instead of penetrating its armor because its warhead simply bounced off instead of exploding.

Kolkhoz: Also collective farm; alleged cooperatively organized farming firm. Kolkhozes were one important component of the Soviet farming sector. In the eyes of the Soviet ideology they were a counter-concept to private family farms as well as to feudal serfdom. In reality kolkhozes were pools of slavery and inequality.

Kubelwagen: German military light vehicle (in German it is Kübelwagen)

KV-2: Specs: Armor plating of up to 110-millimeters thickness, a 152-millimeters howitzer as main gun; ate Tiger tanks for breakfast ... if its crew managed to move that heavy son of a bitch into a firing position in the first place.

Lager: Short for "Konzentrationslager" = concentration camp

Landjäger: Swiss cantonal police

Landser: German slang for a grunt

Larisch embroidery: Old Prussian embroidery forming a certain pattern that was used for collar patches of generals

Leopard: German light tank project that was abandoned in 1943. The full name is VK1602 Leopard.

Luftwaffe: German Air Force

Marder II: German tank destroyer based on a Panzer II chassis

Maus tank: Very heavy German tank that never left development phase. It weighed 188 tons and was armed with a 128-millimeter Pak cannon. Maximum speed was around 20 Kilometers per hour on a street and far less in terrain. By the end of the war two prototypes were build. The correct name is Panzerkampfwagen VIII Maus (= "tank combat vehicle VIII Mouse").

Meat Mount: This is my try of translating the German colloquial military term "Fleischlafette", which means that one soldier functions as a mount for an MG by putting it on his shoulder. At the same time, a second one fires the weapon.

MG 34: German machine gun that was used by the infantry as well as by tankers as a secondary armament. And have you ever noticed that some stormtroopers in the original Star Wars movie from 1977 carry nearly unmodified MG 34s around?

MG 42: German machine gun that features an incredible rate of fire of up to 1 500 rounds per minute (that's 25 per second!). It is also called "Hitler's buzzsaw", because a fire burst literally could cut someone in two halves. Its successor, the MG 3, is still in use in nowadays German Armed Forces (Bundeswehr).

Millimeter/centimeter/meter/kilometer: Since Germans make use of the metric system you will find some of those measuring units within direct speeches. Within the text we mostly transferred distance information into yards, miles or feet.

Modi: Swiss-German word for girl

Moin: Means: good morning. "Moin" or "Moin, Moin" are part of several dialects found in Northern Germany. Pay this region a visit and you will hear these greetings very often and actually at EVERY time of the day.

MP 40: German submachine gun, in service from 1938 to 1945

Nebelwerfer: Series of German mortars (the latter variants fired salvos of rockets). The designation translates with "smoke mortar" because the first weapons of this series were developed when Germany still officially tried to meet the Versailles Treaty requirements. However, the Nebelwerfers were initially thought to fire chemical ammunition, which Germany was not allowed to have or use after World War 1.

NCO corps: This was a hard one to translate, since we did not find any similar concept in any English armed force. The NCO corps (= Unteroffizierskorps) refers to the entity of German noncommissioned officers. It is nor organized not powerful by any means, but more of an abstract concept of thought.

Nordsee: Nordsee is the German term for the North Sea, but is also the name of a German restaurant chain selling sea food.

Officer corps: Same thing as in NCO corps. The officer corps (= Offizierkorps) refers to the entity of German officers. It is nor organized not powerful by any means, but more of an abstract concept of thought.

Pak: German word for anti-tank gun (= abbreviation for "Panzerabwehrkanone")

Panje Wagon: Small-framed two-axle buck car, which was pulled one-piece by a horse. Typical vehicle for eastern European and Soviet agronomies.

Panther: Many experts consider the Panther to be the best German WW2 tank. Why, you may ask, when the Wehrmacht also had steel beasts like the Tiger II or the Ferdinand at hand? Well, firepower is not everything. One also should consider mobility, production costs and how difficult it is to operate the tank as well as maintain and repair it on the battlefield. While the hugest German tanks like the Tiger II suffered from technical shortcomings, the Panther was a well-balanced mix of many important variables. Also it featured a sloped armor shape that could withstand direct hits very well. Since the Panther tank development was rushed and Hitler personally demanded some nonsensical changes the tank finally also suffered from some minor shortcomings, nevertheless it proofed to be an effective combat vehicle after all.

Panzer 38(t): Or Panzerkampfwagen 38(t) was a small Czechoslovak tank adopted by the Wehrmacht after it occupied Czechoslovakia. The 38(t) was no match for Russian medium tanks like the T-34 and was only adopted, because the German Armed Forces desperately needed anything with an engine in order to increase the degree of motorization of their troops.

Whenever you find a letter in brackets within the name of a German tank, it is a hint at its foreign origin. For example, French tanks were given an (f), Czechoslovak tanks an (t). Since the 38(t) was riveted instead of welded, each hit endangered the crew, even if the round did not penetrate the armor. Often the rivets sprung out because of the energy set free by the hit. They then became lethal projectiles to the tankers.

Panzer II: Although being a small and by the end of the 1930s outdated tank, the Panzer II was the backbone of the German Army during the first years of the war due to a lack of heavier tanks in sufficient numbers. With its two-Centimeter cannon it only could knock at Russian tanks like the T-34, but never penetrate their armor. The full name is Panzerkampfwagen II (= tank combat vehicle II).

Panzer III: Medium German tank. Actually the correct name is Panzerkampfwagen III (= tank combat vehicle III). Production was stopped in 1943 due to the fact that the Panzer III then was totally outdated. Even in 1941, when the invasion of Russia started, this panzer wasn't a real match for most medium Soviet tanks anymore.

Panzer IV: Very common German medium tank. Actually the correct name is Panzerkampfwagen IV (= tank combat vehicle IV). I know, I know … in video games and movies it is all about the Tiger tank, but in reality an Allied or Russian soldier rather saw a Panzer IV than a Tiger. Just compare the numbers: Germany produced around 8 500 Panzer IVs of all variants, but only 1350 Tiger tanks.

Panzer Badge: German military award for tank crews that participated in three armored combat operations on three different days (= Panzerkampfabzeichen)

Panzergrenadier: Motorized/mechanized infantry (don't mess with these guys!)

Panzerjäger I: First German tank destroyer. It featured an 4.7-centimeters gun. The name literally translates with "Tank Hunter 1".

Papa: Daddy

Penalty area: Soccer term for that rectangular area directly in front of each soccer goal. When a rival striker enters your team's penalty area, he or she impends to score a goal against you. By the way, soccer is an enhanced, more civilized version of that weird game called "American Football" – just in case you wondered ;)

Piefke: Austrian nickname for Germans, often meant in a denigrating manner

Plan Wahlen: A plan that was developed by Swiss Federal Council Wahlen in order to ensure food supplies for the Swiss population in case of an embargo or even an attack of the Axis powers. Since Hitler had started to occupy all neighboring nations he considered to be German anyway, a German attack on Switzerland felt very real for the Swiss. Because of the war they suffered supply shortages and mobilized their army. They even suffered casualties from dogfights with misled German and Allied bombers, because Swiss fighter planes attacked each and every military aircraft that entered their airspace (later they often "overlooked" airspace violations by allied planes though). Switzerland also captured and imprisoned a good number of German and Allied pilots, who crash-landed on their soil.

Since the war raging in most parts of Europe influenced the Swiss, too, they finally came up with the Plan Wahlen in 1940 in order to increase Swiss sustenance. Therefore every piece of land was used as farmland, e.g. crops were cultivated on football fields and in public parks.

I think, the situation of Switzerland during the war is a very interesting and yet quiet unknown aspect of the war. I therefore used the Taylor episode to explore it.

Potato Masher: Nickname for German stick hand grenades which look alike a potato masher a lot

Order of Michael the Brave: Highest Rumanian military decoration that was rewarded to some German soldiers, since Rumania was one of Germany's allies until August 1944.

Ratte tank: 1 000 tons tank concept, called land cruiser or landship. Ratte should feature more than ten guns of different calibers and a crew of over 40 men. The project never saw prototype status. Ratte means rat.

Reichsbahn: German national railway (Deutsche Reichsbahn)

Reichsheini: Mocking nickname for Heinrich Himmler (refers to his function as "Reichsführer SS" (= Reich Leader SS) in combination with an alteration of his first name. At the same time "Heini" is a German offensive term used for stupid people.

Reichskanzler: Chancellor of the German Reich

SA: Short form for "Sturmabteilung" (literally: storm detachment); it had been the Nazi Party's original paramilitary organization until it was disempowered by the SS in 1934.

Scheisse: German for "Crap". Actually it is spelled "Scheiße" with an "ß", but since this letter is unknown in the English language and since it is pronounced very much like "ss", we altered it this way so that you do not mistake it for a "b".
Same thing holds true for the characters Claasen and Weiss. In the original German text both are written with an "ß".

Schluchtenscheisser: German slur word for the Swiss. The translation would be "someone who poops in a canyon."

Scho-Ka-Kola: Bitter-sweet chocolate with a lot of caffeine in it

Sd.Kfz. 234: Family of German armored cars

Secret Field Police: Secret military police of the Wehrmacht

Sepp: Short form of Josef, nickname for Engelmann

Sherman Tank (M4): Medium US-tank that was produced in very large numbers (nearly 50 000 were built between 1942 and 1945) and was used by most allied forces. Through the Lend-Lease program the tank also saw action on the Eastern Front. Its big advantage over all German panzers was its main gun stabilizer, which allowed for precise shooting while driving. German tankers were not allowed to shoot while driving due to Wehrmacht regulations. Because of the missing stabilizers it would have been a waste of ammunition anyway. The name of this US-tank refers to American Civil War general William Tecumseh Sherman.

Let's compare the dimensions: The Third Reich's overall tank production added up to around 50 000 between the pre-war phase and 1945 (all models and their variants like the 38 (t) Hetzer together, so: Panzer Is, IIs, IIIs, IVs, Panthers, Tigers, 38(t)s, Tiger IIs and Ferdinands/Elefants combined)!

Sicherheitsdienst: Intelligence service of the SS

Sir: Obviously Germans do not say "Sir", but that was the closest thing we could do to substitute a polite form that exists in the German language. There is no match for that in the English language: In German parts of a sentence changes when using the polite form. If one asks for a light in German, one would say "Hast du Feuer?" to a friend, but "Haben Sie Feuer?" to a stranger or any person one have not agreed with to leave away the polite form yet. During the Second World War the German polite form was commonly spread, in very conservative families children had to use the polite form to address their parents and even some couples used it among themselves. Today the polite form slowly is vanishing. Some companies like Ikea even addresses customers informally in the first place – something that was an absolute no-go 50 years ago.

In this one scene where the Colonel argues with First Lieutenant Haus he gets upset, because Haus does not say "Sir" (once more: difficult to translate). In the Wehrmacht a superior was addressed with "Herr" plus his rank, in the Waffen SS the "Herr" was left out; a soldier was addressed only by his rank like it is common in armed forces of English-speaking countries. Also one would leave the "Herr" out when one wants to disparage the one addressed, like Papendorf often does when calling Berning "Unteroffizier" instead of "Herr Unteroffizier".

SS: Abbreviation of "Schutzstaffel" (= Protection Squadron). The SS was a paramilitary Nazi-organization, led by Heinrich Himmler. Since the SS operated the death camps, had the Gestapo under their roof as well as had their own military force (Waffen SS) that competed with the Wehrmacht it is not easy to outline their primary task during the era of the Third Reich. Maybe the SS is best described as some sort of general Nazi instrument of terror against all inner and outer enemies.

Stavka: High command of the Red Army

Struwwelpeter: Infamous German bedtime kid's book that features ten very violent stories of people, who suffer under the disastrous consequences of their misbehavior. Need an Example? One story features a boy, who sucks his thumbs until a tailor appears cutting the boy's thumbs off with a huge scissor. The book definitely promises fun for the whole family!
(Nowadays it is not read out to kids anymore, but even I, who grew up in the 90s, had to listen to that crap). In the U.S.A. the book is also known under the title "Slovenly Peter".

Stahlhelm: German helmet with its distinctive coal scuttle shape, as Wikipedia puts it. The literal translation would be steel helmet.

Stuka: An acronym for a dive bomber in general (= "Sturzkampfbomber"), but often refers to that one German dive bomber you may know: the Junkers Ju 87.

Sturm: Among other things Sturm is an Austrian vocabulary for a Federweisser, which is a wine-like beverage made from grape must.

Sturmgeschütz: German term for assault gun

Tank killer: Tanks specifically designed to combat enemy tanks. Often tank destroyers rely on massive firepower and capable armor (the latter is achieved by a non-rotatable

227

turret that allows for thicker frontal armor). Also called tank hunter or tank destroyer. The German term is "Jagdpanzer", which literally means hunting tank.

T-34: Medium Russian tank that really frightened German tankers when it first showed up in 1941. First the T-34 was superior to all existing German tanks (with the exception of Panzer IV variant F that was equipped with a longer cannon and thicker armor). The T-34 was also available in huge numbers really quick. During the war the Soviet Union produced more than 35 000 T-34 plus more than 29 000 of the enhanced T-34/85 model! Remember the Sherman tank? So the production of only these two tanks outnumbered the overall German combat tank production by a factor of more than two!

T-34/85: Enhanced T-34 with a better main gun (85-millimeters cannon) and better armor. It also featured a fifth crew member, thus the tank commander could concentrate on commanding his vehicle rather than have to aim and shoot at the same time.

T-70: Light Soviet tank that weighted less than 10 tons. Although it was a small tank that featured a 45-millimeters main gun, one should not underestimate the T-70. There are reports of them destroying Panthers and other medium or heavy German panzers.

Tiger tank: Heavy German combat tank, also known as Tiger I that featured a variant of the accurate and high-powered 88-millimeters anti-aircraft cannon "Acht-Acht". The correct name is Panzerkampfwagen VI Tiger (= tank combat vehicle VI Tiger).

Tin can: During World War 2 some German soldiers called tanks tin can (= Büchse), so we thought it would be nice to keep that expression in the translation as well.

SU-122: Soviet assault gun that carried a 122-millimeters main gun, which was capable of destroying even heavy German tanks from a fair distance.

Vaterland: Fatherland

Viktor: Word of confirmation among German Luftwaffe pilots

VK4502(P): Heavy tank project by Porsche that never got beyond drawing board status despite some turrets, which were produced by Krupp and later mounted on Tiger II tanks.

Volksempfänger: Range of radio receivers developed on the request of Propaganda Minister Goebbels to make us of the new medium in order to spread his propaganda. It literally translates with "people's receiver" and was an affordable device for most Germans.

Völkischer Beobachter: Newspaper of the NSDAP that was full of propaganda and agitation against minorities and enemy warring parties

Waffen SS: Waffen = arms; it was the armed wing of the Nazi Party's SS organization, which was a paramilitary organization itself.

Waidmannsheil: German hunters use this call to wish good luck ("Waidmann" is an antique German word for hunter, "Heil" means well-being). As many hunting terms, Waidmannsheil made its way into German military language.

War Merit Cross: German military award issued by Hitler in 1939 in 2 different classes (= Kriegsverdienstorden in German)

Wochenschau: German newsreel that was produced for watching in cinemas and transported the Nazi propaganda to the people

Wound Badge: German decoration for wounded soldiers or those, who suffered frostbites. The wound badge was awarded in three stages: black for being wounded once or twice, silver for the third and fourth wound, gold thereafter. US equivalent: Purple Heart.

Zampolit: Political commissar; an officer responsible for political indoctrination in the Red Army

Wehrmacht ranks (Army)

All military branches have their own ranks, even the medical service.

Rank	US equivalent
Anwärter	Candidate (NCO or officer)
Soldat (or Schütze, Kanonier, Pionier, Funker, Reiter, Jäger, Grenadier … depends on the branch of service)	Private
Obersoldat (Oberschütze, Oberkanonier …)	Private First Class
Gefreiter	Lance Corporal
Obergefreiter	Senior Lance Corporal
Stabsgefreiter	Corporal
Unteroffizier	Sergeant
Fahnenjunker	Ensign
Unterfeldwebel/ Unterwachtmeister (Wachtmeister only in cavalry and artillery)	Staff Sergeant

Feldwebel/ Wachtmeister	Master Sergeant
Oberfeldwebel/ Oberwachtmeister	Master Sergeant
Oberfähnrich	Ensign First Class
Stabsfeldwebel/ Stabswachtmeister	Sergeant Major
Hauptfeldwebel	This is not a rank, but an NCO function responsible for personnel and order within a company
Leutnant	Second Lieutenant
Oberleutnant	First Lieutenant
Hauptmann/Rittmeister (Rittmeister only in cavalry and artillery)	Captain
Major	Major
Oberstleutnant	Lieutenant Colonel
Oberst	Colonel
Generalmajor	Major General
Generalleutnant	Lieutenant General
General der ... (depends on the branch of service: - Infanterie (Infantry) - Kavallerie (Cavalry) - Artillerie (Artillery) - Panzertruppe (Tank troops) - Pioniere (Engineers) - Gebirgstruppe (Mountain Troops) - Nachrichtentruppe (Signal Troops)	General (four-star)
Generaloberst	Colonel General
Generalfeldmarschall	Field Marshal

LEOPARD TANKS IN ACTION

Variants and Combat Operations of the German
Leopard 1 & 2 Main Battle Tanks

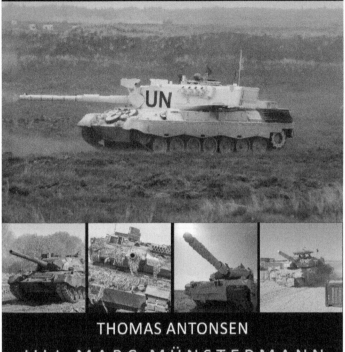

THOMAS ANTONSEN

JILL MARC MÜNSTERMANN

Dive deep into the fascinating world of German tanks in this definitive textbook about the Leopard 1 and 2. Known as one of the most for their prominence in peacetime, there's more to these trusty machines than meets the eye. Follow them on their journey around the globe as we guide you through **every combat mission ever** ventured upon by the mighty machines. **The wide range of conflicts they have been in creates a fascinating reading experience for history lovers and war fanatics.**

Read in raw, uncut detail the savage battle reports from these fierce tanks as you're taken deep into each conflict they took part in. From being pitted against Bosnian Serb battle tanks to their involvement in the invasion of Kosovo, this book covers the complete combat operation history of the Leopard 1 and Leopard 2. Also, their deployments in more modern times are discussed, with them being used to fight against the Taliban in Afghanistan and ISIS in Syria. The amount of missions these tanks have embarked upon is endless, and you will learn about them all in this definitive book.

This is the only book of its kind. A one-off concise guide outlining everything you would ever need to know about the Leopard 1 and 2. First, we go into the history behind the German panzers from its beginnings in World War I as well as an insight into all the upgrades and user states. In the conclusion, we explore the significance of the Leopard tanks in modern warfare. Finally, in the afterword, Danish tank expert **Thomas Antonsen** graces us with a few thoughts. Brimming with umpteen references and sources, this is one book tank enthusiasts don't want to miss out on.

Leopard 1 and 2 main battle tanks took part in combat operations under the flag of **Canada, Turkey, Germany, the Netherlands, Belgium, and Denmark.**

Published by EK-2 Publishing GmbH
Friedensstraße 12
47228 Duisburg
Germany
Registry court: Duisburg, Germany
Registry court ID: HRB 30321
Chief Executive Officer: Monika Münstermann

E-Mail: info@ek2-publishing.com

All rights reserved
Paperback printed by Kindle Direct Publishing
(Amazon)

Cover art: Peter Ashford
Author: Tom Zola
Translation: Martina Wehr
Proofreading: by Jill marc Münstermann
German Editor: Lanz Martell
Innerbook: Jill Marc Münstermann

Paperback ISBN: 978-3-96403-122-8
Kindle ISBN: 978-3-96403-121-1
1st Edition, February 2021

Made in the USA
Las Vegas, NV
22 May 2021

23453502R00142